F Callaghan
Callaghan, Carrie.
Salt the snow

3/20

SALT THE
SNOW

SALT THE
SNOW

CARRIE CALLAGHAN

AMBERJACK
PUBLISHING

CHICAGO

Amberjack Publishing
An imprint of Chicago Review Press Incorporated
814 North Franklin Street
Chicago, Illinois 60610

10 9 8 7 6 5 4 3 2 1

Book design by Aubrey Khan, Neuwirth & Associates

Publisher's Cataloging-in-Publication data available upon request

ISBN: 978-1-948705-64-6
E-ISBN: 978-1-948705-65-3

For my parents

PART ONE

I wouldn't have been born a hundred years
ago for a hatful of gardenias. Would you?
—MILLY BENNETT

Now

February 27, 1934

CRAMMED INTO THE back seat with two other reporters, Milly wished the chauffeur would drive faster.

Instead, the automobile slowed as it turned onto Pushechnaya Street. Outside, only a few lights blurred past, their glow amplified by the white snow piled high on the sidewalks. Inside the chauffeured Ford, the raucous voices seemed to get louder.

"Pipe down, you drunkards," Milly said. She wasn't nearly as tight as the rest of the group, though sure, she'd had a few dishes of vodka. "You'll wake up the block." If she was lucky, Zhenya would still be awake, waiting for her in the small room he shared with his mother. Not that she had any real hopes of getting a tumble out of him.

Seema, who was sitting between Milly and another American newspaperman who'd been at the party, reached over to ruffle the black frizz of Milly's hair.

"All that glorious hair." Seema giggled. Her own black hair was straightened and pulled into loose finger waves, prettier even than Josephine Baker's.

"Old ladies like me have to have something to keep our spirits afloat." Milly hoped she sounded more witty than self-pitying.

It didn't bother her to be thirty-seven; she just liked making cracks about it.

The chauffer pulled the Ford over to the curb.

"You're lucky I put up with you rotten louts," Milly said, then opened the door. The brutal Russian cold flooded into the car. She swung her legs carefully onto the icy street, stood, and snapped the door shut. Before she could tap a farewell on the window, the automobile rolled off.

She had her boots on, so she stepped right through a dip in the snowbank and onto the sidewalk. The cold burned her nose and made her glasses fog up, and yet there was still something beautiful about a Moscow night. As soon as the weather warmed, she and Zhenya would have to go for one of their nighttime walks again. It had been so long since they had, and by springtime he would have fewer opera rehearsals to occupy him. She cleared her glasses with the wool of her gloved fingertips.

There, parked a little way down from where she stood, was a black automobile. Milly's breath caught. None of Zhenya's neighbors owned a car—no ordinary Russian did. The Soviet Union was still learning how to make cars, and there weren't enough imports to go around for anyone except the government. The light of the single streetlamp caressed the smooth curves of the Ford. A shiver even colder than the winter air drilled through her.

She hurried inside the building's unlocked exterior door and shook the snow from her boots while the snoring of one of the first-floor residents droned down the hallway. Then she hurried up the flight of stairs to Zhenya's floor. By the top, she was taking the steps a wobbly two at a time.

Then, when she reached the top, she froze. The door to the apartment containing Zhenya's room was open, and light spilled out into the dark hallway.

The building was quiet.

Milly walked slowly inside. From the front room, filled with the cot and belongings of Luba, a Ukrainian student assigned to the subdivided apartment, Milly could see inside Zhenya's room, but she couldn't see him. A man in a brown uniform with a peaked cap stood by Zhenya's open door. Inside, Zhenya's mother, Olga Ivanova, sat on the edge of her couch, her chin in her hand and her eyes on something to her left.

"What's going on?" Milly asked in Russian as soon as she entered the small bedroom. Zhenya stood in the corner, his fine skin smudged with weariness.

A second uniformed man was on his knees, peering into Zhenya's wardrobe. He stood.

"Who is this?" he said to Zhenya, next to him. Luba and Victor Pavilovich, Zhenya's closest friend and fellow actor in the opera, sat solemnly on the bed, Luba's flaxen-haired head resting on Victor's slim shoulders. Milly had never seen the room so crowded.

"My wife," Zhenya said. "She doesn't live here though."

Milly's legs felt weak.

"What does this mean?" she asked Zhenya in English.

"An OGPU search." He answered like the scene was just as confusing to him. His gray eyes were wide, and his blond hair was still slicked back with the pomade he used for the stage. He looked both devastatingly handsome and fragile. Milly reached for him without moving closer, but he kept his arms hugged around his chest.

"Search? What for?" Milly let her hand fall and looked around the small room again. A photograph of Zhenya and her at the dacha was pinned above the bedside table. She hadn't minded that photo as much as she usually did with pictures. In this one, her jutting chin and overbearing front teeth were muted, and she looked happy. Happy to feel Zhenya's arm around her waist and the warm sun on her hair. The paper curled up at its scalloped edges.

The officer had gotten back down on his knees to search under the wardrobe, and he scowled up at her.

"Don't speak in any foreign languages. Speak in Russian."

"Her Russian isn't very good," Zhenya said, and Milly glared at him. That wasn't true; she could get by fine.

"Then she doesn't have to speak," the officer concluded. He pulled out a pair of shoes and shook them upside down.

"Has he got a warrant?" Milly didn't bother to speak quietly, or in Russian.

"Yes. He has a warrant for me." Zhenya's fingers tapped at his chest.

That didn't make any sense. "You've seen it?"

"Yes."

Milly turned to the officer and flung the wardrobe door wide open, narrowly missing his head.

"What are you looking for?" she asked in her accented Russian.

He pressed his hands against a shelf and stood, then brushed his palms together.

"Guns." He smiled.

Milly almost laughed. Surely he was joking. Zhenya, her gentle opera supernumerary, with his eager smiles and graceful fingers, stockpiling guns? But the cold lead snaking through her gut reminded her that the secret police were no joke. Especially not when they came after midnight.

The officer closed the wardrobe door quietly, then turned toward the large green trunk wedged under the window. He lifted the latch.

"That's mine." Milly almost reached out to grab his hand, but she restrained herself. She was nervous, she knew, and when she got nervous, she grew uncontrollable. She needed to be careful.

He looked at her and smiled again, and this time she noticed the sizable gap between his front teeth.

"I have a warrant."

"But that trunk's mine! You can't search my things."

His eyes narrowed. "You are his wife. It counts."

She had nothing to hide, no guns certainly, but still, it wasn't right that this ham-handed officer with hair curling up from the top of his shirt collar could rummage through her underwear.

"Don't tear those stockings," she muttered. "I only have three pair."

He gave her a sideways look but otherwise continued uninterrupted. To his credit, each item he removed he replaced as carefully folded, or more so, as he left it. But he seemed to be inventorying her items with more attention than he paid to Zhenya's clothes. The hairs at the back of her neck prickled.

Milly glanced back and forth between Victor, slender and hunched like a willow, and Luba, stocky and straight, who sat together silently on the bed, while Zhenya stood staring out the window as if he were admiring the snowfall. The guard by the door peered into the room, but he looked bored.

"See? Nothing!" she said when the officer closed the trunk. Victor looked up, as if surprised at her conclusion, but otherwise no one else paid her any attention. She wondered if they were scared or simply resigned.

The officer likewise ignored her, and next turned to the cabinet they had once used to store what little food the three of them could accumulate, before they had decided to store things in the apartment's small kitchen. Milly didn't sleep in this room, not usually, but she had meals with Zhenya and his mother when she could. Olga, whose arthritic hands kept her from working, couldn't qualify for her own meal ticket book, so it was easier for Zhenya to feed her if Milly pitched in. Plus, Milly enjoyed the older woman's calm determination.

"Look out," Milly said to the officer, who reached his hand into the cabinet. "There's been a mouse in there for a while."

"I'm not afraid of mice."

"Oh, no. I was thinking of the mouse."

The officer turned to face Zhenya.

"Why is your wife so rude? I'm being very quiet about the whole business."

Zhenya shook his head. His lips, Milly saw, had turned pale, and he didn't speak.

"I'm not rude," Milly said, though she knew she had been, and she wished she could stop. "I'm not the one going through people's underwear."

"Look at the other citizens." He gestured at the three seated figures. "They don't complain."

"They're Russian. I'm American." And she'd had a few swallows of vodka, but that probably didn't matter.

He blew out a puff of air, shook his head, then closed the old cabinet. He turned next to the pile of books on the floor, all of which were Milly's, and he picked up each one, gave it a shake, then replaced it. On top he put *Penguin Island* by Anatole France upside down. That seemed fitting, so she left it.

He got down on his hands and knees again and peered under the bed. He pulled out a box.

Inside were fistfuls of worthless tsarist rubles. Olga gave a little chirp, then tucked her gray-blond hair back under her kerchief.

"Necessary to burn these, little mother," he said.

She stood, without a word, and took the box from him. Then she sat again, with the box on her lap under her veined hands.

The officer shook his head but turned away from her and resumed his search.

"When did they come?" Milly asked Zhenya in hushed English.

"Before you."

She wanted to ask him why he thought this was happening, and what he—or she—had done to deserve it. But he turned away to look out the window again. As if she embarrassed him.

The officer ran his finger down the spines of Milly's notebooks, resting on a table near the bed, and she wondered if the secret police had meant to come while she was out, to catch her unawares. She still had her American passport, and they probably wouldn't have been able to obtain a search warrant for her. But they could access her belongings, the ones here at least, through Zhenya. She tried to remember through the haze of the night's vodka if any of the stories she had written recently, for either *Moscow Daily News* or one of the wire services, had been inflammatory. She didn't think so, but maybe her carbon copies of her stories would prove differently.

"Have you been to the New Moscow Hotel too?" She'd been staying there since November.

The officer ignored her and continued to page through the notebooks, filled with her scribbles from Russian lessons with Luba. Verb conjugation, sentence construction, vocabulary for going to the market. She let out a quick exhalation.

"No need to study," Milly said. "I'm sure you learned all this long ago."

He turned the next page even more slowly.

"Truthfully, there's nothing there. Just my last six months of lessons. See how badly I learned?" Her accent flattened the Russian words into uniformity, and she knew she often mangled verb tenses.

He continued to ignore her. Every few pages, he would suck a hiss of air through his teeth, though whether it was in recognition of something subversive or disappointment at her abuse of his language she couldn't say.

She stepped over to Zhenya and slipped her hand into his. As usual, he lifted her fingers to his lips to kiss them and then dropped her grip. He had dark shadows peering through the fair skin under his eyes. She wanted to kiss his angled nose.

The officer began to flip the pages of her Russian lessons more quickly, but he frowned as he did so, as if disappointed not to find what he was looking for. Milly's neck felt constricted, and she realized she still wore her heavy coat, though the heat inside was stifling. She rushed to peel the garment off. She threw the coat on the bed, behind Victor, who flinched, then looked at her again with some inscrutable question. The officer tossed her notebook back onto the pile, then reached down to straighten it.

"I'm in room 512 of the New Moscow Hotel," Milly said. "Most of my papers are there. Many more papers to look at than here."

She didn't want the filthy secret police to go pawing through all her letters, all the carbon copies she'd been keeping for the past three years so she could use them to write her novel some-day. But if the police were going to harass Zhenya only because he was married to an American newspaperwoman, let them bother her, she could take it. She hoped.

"Are you inviting me?" The officer stood up from his crouch. "As a guest?"

"No, not like . . ."

"Don't say things you don't mean." He turned and picked up the *New Yorker* from last December, which was lying on the side table.

"It's a humor magazine. Like your *Krokodil*, but on better paper."

He glared at her, then flipped slowly through the pages he surely couldn't understand. He replaced it exactly from where he had taken it.

The search continued. Milly's legs trembled from nerves and exhaustion, so she sat on the small couch with Olga and took the other woman's hand in her own. Olga was probably around sixty, but she looked older, with her narrow shoulders slumped. Olga's free hand continued to clutch her box full of worthless rubles. They had never spoken of it, but Milly assumed Olga dreamed that someday everything would be restored to her:

her tsar, her bourgeois wealth, the large home Zhenya claimed they had once lived in. Maybe she would settle for receiving this entire apartment back. At least Zhenya's dreams were reasonable: he had a chance of singing tenor at the Bolshoi. More chance than his poor mother did of spending those rubles.

It was past three a.m. when the officer finished his search, and by then Milly was bleary and sagging. The buzz of the dinner party and the vodka she'd drank had long ago fizzed away, leaving only her drooping stockings and eyelids. Through it all, Zhenya stood.

The officer pulled a paper from a folder the other officer held, then sat down at the desk to write. Milly wanted to make a quip about writing a letter to his granny about his good work, but she was too tired to muster the Russian words. They all watched in silence as his pen scratched its way to fill an entire page.

"Excuse me," he said, then took the page and left the room, then stepped out of the apartment. With the door open, he picked up the shared phone in the hallway, rattled off the six numbers to the operator, and had a hushed conversation. No one else in the room moved, and the Russians all kept their eyes to the ground. Milly darted her gaze back and forth among them, hoping that someone would look at her and, in that way, explain what was happening. In the apartment above, something fell and thudded on the floor, and Olga startled. Still, no one spoke.

The officer walked back in. He sat down at the desk again, wrote a few more lines, then called Zhenya over.

"Nothing is out of order in this room, correct?" The officer waved a hand around. "Evgeni Ivanovich, you have no complaints, correct?" He held up the paper and jabbed his finger at it. It must be a record of the search.

"It's all fine," Zhenya said in his gentle way, as if it were the officer who needed reassuring.

Without realizing she had decided to do so, Milly stood.

"Evgeni Ivanovich Konstantinov, you are under arrest." The officer turned and handed Milly the handwritten record. Her mouth gaped, and she almost let the paper fall to the floor but remembered to grasp it in time. Everyone else in the room was still and silent, like mice hiding from a raptor circling overhead.

She reached for Zhenya, and he gave her a quick kiss on the cheek before pulling away. He turned to look at each of them in the room, one at a time, then followed the OGPU officer out the door, past Luba's cot and her neatly folded clothes, past the dried white flowers Luba kept in a vase stacked on top of a volume of Lenin's speeches. Zhenya picked up his coat from the hook by the door, then followed the first officer out.

The second officer closed the door behind him, and they were gone.

Olga Ivanova began to weep quietly, so Milly sat down next to her again and pressed the woman's wet cheek against her shoulder. Olga's sobs cut into Milly's chest, and soon she was crying too.

This was all her damn fault.

Before

February 1931

Sitting in her cramped ocean-liner cabin, Milly grimaced at her headache. Her first night into her new life in Russia and already she was hungover. She lifted the long-stemmed pink rose to her face and sniffed. Even with the waves of gin on her breath and the salt water musk rising from the cabin carpet, she could smell the rich scent. Too rich, her coiled stomach told her, and she placed the rose carefully back in its box. It was swell of her friends to have surprised her onboard last night before the ship set off from New York, but now she was paying the price. She pressed her fingers to her lips, then went to open the cabin door. Maybe that would get some fresh air in here.

"Steward!" she called when she spotted the man down the hall. While he approached, she stepped back into the cabin to run her fingers through her sleep-tossed hair. Some good that would do.

"Mrs. Mitchell?" he asked. She'd booked her passage to Germany, en route to Moscow, under her legal name, though she still smarted at the reminder of her failed marriage to Mike. No matter that they'd divorced five years ago: passports were passports.

"Could you clear out this mess?" She pointed at the empty bottles and boxes of crumpled green paper with daisies and carnations spilling from them. "I'd be grateful. Oh, but those roses, those'll be for my table. Can you do that?" She should throw the whole mess out, but she couldn't bear to part with the ones from Fred, her married lover. No, former lover, and she should toss those flowers straight into the can.

But she wouldn't.

She dug for two quarters in her change purse, then dropped them in the steward's hand with what she hoped was an appreciative smile.

"My pleasure, Mrs. Mitchell."

"You're a champ. Now, give me a minute to put myself together."

He stepped out of the cabin, and as soon as she latched the door, Milly turned to collect the blue telegram slips she'd left scattered across the table. One by one she wedged them into the frame around the mirror: Esther, LooJo, Grace. When she got to Fred's, she paused. *Don't do anything I wouldn't do best wishes Fred.* The tears welled up again. She still loved the bastard, but she was glad to be rid of him. He'd made it clear he had chosen his wife over her, and that was that. Or, Anna Louise Strong had offered her a job in Moscow, the fascinating new socialist world of Moscow, and that was that. Milly pressed her knuckles into her damp eyes and tried to believe she was chasing the intellectual thrill of seeing a new way of organizing society, not fleeing the age-old story of a broken heart. Ever since Hawaii, all she seemed good at was running away from her problems. Especially when those problems were men.

Quickly Milly stuffed Fred's note into one of her notebooks, then pulled on her stockings, snapped the garters over them, and fluffed her skirt into place. She looked like a rotten onion, splotchy and out of sorts, but she had to go above deck. This morning she had missed the receding New York skyline. The least she could do now was to get her poor, sour stomach some damned air.

She gave the waiting steward another enthusiastic thanks and then ascended on wobbly legs to the deck, where the cold sea wind buffeted her ears and sent her scurrying back inside. So much for that. Next time she'd remember her coat, she scolded herself. Typical Milly Bennett. She stood by the window and tried to make out the horizon in the distance, but the dividing line between the ocean and sky blurred. She frowned, and the ship's engine hummed as if burrowing into the waters beneath her feet.

At dinner that night her beautiful long-stemmed roses were arranged in a vase in front of her place setting, their soft blooms pouting like flirtatious girls.

"You've already got an admirer, I see," said the man seated across from her at the small table. He spoke with a crystalline British accent and held his cigar between large fingers.

Milly laughed.

"They're from my old boss out in San Francisco." It wasn't true, but she wasn't about to tell a stranger they were from her married lover. Ex-lover. "Sweetest old man you ever saw."

"I didn't see you at lunch." He put out the cigar, then looked at her, holding her gaze. "Though I can tell you, you didn't miss much."

She stared back at him. He had high cheekbones and a carefully combed shock of blond hair, and he was enough to give her a tremor of pleasure instead of sea sickness. "I was still sleeping off the farewell party. So, you're to be my meal companion?"

"My good fortune." He smiled. She knew he was flattering her; no one looked at her face and called himself lucky, but she wanted to be flattered. "Much better than my fortune with lunch, when these Germans"—he gestured at the ship—"subjected us to boiled meat and sticky bread. Cheapskates."

Milly flinched at the insult but, wanting to be polite, nodded and lifted a spoonful of green pea soup to her lips.

"You know, I don't think I can handle this mess either," she said. "I'm usually a good sailor, but . . ."

"Shall I get them to serve you something else?" Without waiting for her response, he turned to flag a waiter, and the yellow light from the wall sconces glistened on the slick of his hair.

"No, no," she said. "Thanks though." She'd never sent a meal back, not once in her life. She picked up a crust of bread and nibbled at it. Bread should help settle her stomach.

He clucked his tongue, then raised his hand again to signal the waiter.

"This won't do," he said when the red-faced waiter arrived. "Bring a bowl of consommé for the lady please."

"Sir, I'm afraid we don't—"

"With how much we're paying for tickets, there is no *don't*. Some consommé for the lady, if you please."

"I'm fine," Milly protested. She was starting this journey to help workers, not beleaguer them. The waiter looked back and forth between them, his chapped hands tugging at his sleeves.

"She's being polite," her dining companion said, then added in marbled German, "A better soup." The waiter's eyebrows pinched as he looked at them, then he gave a short exhale and walked away.

Milly set her spoon down and regarded her dinner companion, who was smiling broadly at her. She didn't want a better soup.

"That poor man's going to get in trouble," she said. As usual, her complaints came too late.

"Trouble?" Her companion tapped a finger against his lips. "Seems unlikely. He'll get a tip from me for doing his job properly."

She looked at the tablecloth.

"You promise?" She didn't want to fight with this handsome man, even though a small voice at the back of her mind said she should.

He waved a hand. "Of course."

"I guess I ought to appreciate your effort." She sighed, defeated. Later, she would check on the waiter, make sure he was all right.

She pushed the bowl of green sludge away, and it gathered up a fold of white tablecloth as she did so. The Brit reached across the table to straighten it out. Once he did, he grasped her fingers lightly between his.

"The name's Caldwell," he said. "I don't believe we've introduced ourselves."

"Milly Bennett." She smiled, and her hungover stomach felt a little better. He was a cad, sure, but a good-looking one. She squeezed his fingers then withdrew her hand.

The next day, he rearranged his deck chair assignment to sit next to her and brought her a heavy rug to withstand the bracing sea air blowing past.

"For the lady," he said with a mock bow. "Though I'm sure she looks better with far less," he whispered.

Milly laughed, and was tempted to tell him he was most certainly right—her full breasts and curved hips were a far better feature than her face—but she didn't have the courage. In the twenties she had learned how much fun it was to let a man rattle her bones, but that was San Francisco and Prohibition, when the rank grape smell of fermentation wafted up Telegraph Hill while a sharp-witted man nuzzled her neck.

"Did you tip the waiter?" she asked instead.

"The waiter? I'm sure." He settled into his chair and pulled out a book.

Milly frowned. She would have to leave a tip in the dining room herself, though heaven knew she couldn't afford it. She brushed her windblown hair behind her ear and peered at the title. *The Well of Loneliness.*

"You won't like that one," she warned him. The girl in that novel loved other girls and had no need for men; Caldwell wouldn't know what to make of such a character.

"Maybe I shouldn't read it, then." He laid the book open on his lap. "Why is a young woman like yourself going to Germany? Or are you getting off in England?"

"To Moscow. To work on a newspaper," she said. "A woman I sorta know runs it, and she said she needed an experienced hand. And who could resist finding out what new world they've got up and running there? We're washed up here." She gestured behind her, as if New York, its stock market crash, and its lines of desperate beggars were over her shoulder.

"If you say so," he said casually, and returned his gaze to his novel.

❀

When the ship docked in Southampton, Milly stood on the deck and waved at Caldwell as he disembarked. She never had learned his first name, and in the end, that seemed fitting. It wasn't the old world that she wanted to discover.

3

Now

February 28, 1934

After the OGPU officers took Zhenya away, Olga cried quietly for a few minutes while the rest of them puttered around the cramped room, looking for books to straighten or shirts to refold. But everything was in order. Milly alternated between holding Olga's hand and rereading the mundane arrest receipt. Then, by silent agreement, they tried to sleep. It was too late for Victor to go home, so Luba gave him her cot and shared Zhenya's small bed with Milly.

When Milly woke, probably a couple of hours later, a light glitter of snow fell from the bright sky, and a truck rumbled past. Next to her, Luba slumbered, her eyelids tight and twitching, and beyond her, Olga's breath gave a growl each time she exhaled. Milly pinched her eyes shut and tried to fall asleep again, but all she could think of was Zhenya's lean body, curled up somewhere and shivering.

She rolled over, turning her back to Luba's warmth, and hugged herself, staying under the blankets as long as she could, until the pressure of her bladder forced her out. She searched for Zhenya's slippers but gave up, and she tiptoed across the painfully cold floor and down the hallway to the shared floor bathroom.

There, one of the neighbors shuffled out the bathroom door as Milly approached. He looked at her, closed the door, and stood blocking the entrance. Milly crossed her arms. He raised an unruly brown eyebrow, and she knew he had heard at least something of what had happened last night. Nonetheless, he had obviously slept better than she had. His left cheek bore the red marks of the pillow. The wooden floorboards were cold and rough beneath her bare skin, but Milly remained, arms crossed. If he wanted to know something he could ask. Not that she would tell him about Zhenya anyway.

"Excuse me," she said in Russian, though her exhausted voice came out as a croak.

He smirked.

"I could pee on your floor if you want," Milly added.

He huffed and stepped out of the way.

Back in the apartment's tiny kitchen, she wet a rag in the pot of water they kept for cleaning and washed her narrow feet. She sighed and wrung out the rag in the empty sink basin.

She pulled on an extra pair of socks and one of Zhenya's sweaters, then buttoned herself into the pretty reindeer coat she'd bought last fall. Worth every ruble that coat was, now that bitter winter once again had its teeth in the city. She wrapped her scarf around her neck and head and trundled, as quietly as she could, out of the room.

Outside, a few snowflakes still sprinkled the morning sky, and her glasses fogged up. Without breaking stride on the slippery sidewalk, she pulled the glasses off, wiped them down, and replaced them on her nose before she could trip. She had enough times in the past, god knows. Now, with her glasses cleared, she could see the fine ornamentation on the buildings on Zhenya's street, and she strained to see past the iron gate closing an arched passageway between two buildings. Here,

Moscow felt like Europe, and she let herself be charmed by the decorative touches some architect had added in hopes of welcoming people into his building. She imagined how she would describe each archway and windowsill if she were to write a story. Better that than thinking about Zhenya.

When she reached her miniscule room in the New Moscow Hotel, about fifteen long minutes later, Milly examined her notebooks. Nothing, it seemed, had been touched, and there was no sign of a search here. Still, she pulled a few particularly critical pages from her notes and burned them in the trash can, next to an open window to dissipate the smoke. She hurried to rush her still-cold fingers through undressing, ditching the dinner dress and stockings, even Zhenya's sweater, and pulling on sensible trousers and wool stockings beneath them. Today, she would start to right what had gone wrong. She picked up her enameled hairbrush and yanked it through the knots in her unruly black hair. She scowled at her displeasing reflection in the mirror, then slashed on some red lipstick anyway. So what if lipstick was bourgeois; her poor mug needed all the help it could get.

But that day all she could do was get a number from the old woman at the front of the OGPU precinct building, a card that gave Milly a place to stand in line the next day. Number seventy-one for the package line. She called Olga to tell her on the shared telephone, and the older woman thanked her in a tiny voice. Then Milly rushed to the Moscow Daily News newsroom in the former ballroom of a requisitioned mansion to edit the two stories she was responsible for that night. She did her work without saying a word to anyone, not even Seema, who tapped a questioning finger on Milly's desk when she passed. When her editing was finished, Milly had no time to walk all the way to Olga's, so she ran to the store and bought what she could for Zhenya's package. There was a ten-kilo limit—she had overheard one of the Russian translators say so a few weeks ago—but she didn't know what he would need. She spent the waning hours of the night arranging and rearranging the items in her box until she stumbled to bed.

For the second night in a row Milly got only a few hours of sleep, and she awoke groaning in the still-dark morning. She pulled on her same wool stockings and trousers, attire that made her almost immediately identifiable as an American, since the Russian women wore skirts no matter how cold it was. She grabbed the package she had put together for Zhenya and went outside to stand in line.

By now, dozens more anxious women, and a few men, milled around in the street. Milly heard people mentioning line numbers as high as two hundred. She clutched the brown paper package to her chest and shivered. No one spoke to her, which was fine. She needed to think. She ran over in her mind the stories she had overseen or written in the past few months, or at least what she could remember. The interview with the Lunts, the yarn on the tractor factory, the countless translated pieces about five-year plans and collectivization. It had been months, even years, since she had written anything that had so much as made the newspaper's leadership frown. Sure, they had been upset over the typewriter incident, but that wasn't reason to call the secret police. It didn't make sense that the OGPU had targeted Zhenya because of her, but it made even less sense that he had any political clashes while rehearsing for the opera or taking singing lessons.

At ten o'clock the office door unlocked, and the crowd merged then distended in the shape of a line. People murmured as they compared numbers, but said little more. Their strained faces did more talking. An old woman in front of Milly balanced three packages, and each time she shuffled forward the top box wobbled. Milly thought of asking the woman, who had a shadow of a mustache on her crinkled upper lip, what she had packed. With three packages to send, the woman must know what prisoners needed. Milly gripped the wrapping on hers until the box began to dent inward. She hoped the food would make it to Zhenya, and she wondered, with a sick feeling at the pit of her stomach, what he had been eating for the past day.

By the time Milly made it into the cramped building and to the glass window where they accepted the packages, it was early afternoon and her stomach was growling. A stern man with a bulbous nose and brown hair streaked with gray waved for her to approach the window's ledge. He remained seated, with a card catalog box in front of him.

"Let's see," he said, reaching for the parcel.

She pushed it through the opening. He moved to untie the string, but then looked at the name on the exterior and frowned.

"No location?" He raised an eyebrow at her.

"I don't know where he is," she said, articulating the Russian words.

The man huffed. He set the package aside and began flipping through the cards. He reached the middle of the box, stopped, and reversed course.

"Sorry," he said. "No Evgeni Konstantinov here."

Milly's hands felt detached from her wrists, as if they were about to dissolve.

"What in the hell," she said in English, then switched to Russian. "He's got to be here. He hasn't vanished."

He turned to his right. "Natalia! You have an Evgeni Konstantinov?"

Milly pinched her eyes closed. The air around her stunk of wet wool and human sweat, but every time she started to complain to herself, she remembered Zhenya. Who was probably freezing or starving or maybe even hurt. She took a deep breath. She wouldn't cry in front of this man.

"Evgeni Konstantinov," he repeated. Milly opened her eyes, and he was writing something on the package. "You're lucky Natalia had the new records. Now, let's see what we have here."

He untied the string, folded back the brown paper, and lifted the lid from the box. One by one he removed the loaf of bread, chocolate bar, extra sweater, cooked chicken breast, wrapped pouch of coffee, boots, and pair of wool socks.

"I didn't know . . ." Milly began, but her tongue tripped on the rest of the Russian words. Know what? What to pack for her husband in jail, or that he was going to be arrested? That he could be punished for knowing her? The tears welled up again, and she looked at the floor.

"I should have packed more," she managed.

The man gave a small nod, and she couldn't tell if he agreed or was dismissing the comment. He repacked the box and wrapped everything up again. He handed her a receipt with each item listed.

"I don't have any more information," the clerk said. "Come back in three or four days. Then they'll have his case files."

Milly wanted to give a sharp retort, but again, her Russian failed. She nodded. For now, she'd be the obedient little wife, if that's what would save Zhenya.

She took a deep breath of the humid, onion-scented air of the office, nodded, and walked back through the biting cold to Zhenya's apartment. When she opened the door, Olga's face lit up, only to fall in disappointment when she saw Milly was alone.

"I was sure you would get him out," Olga said. Milly had to curb her irritation; Olga's ignorance was frustrating, but it wasn't the old woman's fault. She hardly left the house, and had no one to talk with except Luba, Victor Pavilovich when he visited, and whomever else was registered to the apartment at the time. Olga stood from the chair in their makeshift kitchen space and went to light the single-burner primus stove. "Soon though, yes? Until then, some tea."

Milly nodded, then pulled off her boots. Exhaustion hung on her back like a load of firewood, begging to be burned, but she had nothing to do with it but collapse. She sat in the other chair by the small table and waited until Olga delivered the steaming black tea to her cold hands.

"No one has asked to search my belongings," Milly said.

Olga frowned. "Why would they?"

"Zhenya was arrested because of something I've done. It must be. A story I wrote, or something I said. I can't think of any other explanation."

"Millichka, if you were the problem, you'd be arrested. Or have your permission revoked." Olga clucked and sipped her tea.

"You mean you think Zhenya actually did something wrong? Had guns?"

Olga placed her tea glass on the table.

"We both know he had no guns. But as for what else he did . . . Did you watch him every moment?"

There was no answering that. Milly and Zhenya hadn't looked for a partnership that bound them tightly—that wasn't what they sought in each other. Or, that's not what they ended up with. Milly took a large swallow of the scalding drink.

A knock banged on the door, and they both leapt to their feet. Olga opened the door, but it was only Victor, returning to share their vigil.

Olga poured him hot water from her tarnished samovar, then added the concentrated tea, and they waited, Victor leaning against the wall while the two women sat. Behind the wall the pipes clanked and moaned in the cold. Milly looked at Victor, and she wondered.

IT WAS FOOLISH, but Moscow was colder than she had expected. At Anna Louise's kitchen table, Milly took her teaspoon and tapped it against the ice that had formed over the pail of milk until the layer splintered and bobbed in the creamy white.

"What a girl has to do to make a decent cup of coffee around here," she said.

Anna Louise Strong, the newspaperwoman who had hired her and with whom she'd been living for a month now, glanced up from the notebook in which she was writing.

"Stop complaining," Anna Louise said. Her handsome face frowned. "The proletariat have no coffee."

Dasha, Anna Louise's maid, shrugged and continued kneading the dough for pelmeni. Flour caked the woman's forearms, and Milly's stomach grumbled, even as she shivered.

"They ever turn the heat on two days in a row here?"

"No," Anna Louise said without looking up. She had a pencil tucked behind her ear and another twirling in her fingers, and her lips were pursed with humming some unending, tuneless song. She was about ten years older than Milly, and, Milly thought, about ten times louder. Which was saying something. But still, Milly was grateful for the place to stay, even if it was frigid, and she was more than grateful for the food to eat. Elsewhere in Moscow people were sleeping under staircases or in hallways, so cramped was the city with newcomers fleeing the countryside. And elsewhere people had to line up for hours to get what little food they could find. Anna Louise, at least, had a prized foodbook, entitling her to access to the class store for journalists and writers. There, they could buy milk deliveries. Even if the milk froze overnight.

"Don't you have work to do?" Anna Louise said, her large, deep-set eyes fixed on her notebook. Without waiting for an answer, she resumed her humming.

Milly harrumphed and finished her coffee as slowly as she could. The last three sips were cold. Anna Louise continued to scratch away at her notebook, and the midmorning winter sky outside the small kitchen window was still dark. Milly dug her elbows into her ribs as she hugged herself, watching Anna Louise write. She wished she could write about herself with the ease Anna Louise did. The woman had a handful of books already to her name and was publishing two more this year alone. Milly had a heart full of ambition and a closet full of news stories—about other people.

"I'll get to it, then," she said in a low voice. Anna Louise didn't seem to hear.

In the cruel cold, the ten-minute walk to the office on Petrovsky Pereulok felt three times as long. *Moscow Daily News* occupied most of a sprawling nineteenth-century mansion that Mikhail Borodin, their chief, had somehow managed to find. One side of the building held the printing presses and the workers' lunch counter, converted from a once-regal bathroom, and there Milly could at least be guaranteed a lunch.

Inside, Milly walked up the perpetually muddied white marble steps of the grand foyer and turned down the hallway until she came to the wide double doors leading to what used to be the mansion's ballroom, once as wide-open as a meadow but these days crammed with reporters, translators, editors, and all their desks.

Though it was quiet now, she knew that wouldn't last. Fortunately. There was no place like a bustling newsroom. Men with their shirtsleeves rolled up smoked endless cigarettes, while women cursed like sailors and banged their fingers against the clattering typewriters. Often in Milly's first month she had seen a young American or Brit or Canadian wander in, wide-eyed and hungry, hoping to land a job by dint of their native tongue and enthusiasm to see Bolshevism's "great experiment."

She didn't speak any Russian, though she was working on it, so she stuck to writing stories about the Americans who came to town. Meanwhile, she tried, and mostly failed, to ingratiate herself with the foreign press corps. Those chummy boys who hired drivers to take them from meeting to office to Russian mistress, and who looked down on the *Moscow Daily News* crowd for being too credulous. As if the rich newspaper owners like Mr. Hearst had ever looked beyond their fancy croquet lawns, tried to see why people suffered and if there might be a better way. Reflexively scorning Soviet efforts was its own form of credulity, she wanted to tell the other newspapermen. But she still wanted to be invited to their parties.

Today, she was in the rotation to stick around and make sure the paper went to bed without any problems. She pulled out the chair by her desk, sat down, then leaned back on the chair's rear wooden legs and kicked her feet up on the desk. She hadn't had her own desk in any of her previous gigs, unless she counted when she was running the paper in Shanghai out of her house for fear of discovery by the authorities. And she didn't count that. Her desk here had her own typewriter, which she had already used to write dozens of letters to her friends back in San Francisco.

"Milly."

Jack Chen, dear boy, stood at the entrance to the room she shared with a few other desks, now empty, and he frowned. His dark curly hair, the legacy of his deceased Guyanese mother, spilled over his forehead.

"You'd better talk to the printer," he said. "He won't listen to me, and they're about to start the press run."

"Again?" Milly craned her head back, so she could see the stains coloring the plaster ceiling, then stood. The team of printers, imported tough guys from Brooklyn, might have been as happy tossing block letters at the printing press as trying to arrange the stories in a reasonable fashion, and their haphazard approach was one of the reasons the foreign correspondents writing for the big papers back home looked down their noses at *Moscow Daily News*.

"We'll sort them out," she told Jack as he led her down the hallway toward the print room.

❖

FIVE MINUTES LATER, Milly stormed out of the print room and, from the hallway, she tossed an angry curse at the stubborn printer over her shoulder.

"I'll call Axelrod!" he yelled back at her. Axelrod, the Russian editor in charge of the operation, could have Milly sent home in a blink.

"Go ahead," she muttered, though she didn't mean it.

Jack looked at her mournfully.

"You tried," he said.

They walked back to the former ballroom, past at least a dozen disconnected porcelain sinks lining the dim hallway.

Milly stepped aside to let one of the translators pass, and she bruised her shin on a porcelain rim.

"Dammit. When're they going to finally clean these?" she asked, rubbing her leg. The sinks had been there since she arrived, awaiting some deep clean that someone thought couldn't be accomplished without removing the sinks from the bathrooms where they had been installed.

Jack shrugged. He had been in Moscow a couple of years and didn't seem to have her neophyte need to find an explanation for everything.

Back in the ballroom, she started to walk toward her desk, then stopped at the coatrack.

"Thank god Charlie Malamuth is tossing a party tonight," she said, and exhaled, trying to shake off the nerves. "You going?"

"Not my scene." Jack ran his fingers through his hair. "Too many Americans and their Russian mistresses."

"I don't have a Russian mistress yet, and I'm going." Milly grabbed her coat from the rack and pulled on her heavy boots. The narrowed looks Jack's dark face elicited from some of the white Americans probably had something to do with his reticence too, but Milly hoped he would come anyway. "Think about it, kid. I hear vodka's tasty. Anyway, I need a walk. I'll be back for the editorial meeting."

Outside the palace, Milly stepped carefully as she walked, avoiding dark patches of ice and frozen lumps of dog shit. A few blocks from the office, she slowed. The cold clawed through her terrible jacket, and her skin tightened as if to block the chill out, but she didn't mind the shivering for a few minutes. She stood on the same block as a bathhouse, where Moscow's many cramped residents fled once a week to try to scrub the stench and grime of communal living from their skins. Three old women with lined faces peeping out from their wrapped heads stood in front of the building, and when people turned toward the bathhouse's double doors, the women would hold up their baskets. A broad-shouldered man with gray encrusting the fringe of his black beard approached one of the women. He pulled off his dirty glove and reached into her basket, from which he extracted, between his thumb and one finger, a sliver of soap. He sniffed it, then replaced it and fished out a second. That one he also sniffed, twice, before returning it. The old woman waited with her face blank, while the woman next to her extended her basket to a mother and her young son who approached. The man finally found a scrap of soap that met his satisfaction, grabbed a coarse wooden bath brush, and handed over his three rubles. About $1.50, Milly knew, enough for lunch back in San Francisco. All for a cake of soap that couldn't sud. Milly's teeth clattered with the cold, and she turned back to the office.

A boy with a dog with matted brown fur stood at the corner. He wasn't begging, exactly, but it was too cold for any child to spend time outside unless he was desperate. Milly shoved her hand into her pocket. She had only one fifty kopek coin, which she had planned to use to buy a cup of tea after work. She would have preferred beer, but she couldn't afford that, and she wouldn't get paid for two more days.

She pinched the coin with her gloved fingers and handed it to the boy. He stuffed it into his pocket without looking at her, but mumbled his thanks, loud enough so she could hear, but quiet enough that no one passing by could accuse him of begging.

She wanted to tell him to hold fast, to believe in the change his country was building. Someday his country would provide a new example to the world, and he and his mutt wouldn't have to shiver on the street corner. Even now, he was better off than the beggars jumping off of bridges in San Francisco. But she didn't have the Russian words, so instead, she gave him a bright smile and walked away, back to the office, where the smile lingered on her face.

❦

BY THE TIME the editorial meeting about the next issue was over and the printing well on its way to being completed, probably with the wrong stories on top, Milly was so tired she wanted to collapse into bed or drink her way into the arms of a charming man.

"Come on, Jack," Milly said as they wrapped themselves in scarves and mittens before leaving the office. "Come to Malamuth's party, it'll be swell."

Jack shook his head.

"Don't laugh, Milly."

"Me, laugh?" She buttoned up her coat and winked.

"I have a study group. I'm going to tackle Marx, really get to understand it. You should come."

"Have you seen those books?" Milly smiled, then took in a deep breath of the office's warm air. "You're right. But I don't usually do what I should. Instead I'm putting on my good hat and finding my way to Malamuth's." For the two years Milly had gone to college, she'd never been any good at keeping up with her homework. Not when dancing on the beach was an option. And now she needed a twirl around a dance floor.

"I can hardly see how that's more fun." Jack held the office door open for her, and they walked down the hallway, past the sinks, and down the stairs. "Maybe once you're ready, you'll join our group. It's like we're learning to see right to the heart of the world."

Milly grasped his hand in her mittened one and shook it.

"That sounds nice, Jack Chen. I hope I learn to see that too."

He laughed and withdrew his hand.

"Have fun at the party tonight." He turned to walk toward the streetcar he took back to the hotel where he and his sisters lived.

"I shall!" Milly yelled to him, causing a few of the passing pedestrians to glance up from their feet as they hurried by.

She wondered if he believed her.
She wondered if she did.

❧

She was wearing her best hat, a sharp black number cocked to the side, when she walked up the steps of the old palace where Charlie Malamuth lived.

"This second husband to Jack London's daughter does all right for himself," Milly whispered to the man ascending the stairs next to her. He was a new international correspondent, if she had to guess, and he nodded. She smiled back. Maybe the new guy would be willing to socialize with her, even if she was with the lowly *Moscow Daily News*. But he kept walking, outpacing her.

Charlie stood at the top of the stairs with a tall woman on his arm and a dinner jacket as black as his slicked-over hair. He greeted first the man ascending the stairs ahead of her, then Milly.

"This is Katya." His companion nodded on cue. "She doesn't speak much English, but isn't she gorgeous? Anyway, come in, make yourself at home. I did!" He laughed, an ugly, proprietary laugh, but Milly loved the honesty of it, so she laughed too.

Inside, the palace was almost as cold as outside, but she stripped her boots off, popped on her heeled shoes, her only nice party shoes, and placed the boots along the wall. A servant took her coat, and Milly shivered and rubbed the goose bumps on her bare arms. She hadn't expected servants here in socialism, but apparently the diplomats and foreign press corps lived by different rules. She wanted to scorn them as cowards, and yet she stood by the coat check touching up her lipstick and hoping her stockings didn't have a run in them. Somewhere in the mansion performers played a folk tune, while guests in the foyer clinked glasses beneath the sparkling French chandelier.

She wished Jack had come, so she'd have at least one friendly face.

She inhaled, plucked a brimming champagne coupe from the tray of a passing servant, and walked toward the sounds of the mandolin coming from down the hall. In the grand ballroom, lights glittered off the gilded mirror walls and winking crystals above. A correspondent she knew waved at her from across the crowd then threaded his way through the ballroom to her side.

"This poor room," Milly said after he'd kissed her cheek.

"What do you mean?" The correspondent, an American named Joe Steinman, drew his thick eyebrows together in an expression that made Milly laugh.

"A room this luscious deserves better than a snaggle of grubby newspapermen. What parties this room has seen." She gave a theatrical spin, then took another sip. She hoped it looked like she was having fun. No one liked a lady who was a drag.

"There's more than newspapermen here, you know. And we're not all grubby." Joe gave a defensive tug to the hem of his dinner jacket. "Over there's the first secretary of the British embassy, and then the fellow in the gray jacket, he's a theater director, and—"

"Cut it out, Joe, I was kidding." Milly placed her empty glass on another servant's tray. The band rolled from its folk tune into a semblance of a waltz, and Milly hauled Joe out onto the dance floor, where he danced better than she'd expected from his thick fingers and big feet, though he was too short for her to want to partner with for long. He'd give her a backache before the party was halfway over.

When the song finished, they went to stand by a few other correspondents, and Charlie Malamuth himself came by with a tray of drinks, but without his curly haired Russian beauty. Milly took one of the small glasses and sniffed it. Clean, with a spark of fruit, almost cherry.

"Vodka," Joe said, holding his own glass. "Haven't you read my book? The drink's not for ladies, it's—"

She poured the bright liquid down her throat.

"Now, that's fine," Milly said, forcing a smile. "How about another dance, Joe?" The new warmth in her stomach felt like it was sparking a fire. That was an improvement.

He frowned, and there, on the uncertainty marking his plain face and the hesitation in his response, Milly saw her loneliness. Her hours hoping for more affection than Anna Louise's rants about some new injustice; her cold walks through this closed-up city that bristled with impenetrable defenses; her afternoons writing letters that no one seemed to receive, or care enough to reply to. Even a grubby newspaperman didn't want to dance with an obviously lonely woman.

The performers switched back to a mournful Russian tune, and Joe shrugged. Milly shrugged too, trying to look indifferent.

Another press man, Tom Uplands, sauntered over and shook both of their hands. He was very drunk.

"Now, this is better than Warsaw," he said as he snatched a glass from a passing servant. Milly replaced her empty one with a full one, but she didn't drink it yet.

"Moscow's a bed of cockroaches, one fat bed of cockroaches," Tom continued. "But at least Charlie knows how to toss a party. He must be making good money writing for those fancy magazines."

"I wouldn't know about fancy magazines," Milly said, then regretted her bitterness. She shouldn't care that the American papers didn't want her writing; what mattered was that the foreign workers here did. The workers here needed her English-language news more than the gentlemen sipping coffee at their breakfast tables in New York.

Tom seemed to ignore her.

"I've got a story for you," he said, his eyes bright. Milly glanced at Joe, who shrugged. "That ugly man there, the one with the whiskers and the bottle in his hand, he's the kind of revolutionary you'd be interested in. Imprisoned in an American jail for being an abortionist! So now he's a hero over here."

Milly tightened her grip on her glass and took a sip. It was two years since she'd had the abortion that had hurt her heart and her womb, far more than she'd expected. Not that she regretted what she'd done, and not that she blamed the doctors, but she wasn't going to champion them either. The room was still cold. Around them swirled laughing couples and plumes of smoke from the cigarettes dangling from elegant fingers.

"Maybe this is the revolutionary story right here," she said. "The revolution that feeds the capitalist bellies of American newspapermen while Russian peasants try to hold their pants up with string, sacrificing to build something better."

"Oh hell." Tom nudged her shoulder. "Don't get serious on us, *Moscow Daily News*."

"Why not?"

He looked at her trying to figure out if she was serious, and she wondered too. She meant what she'd said, but she didn't want to alienate the few American journalists who would talk to her. She rolled her eyes, then gave him a sweet smile in hopes of making up for her outburst.

"I'd better get some fresh air," she said.

Out in the hallway she leaned against the papered wall and rubbed her eyes to ease the sting from the smoke. She had once known how to have fun at a party, hadn't she? Certainly in Hawaii, staying up until dawn drinking and swinging her hips to the music and the surf. Even in San Francisco, at the gin joint. Before Fred told her he and Ann were moving away. Leaving her alone with her scars.

She walked into the billiards room, which was crowded with people talking and no one playing. A smattering of billiard balls lay scattered over the table as if abandoned in the middle of a game. Maybe she could find someone to teach her how to play.

"Have you read my book on Lenin? The second one," a thin man was saying to a blonde woman obviously trying to escape him.

Milly shook her head. Some things never changed.

Joe and Tom had wandered into the room. Milly sighed, and with no one else to talk to, she rejoined them. From the ballroom came the strains of guitar and mandolin, and a mournful voice swinging through the cadence of the song.

"Isn't Gypsy music prohibited?" Milly asked. Maybe they would forgive her the earlier outburst.

"Yes," Joe said. "It creates thoughts." He waggled his eyebrows, and Milly laughed.

"The Party is against Gypsy music, yes," said a man behind her in accented English. Milly turned. A tall Russian man with a lean face and broad shoulders was leaning on the marble mantle. In his loose Tolstoy blouse, he looked like a sculpture of Russian youth. "But the words, you know, are Pushkin." His eyes brightened, and he raised a hand to almost touch his chest. "'In farewell, bind my shawl around me, weave the ends together, as we have been together and now must part. For who can foretell my fate?'"

He gave a flourish with his hand and a small bow.

"Bravo!" Milly clapped. She tried to think of something to say, something about Pushkin or music to ask him about, but he quirked his luscious mouth upward then walked away to join a young man with brown hair.

"I'm starving," Tom said, scanning the room. He beckoned at a servant holding a plate of small sandwiches.

But as she ate, Milly felt the Russian man's gaze on her. Her midsection warmed even more pleasantly than after she'd had the vodka. She took another glass.

There was a piano in the corner of the room, and the Russian began to play. She watched while Joe and Tom compared stories about filthy Moscow hotel rooms and frozen pipes bursting. The Russian sang to his own accompaniment, with a voice that was thin but sweet. Milly sighed, her shoulders sagging from the liquor, the late hour, and her aching feet, and she went to sit in a chair near the piano. There, he couldn't see her while he played. The music, at least, was reason enough for having come to this party.

When he finished, he turned to look at her.

"Americans are not supposed to be unhappy," he said with a half-smile. He had cropped blond hair with loose, handsome waves at the top, and a square chin below his curved lips. His accent rounded out the words, but he was easy to understand.

"And all Americans are supposed to live in New York. Isn't that true too?"

"I only hope all Americans have beautiful parties like this." He swept his arm around.

"I thought building socialism meant ditching brawls like this." She raised an eyebrow, wondering if he would find her provocative, but he smiled again.

"No. This is the life I want. I study and work in the theater so someday I'll live this life. Maybe I'll be a star, like my friend Vera Yergenovna." He pointed at a short, buxom woman standing on the other side of the room.

"You do have a nice voice," Milly said. He did, and she found herself wanting to praise him, to bring the warmth of his gray eyes back to her.

"Do you like music?" He leaned toward her.

"Sure I do. I miss it. The music is the best reason to come to these parties." She blushed at her unexpected honesty, but her companion didn't seem to notice. Instead, he was fishing through the pocket of his dinner jacket.

"My name is Evgeni Konstantinov." He handed her a card. "I will get you a ticket to see the Mussorgsky performance at the end of the month. I'm a super, how do you say it, supernumerary." He pronounced the syllables slowly. "I have always wanted an American friend."

"I'd love to go."

Milly took the card, and when her fingers brushed his, she smiled.

Now

March 3, 1934

It was still dark out as Milly stood in line outside the OGPU building, this time closer to the front. Her feet had numbed inside her boots and layers of stockings, and her efforts to cover her face with her scarf only brought ice crystals to her lips. Her throat burned with cold. She watched the other women, and the few men, and imagined she was doing an article about the lines. She would introduce herself, ask about their feet, offer a slice of sausage. Eventually she'd ask for whom they were carrying twine-wrapped parcels. She glanced over her shoulder at the hunched woman behind her, the woman's black knit cap pulled down to her auburn eyebrows, her eyes dull as she stared at the pavement. Milly grimaced. No one here would talk to a newspaperwoman. And this newspaperwoman was too afraid to write such a yarn anyway; a stunt like that would get her kicked out of the country. Now, more than ever, she needed to stay. No matter what had gotten Zhenya into prison, Milly would certainly be his best advocate for getting out. His Russian friends could do even less.

The sun coughed its way through the heavy clouds, and the line finally began to move.

She had brought some bread and a cold roasted potato, and she ate as the line shuffled forward. No one spoke to her, not even to ask for some of the food, which she would have shared. A streetcar stopped to pick up a crowd of people, and before the mass had finished slithering into the trolley's small mouth, a woman in house slippers with her hair wrapped in curlers came running down the street, shouting at her no-good, cheating, son-of-a-bitch husband. A man with a hat pulled down low pushed onto the trolley, and the doors closed before the woman could reach the car. Someone near Milly gave a small grunt of laughter, but no one else reacted. Milly could understand why. The woman was lucky to have a husband to run after and curse. Still, she found herself grinning. No matter what troubles she and Zhenya had had, no one would find her running down the street with her hair in curlers. Nor was Zhenya the cheating kind, not really. Not like that. Milly kicked a pebble across the sidewalk and into the icy street.

The line's movement stalled once Milly made it inside the building, and she was waiting so long in the cramped hallway she began to sweat under her coat. She took it off and mumbled an apology to the old woman she nearly punched in the process. The woman didn't reply. Once again, Milly wondered what the rules were. After three damn years in the country she still couldn't figure out how to interact with Russians, who seemed both boorish and refined, stoic and dissolute.

Then it was her turn. The clerk frowned and searched three card boxes before finding Zhenya's record.

"I want to see him today," Milly said in Russian. "Three days ago, they told me I could see him today." That wasn't exactly true, but close.

The man with a curly beard behind the window shrugged.

"It is not permitted."

"When can I see him?"

"Come back in four days."

Milly cursed, though she had the presence of mind to do it under her breath and in English. The clerk remained impassive, working with his tongue inside his mouth, probably trying to pry food from his teeth.

"There's been a mistake," Milly said. "I write for the *Moscow Daily News*. I'm here in good standing. Let me explain to someone, anyone, about my husband's case."

The clerk began to write. Milly sucked in a hopeful breath and leaned over to read his note. But he was merely filling out the office's address on an empty card, awaiting the next record, the next crime against the state.

"I want to deliver these to Zhenya," she said. She held the parcel up to the window.

"Down the hall." The clerk pointed with his pen.

Milly pressed her glasses down against her nose, then walked away.

That afternoon, the packages handed over, she returned to the newsroom, where she was overseeing half the large translation team. After correcting one translation's many spelling errors, she threw her pen down and went into Borodin's office. His office was a spacious, wood-paneled room, probably formerly a small library or study, adjacent to the ballroom. It had a window onto Petrovsky Pereulok, from which he could see the gorgeous redbrick theater across the street. She shut the door behind her, and he looked up from his typewriter with one bushy eyebrow raised.

"I'm petitioning the Glavlit about the story they brutalized last week," he said. "Striking out sentences, demanding we publish that cauterized mess of a story. They misunderstood. They can't even read English, and I hate to think they'll start worrying we're counterrevolutionary.

He had dark circles under his light brown eyes, and Milly noted gray hair in his mustache. She had known and admired Mikhail Borodin since they had met in Hankow in 1927, where they were both supporting Sun Yat-sen. Milly had thought then that nothing could be more thrilling than running a newspaper during China's civil war.

"I'm still mad about that swell funny story of mine they threw out," Milly said. She collapsed into the chair facing his desk.

"Which one? You've got a 'swell funny story' every month, Milly, and I swear half of them are removed for good reason."

Milly shrugged and winked. A dot of moisture licked her cheek, and she raised her fingertips to her face, where some snow from her hat was melting. Still, she kept the hat on. It was flattering, much better than her wild hair.

"The coldest winter since Lenin died," Borodin said sadly. Milly looked up, and he was staring out the window at the gusts of wind swirling old snow. Maybe he already knew about Zhenya's arrest. That would save her the pain of telling him, but if he already knew, that meant someone had told him, that people were talking. Or making inquiries.

"We should do a spring series, Borodin." She placed her hands on his desk. "Some pretty feature stories, you'd like that, wouldn't you? The return of the birds. There must be some old lady who feeds the birds."

"That's cheerful for your tastes, Milly. Why not the starving children this time? What are you up to?"

She looked at her fingers, red and chewed.

"Zhenya's been arrested."

"What?" He sat up straight.

"By the OGPU." She wanted to vomit, saying it out loud.

"Zhenya? But he's not in the Party, not involved in politics. Unless—secretly?"

Milly pulled her glasses from her face and pinched her nose. "I don't know why he was arrested. Maybe it's me. That's partly why I wanted to tell you. In case they think I did something."

"Oh hell." He jumped out of his chair and began pacing. She was relieved he didn't already seem to suspect her, but she worried too. He could ban her from going to the OGPU offices, or even transfer her to Leningrad. They had been talking about opening a bureau there, one that she would lead. She had wanted to, but only if Zhenya would come. She wouldn't start over again with no friends, no lovers.

"You haven't done anything. Have you?" He stopped.

"Of course not. Do you think I'd be here relaxing in your office if I were guilty of some sort of counterrevolutionary plot? You know me."

"I do. And you're a firecracker, Milly. I never know what kind of trouble you'll get me in."

Milly flared her nostrils but let the comment pass. After all, Borodin was scared. She had seen his appearance before the Party last fall, in what they called a cleansing. He had nearly lost his job as the Party threatened to make him pay for sins some five years old, from when they were in China.

"What's Zhenya charged with?"

He paused at the edge of his desk and fingered the rim of the clean glass ashtray sitting there.

"They won't tell me." Milly's voice trembled.

"How can we be sure it's safe?"

"What's safe?" Behind her, in the newsroom, someone yelped in pain and then cursed at one of the couriers for spilling coffee.

"For you to be associated. For us." Borodin's forehead was shining with a fresh sheen of sweat.

"Dammit, Borodin. How is this about us? Zhenya has practically vanished!"

"I have to be careful." He paused. "Would you go into exile with your husband? If that's an option."

"What?" Milly looked at him. Perhaps he was joking.

"If he's exiled," he clarified. "Sent to the camps in Siberia."

"People who aren't locked up can go too? What sense does that make?"

Borodin shook his head, disappointed.

"Even under the tsar, women followed their husbands. Cooked, kept them company."

Milly laughed, to relieve the tension. "You've never had my cooking." She hadn't thought that she and Zhenya could both, in a sense, be arrested together. She looked down at her fingers and imagined them entwined with his, while behind her in the newsroom, one of the typists gave a twinkling laugh in response to a man's joke. She didn't want to leave her life, she didn't want to leave her husband. She didn't want that choice at all.

But Borodin continued to frown and turned to look out the smudged window.

"Young people. No loyalty, no sense of the romantic."

"It's not about following him. It's about getting him out."

Milly stood. He wasn't going to give her carte blanche to do what she needed to find out what had happened to Zhenya, that much was clear.

"Maybe I'll write a story on midnight arrests," she said, placing her glasses back on her face. "Smuggle it out for one of the London papers. Who do you think I should interview?"

"God, Milly." His face blanched. "You'd get us all arrested."

"Just tell me who I should talk to about Zhenya's case."

He shook his head. "I don't know. The prosecutor, I'd guess."

"Will you call and find out who that is?"

He pressed his lips together.

"No."

"And if I write that story?" She put her hands on her hips and tried to look imposing.

"You won't."

She kicked his desk, then closed her eyes and tipped her chin toward the ceiling. A rivulet of melted snow shivered down her neck. "What the hell am I supposed to do?"

"Keep your head down, do your job. These arrests, Milly . . . Things are starting to change here. Don't put yourself—and all of us—at risk. For an opera actor. A man you are sort-of married to, who you won't follow to Siberia."

"The hell with you, Borodin."

She walked out and slammed the door.

Quickly, before he could recover his nerves and emerge from his office, Milly walked over to Axelrod, the Russian editor.

"Borodin wants you to call the OGPU," she said. "To ask who is handling a certain case."

"What?" He leaned back in his chair, his close-set eyes blinking.

Milly shrugged, as if indifferent. She bent down and wrote Zhenya's full name on a piece of paper.

"I think that's it. Could you call now? My Russian's not good enough, they wouldn't answer me."

Axelrod glanced between Milly and Borodin's closed door. Her pulse raced.

"I don't know why he can't do it himself," Axelrod grumbled, then picked up the phone. He gave the operator the numbers for the OGPU headquarters.

Milly held her breath.

BEFORE

MAY 1931

A HINT OF sweet warmth crested the spring breeze, and a stout woman in black carrying an armload of white lilac blossoms took a wary step away from Milly when they passed on the sidewalk.

"Zakaznee, purzhatsda, daitche . . ." Milly continued muttering, now a little louder for the benefit of the woman receding behind her. Perhaps Milly was mad, after all, to try to mail her own registered letter at the Soviet post office. But she wouldn't always have Dasha, Anna Louise's maid, to do the work for her. Lord, she hoped she wouldn't be living with Anna Louise much longer. She needed to figure out how to live on her own. If she could mail her own letters, she could feel freer to write more to her friends back home. And then she'd feel less lonely.

The trees were finally sprouting tentative green leaves, even if city workers were still carving ice blocks out of the river to chill the Muscovite iceboxes and cellars. She seemed to have survived her first Russian winter, and she reveled in the heat that her brisk stride generated. Now that winter no longer pummeled her into submission, she could get out more, and finally find some groundbreaking stories to write about.

Milly crossed the bustling Pushkin Square and headed toward the old Strastnoy monastery, which now housed the Godless Museum. That had been a fun Easter tour, first the Godless Museum with its rotting exhumed saints, and then a quiet Orthodox ceremony in a church at the top of a hill. If only the censors had let her publish that write-up, with its delicious contradictions, the state that disdained religion and yet permitted it. Milly had loved the complexity in that story, the notion that the Bolsheviks couldn't stand religion, yet they cared enough for the people to let them retain their rituals. Well, they hadn't let her publish it, but she kept the story's draft. Maybe she could get the story out to an international paper somehow and publish it anonymously.

The post office was in a small building behind the monastery, and she recited her memorized words one more time before pushing the door open. Learning how to get around was the first step in understanding this new world.

But when she entered, nothing looked as she remembered. The wire wicket enclosing the postmaster's perch was torn down, and instead of the red-cheeked man with the brown mustache, a young woman sat behind a desk. A drawing of a rodent with soulless eyes hung on the otherwise bare wall behind her.

"Post office?" Milly mumbled in Russian.

The young woman shook her head sadly.

"No," she said in accented English. "The post office it has moved. This is Soviet Mousetrap Commission."

Milly giggled.

"That figures, doesn't it," she said to the bewildered woman in English. The Soviets had a commission for everything, and she loved their ambition to solve even the smallest problems. She switched back to Russian and asked, as well as she could, where to find the current location of the post office. After a few confusing exchanges, the woman wrote down an address on Marx and Engels Pereulok.

"You see," Milly told Anna Louise when she returned home. "That's Moscow for you. Changing, never fixed."

"Is it?" Anna Louise didn't look up from the letter she was banging out, one finger at a time on the typewriter in her room, where they sat to eat dinner.

Milly bit her lip.

"Can you believe him?" Anna Louise bellowed as she pulled her letter out of the typewriter. Without waiting for Milly's response, Anna Louise leapt to her feet and paced through the room, complaining loudly about some American writer who had criticized her latest book.

Milly waited until the other woman took a breath.

"Anna Louise," she said.

Anna Louise's deep-set eyes skittered around the room, as if unsure where the sound had come from, and then she pinched tight the nostrils on her finely shaped nose. Her best feature, Milly thought.

"Anna Louise, I'm ready to take that trip. That factory you mentioned in Nizhny."

"The Ford factory?" She frowned, and the lines alongside her mouth dug deeply into her flesh.

"Sure, that one." It didn't matter where, Milly just needed to see what was happening with Soviet socialism outside of Moscow. Anywhere where the real revolution in industrialization was taking place.

"I'll talk to Borodin about it."

"Did he tell you the Vorobey story?" Milly continued. Anna Louise shook her head and sat back down at her typewriter.

"We were having lunch at that hole around the corner, you know, the cooperative restaurant where they hand you a spoon when you walk in, and that's all you have to eat with? Then you have to hand it back when you leave. On account of the theft."

Milly watched Anna Louise for a reaction, hoping she would at least smile in acknowledgment of some of the hardships of communitarian living. Milly loved Moscow—the thrill of a new culture, the passion of a people dedicated to building something unprecedented—but hell, it wasn't perfect. For every gaggle of smiling young women reveling in women's newfound rights, there was a bent-backed man going from door to door, looking for a stoop to sleep on since there weren't enough rooms. Anna Louise didn't look up from her typewriter, but merely waved a hand for Milly to continue the story.

"Never mind," Milly said. The story about some silly peasant misunderstanding wasn't worth the disappointment of throwing herself against Anna Louise's indifference. "I'm going out for a stroll. I'll find my former palace dweller, and he'll show me around."

She grabbed her cardigan from the row of hooks along the far wall and stuffed her feet into her favorite pair of comfortable heels, low square affairs that could carry her miles if she had the mind. Her walks with the opera actor past old parks and darkened churches often lasted that long.

"It's late, isn't it?" Anna Louise looked up, blinking like a mole in daylight.

"Moscow's white nights, lovey." Milly splashed a hand toward the window.

With that she left, biting off the retort about Anna Louise's self-absorption and resisting the temptation to bait her roommate with another mention of the formerly bourgeois opera performer she was going to meet. The handsome young man from the party, whom Anna Louise wouldn't approve of, solely because the Soviets didn't approve of him. All because the boy's father was a rich man before the revolution. Milly closed the apartment door behind her, the heavy wood echoing down the hall. She shouldn't get angry at Anna Louise, who had gotten Milly her job, her bed, her food. But still. The other day Anna Louise had told Milly that the true remedy for loneliness was propaganda, because it guides people and gives them a sense of being part of something larger. "Stop trying to make friends. Set your sights on the cause," Anna Louise said while pecking away at the keys on her typewriter at home. It was enough to make a woman spit. Now Milly gritted her teeth, then forced a smile when one of the four young women sharing a room down the hall stepped out of their apartment as Milly passed. Milly didn't have enough Russian yet to talk to her neighbor, not unless Milly wanted to inform her "there is a black cat in the alley." But, someday.

Outside, the setting sun licked the sky and glazed it in a strawberry glow. Milly exhaled, and paused to enjoy the view. Then she did a little shimmy with her hips and went to meet Evgeni.

❦

MILLY HOOKED HER arm through Evgeni's, though his height meant she had to tilt her elbow upward to fit. She smiled looking up at him, and his cheeks glowed as he pointed down the street.

"That's one of the finest baths in Moscow," he said. "The Central Baths. The building was owned by a, how do you say it, cloths maker. The finest dancers in the Bolshoi go there." His eyes glittered in the golden summer light, and Milly pulled his elbow closer to her ribs.

"Have you been?"

"Not yet," he said, more excited than resigned. "Only the right people get permission to enter."

"And someday you will," she suggested.

"Someday. After all my singing lessons, and I get voice roles."

"Are you trying out soon?"

He pointed across the street.

"A famous writer lived there, on the other side of that building." A large arched portico opened to a two-story gallery. "Someday people will note where you lived."

She snorted. "I don't think so."

He stopped walking and released her elbow so he could turn to face her. His young skin was tanned and fine. She wanted to rise up on her tiptoes and kiss his lips, but instead he furrowed his brows at her.

"You do not know what the future brings," he said. "And having a belief in the future is important."

"I do believe in the future," she said, but her voice sounded tinny. "Evgeni, I'm—"

"Call me Zhenya. My friends do." He lowered his chin.

"Zhenya." The name sounded like a breeze on her tongue. "I've seen too much to believe in my future. My first job was writing about murders and fires in San Francisco, and from there it's only gotten bloodier. Until here, that is."

"See?" He waved at the sky. "It is already better. Looking up." He began walking again, and she followed. "It is not as if my life has been easy," he continued, his voice low. "After my father died, I thought my mother would too. We lost almost everything, and we lived in the hallway until the house committee took pity on us. But I am lucky. My mother is happy for me to be in the opera. So why will my luck not continue?"

He didn't wait for an answer, but quickly began pointing out other historical buildings. The Metropol Hotel she knew already, and the mountainous Karl Marx monument as well. But she let him talk, as if his enthusiasm could spin a cocoon around them, and she slipped her hand into his.

※

TWO DAYS LATER, Borodin surprised her with a rail ticket and a pass to the Ford factory in Nizhny Novgorod.

Milly kissed him on the cheek, then laughed at his shocked expression. "I'll bring you back a darling of a story, don't fret." She stuffed the papers into her breast pocket and sped from the newsroom as quickly as possible. She had a suitcase to pack and a train to catch.

In the apartment, she dumped out the contents of her purse onto her hard bed and cursed when she saw the ticket from last night's opera, *Lohengrin*. Her charming Russian friend had been acting in the performance, so he got her a ticket, and she had clapped wildly when he showed up onstage holding the queen's train. She loved how the seats around her were filled with soot-smudged workers and bent-backed grandmothers: people who never would have seen the opera before socialism. Afterward, she told Zhenya he carried a jaunty train for the queen, better than the soprano with the cracked cadence deserved, and though he didn't understand the slang, he laughed and held her hand. She had promised to meet him again tomorrow, but now she would be out of town. She scribbled a quick note on the back of the ticket, then ran out to ask Dasha if she would call him later.

"Please?" Milly asked the exasperated maid. "I don't know how to say the Russian numbers on the phone, and I don't have time now for you to teach me."

Dasha huffed.

"Fine."

Milly rushed to pack, and she made it to the station in time to jump onto the train before the doors closed. She smiled as the train rolled away. Now she would see the real socialism, the real work being done to launch the Soviet Union into the twentieth century and beyond.

When she arrived at the Nizhny Novgorod station, her guide met her on the platform and escorted her silently to the automobile. Milly sat in the front seat like a gaping child, her hand clinging to the door and her forehead nearly touching the cold glass of the window. They passed under the tall brick gate fortifying the entrance, as if the grounds held an ancient castle, not a car factory still under construction.

While she toured the workers' housing and the factory itself, Milly was buffeted by the demands and petty rivalries. The German plumbers wanted her to deliver their ultimatum for higher wages; the American engineers told her she couldn't possibly take that rag *Moscow Daily News* seriously; the Canadian housewives tried to elbow one another out of the way for the best choice of new employee cabins the management had built. A nest of grievances that Milly had to shape into a sculpture of success. Fine, she could do that. She could see what they were aiming for, see the skeleton of productivity beneath the haze of their frustrations. They sought the impossible, in a way, industrializing a countryside forgotten by time and tsars, and the workers were managing it. Milly scribbled notes into her notebook. The more she thought about the story, the more excited she grew. Yes, the foreign workers were facing difficulties. But they were in Russia, sweating to create something the world had never seen before.

While pacing the train platform in Nizhny, waiting for her return train to arrive, Milly ran through the lines of her story. Building a new economy was a challenge, and these workers had grievances to air. But they weren't leaving. Maybe that would be the first sentence of her story. She paused to roll the words around, and she felt a subtle prickling along the back of her neck. She turned.

Behind her stood a tall man with a dark beard cresting his jawline, and he smiled.

"You must be American," he said in accented but easy English as he approached. "So much energy, so much movement." He lazed his hand back and forth in the air, gesturing across the platform.

"You'd better watch out," she said with a wink. "The energy's contagious. Want to try?" She held out her hand before she knew what she was doing, and as her upturned palm waited, and waited, the mild evening air cooling her skin, a heat rushed to her cheeks. She hadn't brushed her hair all day, she remembered, and she had forgotten her lipstick.

She waited, hand extended to a stranger.

He stepped forward and laid his hand in hers.

She tugged him playfully to and fro, then gave him a quick, suggestive demonstration of the hula dance she had learned in Hawaii. When they boarded, she stayed in the crowded train passageway and giggled with him as the farms rolled by. The train was overbooked, and she didn't have a sleeping compartment, so the Russian insisted she take his. He would sleep with the porter, he said.

When she woke up, she found him standing again in the passageway. He was the director of construction at the Nizhny Novgorod plant, he said, and he knew she had come to write about it. But he didn't want to talk about work. He placed a hand on her lower back, and when the train entered a tunnel, he reached up to tuck her hair behind her ear. Her skin tingled where his fingers touched. Then, he kissed her. She ran her hands around the back of his neck to pull him in deeper, but then the train jerked to a stop. She stumbled away from him, and they both laughed.

"Here we are," he said, gesturing out the window at the Moscow platform that seemed to have come from nowhere.

"Fancy a stroll?" Milly asked. She picked up her bag, and they began processing down the crowded passageway toward the train exit.

"Ah, I can't tonight." His face grew grim. She looked at the ground. She knew that look, the I-have-a-wife look.

They stepped down from the train, and there, on the platform, stood her handsome opera actor with a large bouquet of flowers in his elegant fingers. He smiled brightly upon seeing Milly, but the smile faded into confusion when he glanced at the man holding her elbow.

"Looks like you're spoken for, for tonight anyway," the man said in a low voice.

"Who says a girl can't have two escorts?" She was hoping he would laugh and let her feel wanted, but he stayed quiet.

He raised an eyebrow as Zhenya approached, his blond head bowed and his shoulders slumped.

"I guess I do. Especially when one companion is . . . that type. Good day, Citizen Milly."

Milly lifted her chin in a jaunty farewell, then sighed. It was amazing how the bolshies could spot a former bourgeois from a mile away.

"Milly," Zhenya said, then grabbed her hand to kiss it. He traded her the flowers for her valise and nudged her toward the station's exit.

"My broken flower," she said in a low voice, a soft smile on her face as she looked at him.

"You like the flowers?" he replied.

"Sure." Milly linked her free arm in his. "Where to?"

"We take your bag home," he said. "Then, a walk?"

"Only if it ends with a smooch," she said. "I'm dying here."

"Smooch?" He turned the corners of his mouth down as he considered the strange word. They reached the sidewalk outside the station, and a brisk breeze nearly blew Milly's hat from her messy hair.

"That's right. You'll see." She tapped her finger on his smooth chin. At least this man wasn't rejecting her right after a kiss. Not that they had kissed. Yet.

He laughed, squeezed her arm tighter, and led her through the mass of people on the sidewalk.

❖

MILLY MADE IT home in time to sleep hours of fretful dreams where she longed for hands that would never quite touch her. She awoke in a sweat. By her feet, the cat Anna Louise had adopted a few months ago lifted his head and gave her a reproachful look.

"I may as well join the Party if I'm this committed to mortifying my flesh," she said to the cat. He regarded her with wary yellow eyes, then hopped off the bed.

"Even you don't take me seriously," she said.

At the office, she pulled her twenty-two typewritten pages of notes from her trip and sat down with Axelrod.

"I've got a good story in here," she said. She tapped her finger on the pages. "There's practically a little war down there, between the Russians and the Americans. Calling one another dogs and the sort. But they're all sticking with it, you see? Building socialism in spite of the tensions." She spread out the papers across his bare desk, her heart thumping with pride. This was the important sort of story she had come to Moscow to write—how reality was messy, but people still worked hard. No more fluff pieces about visiting movie stars. "What do you think?"

He lifted the glasses he kept hung around his neck and propped them on his nose while he glanced up and down the pages. His brown hair glittered with silver, and she could see where it was thinning into scalp.

"What sort of story?" He looked up and said the worlds slowly, as if with difficulty, though Milly had heard him yell with fluency enough.

"A regular yarn, a story about he said, the other fella said, you know. But ending with inspirational quotes from here." She pulled out the last five pages of notes, where she had compiled the positive things. "Readers will love it." This was her first chance to write something interesting, with real color, something that showed both the difficulty and the hope of industrialization. She nudged one of the pages toward him.

He turned his head down to the notes again, and Milly listened to the hum of the small desk fan blowing from an empty bookshelf behind him. She began to sweat.

"This part." He jabbed a finger.

Milly leaned over. He was pointing to her interview with the vice president of the American company supervising the construction of the facility.

He lowered his glasses.

"These statements are counterrevolutionary. I want to use these notes. Give them to the stenographer to copy."

"What?" The sweat now slicked down her ribs, and certainly through her cotton blouse.

"Emma, the stenographer." He frowned at Milly, his lower lip sticking out in disgust.

She nodded, collected her papers, and stood. She left the newsroom before he could say another word, then rushed down the hall with the notes folded and tucked into her blouse.

She threw open the washroom door, then locked herself inside. The room was dark and smelled of urine. She fished out the interview with the company vice president, tore it to bits, and flushed it down the john with a few tugs of the toilet chain.

When she opened the door, she yelped.

"Lord, Ruth, you scared me. Standing so close."

"I thought that was you in there." Ruth's blue eyes warmed as she smiled. She was just a few years older than Milly, and she had been in the Soviet Union for almost a decade. "Just listening for when you were done."

"Did the boss send you to check on me? To sign me up for espionage?"

"What?" Ruth gave her a screwed-up look. "You're out of your mind. Come on, I heard there were strawberries in the dining room today, and I wanted to give you a shot at them. Let's see if there are any left."

Ruth was one of the few female American writers on the staff, and Milly had sensed a camaraderie almost as soon as Milly joined the paper. But with all the bustle of newspaper life, they never seemed to find time to do more than roll their eyes at each other behind the bosses' backs or laugh when one or the other wadded up a botched story and missed her throw into the wastebasket.

"Sounds swell." Milly glanced toward the newsroom, where Axelrod was standing in the door watching. She waved a hand as if to beg for a delay, then followed the other woman down the stairs. Ruth had spent some eight years in a commune in Siberia, and both her Russian and her sense of irony were sharp.

When they got to the cafeteria, where grease dimmed the white bathroom tiles that lined the large room, the lunch lady behind the counter held up a hand, shooing them away.

"All the strawberries were bought up by earlier diners," she explained, shrugging.

"Some community spirit," Milly grumbled as they stared at the empty lunch counter.

"Those're the shakes," Ruth replied, shrugging. She took a bowl of cold soup from the lunch lady and led the way to a table in the dining room. Milly followed suit. Outside the tall windows, cars and crowds flowed past.

"You're back from Nizhny?" Ruth said, a chunk of black bread in her mouth.

"That's right." Milly groaned. "Fat lot of good it'll do me. Axelrod paid for all that travel for a story he now doesn't want me to write. And now I'm hiding from him. But it's a good story, I know it."

"A Newspaper Enterprise Association fella, he put in an order for an Austin Company story with me. Isn't that the company down there? But I haven't been to the complex yet." She raised a suggestive eyebrow.

Milly laughed. "That sweet face will get you anywhere, won't it."

Ruth smiled. "What do you say, Milly? We'll split it even. Your notes, my NEA order."

"Do I look like I can turn down free money?" Milly pointed at a frayed buttonhole at the top of her blouse. But it was more than the money. If Ruth could help her get this story out, then maybe the trip wasn't a bust. Maybe the story would resonate, garner sympathy for the workers, and Axelrod would see he had been wrong to shackle her.

"A match made in heaven," Ruth said with a smile. She raised her water glass, and they clinked.

"Perfect." Milly drank. "But later, we'll have to seal the deal with something stiffer."

"I know a place." Ruth took another long sip and winked.

THE NEXT MORNING, still nursing her head from the combined assault of the vodka and Anna Louise's early morning yelling on the phone about some lost paperwork, Milly walked into the newsroom.

"Miss Bennett?" The young assistant to Axelrod stood with his hands clasped around a spiral notepad. "Those notes? From yesterday." His English had a British accent layered over Russian, and he blushed as he spoke.

"I lost 'em," Milly mumbled.

"You're sure?"

"Yup."

"I'll have to tell the boss."

"Are you sure?" she asked, but her voice was too low, and he was already gone.

She slunk away to her desk, where she picked up the translation she had to copyedit. It would be her luck to get kicked out of Moscow right when she was starting to make her way. She'd be seeing her opera actor soon, and maybe this idea of Ruth's had wings. Milly pressed her pencil to scratch out a misspelling, and the lead broke. She slid her fingers under her glasses and rubbed her eyes.

Now

March 7, 1934

A string bag weighed down with potatoes hung on Milly's arm while she fumbled with the key to Zhenya's apartment, trying to jam it one-handed into the door.

The door opened, and Olga's lined face lit up with hope then crashed in disappointment at recognizing Milly. Milly's eyes tightened as she fought back tears.

"I've brought potatoes," she said in Russian as she stood. Small recompense for a son's absence, but she wanted to help.

"Come in. Luba was here, but you've missed her." The older woman left the door hanging open as she walked past the curtain marking Luba's private space, and she collapsed into one of the chairs at the shared table. Milly swung the door shut and tried to maneuver between Luba's hanging sheet and the two stacks of boxes to her right. But, as usual, she smashed her knee into the wooden crate that held Zhenya's father's old books.

"For you," Milly said as she laid the string bag of potatoes under the sink basin. A pile of wrinkled onions sat there too. "I'll get the bag back from you later."

Olga waved her hand toward the other chair, then stood up to boil some water on the primus stove.

"They arrested Victor Pavilovich today," she said in a mournful voice. She reached into a cabinet hung above the sink and extracted two teacups. "And Sorokin too. You know him?"

Milly frowned and blinked in confusion.

"Victor? You're sure?"

"Of course I'm sure," Olga said, her voice sharp.

Zhenya's friends shouldn't be caught up in his troubles, not if his troubles were really because of his connection to Milly. Though, it had been over a week since Zhenya's arrest, and no OGPU officer had been to interrogate her or search her room. Not that she knew.

"They're both at the theater. I only know Sorokin a little. I haven't seen Victor since the night Zhenya was . . . They've both been arrested?"

Olga poured the water into a cracked teapot, sprinkled in some tea leaves, and waited.

"I went to see Victor this morning, and the woman on the house committee for his building told me. Then Luba told me about Sorokin, whoever he is. Oh, Millichka." Her voice caught, and she pinched her eyes tight before taking a deep breath and then turning her attention to pouring the hot water from the samovar into the tea. The scent of it was bracing, and when she placed Milly's glass on the scratched wooden table, Milly let the steam curl up and over her eyelids. Her lenses fogged.

"I'm sorry," she said.

Olga sat. "You are blaming yourself."

"What else can I do? They never would have noticed him if he weren't married to a newspaperwoman who's written some . . . well, the censors haven't always liked my stories." Milly took her eyeglasses off and squeezed the bridge of her nose.

THE NEXT MORNING, Milly bundled herself up against the March cold and began the walk to the Lubyanka building, the massive OGPU headquarters down the street from Olga's apartment. Milly hadn't asked if Olga avoided walking past that block and its army of windows and faux columns molded into the yellow brick facade. She would, if she lived a block away.

A newspaper boy strutted past, hawking his broadsheet, and Milly bought one. Perhaps it would distract her if she had to wait. As she walked, she mouthed her way through reading the Russian headlines—she found she could understand things better if she at least pretended to say them out loud. But when she got to the story at the bottom of the sheet, she stopped. Her mouth hung open, until she read it again.

"Anti-Homosexuality Law Promulgated," it read.

Milly balled the paper up and threw it against the stone wall.

MILLY DUCKED UNDER the building's portico, just out of the autumn rain, and yanked one of the store's large double doors open. Inside the Torgsin store, reserved solely for people paying in gold or foreign currency, Milly strutted to the back, where Torgsin stocked their simple wine selection. Tonight, after enduring the stern-faced inquiries of the Party's Writers Union, she deserved a treat. She pointed to a bottle, asked the clerk the price, then took the proffered invoice to a cashier to pay. While she was waiting in line to hand over her precious dollars and then claim her wine, Milly spotted an associate editor from the newsroom. She waved to him.

"Charles! I got in!" She pulled out her Writers Union card and flashed it under his nose. Now, as a member, she would have her own foodbook and access to the subsidized stores. Her chest felt so effervescent with excitement she almost believed she would float away.

"Congratulations." His thick black hair was brushed back from his forehead, and his dark eyes were still. Charles tapped the card with his fingertip. "A celebration is in order, then."

"A celebration?" Milly raised an eyebrow and put one hand on her hip. She was willing to flirt with the stern-faced man, but she was pretty sure he wasn't interested in her—or any dame, for that matter.

"A beef steak and soda pop. A proper soda pop." He wasn't smiling, but his voice was light.

She ran her tongue over her lips. "I haven't had a soda pop in, lord, I don't know how long. I'll accept that challenge," she said. "After I buy this bottle here to make up for what's sure to be a doomed quest. Soda pop in this city . . ." She clicked a mocking disapproval, but Charles merely nodded, then inclined his head toward the waiting clerk behind the counter. Milly paid for her wine.

"You weren't really going home to drink that alone, were you?" Charles said as they stepped out of the store and onto the dark, rainy street. A passing car sent up a spray that mottled Milly's legs with water.

"You assume I have no friends, Charles? Come on." She hoped he didn't notice how her cheeks had flushed. He was close enough to the truth. But maybe, if he was willing to go out with her, her luck might be turning in more ways than earning a spot in the Writers Union.

"No, I don't assume so," he said. He flicked his eyes back and forth between the cars while they waited to cross.

"For your information, I was going to find Ruth." There was at least one friend Milly had, or so she hoped. The women had succeeded in sneaking Milly's story out, and they had big plans for more collaboration. So long as they didn't get caught publishing prohibited yarns. "Going back to my room is a wash, anyway. Anna Louise is lending her other room to a minister, and he's the worst air bag I've ever met. Makes my blood boil."

They crossed, then Charles glanced down a side street, apparently looking for something specific. When he didn't find it, he turned to her.

"Not the religious type?"

"Me? Well, no, but that's not the problem. Do you want to hear what this guy is up to? He's got some nerve." She was talking too much, she realized, but the combination of nerves and excitement had left her mouth utterly off its leash.

Charles took her elbow and steered her down the next cross street. A frisson of attraction buzzed up her arm, into her throat, and she glanced at him. He was thin, like her ex-husband, with long lashes.

"The fellow's gutless, I tell you," she continued.

"Hold that thought, here's the joint I was looking for. Let's see if they have soda pop. Wait here, and I'll check."

Charles had been in Moscow for at least half a year longer than Milly, and his Russian was undoubtedly better. Still, Milly didn't like being left behind. She tapped her foot on the damp pavement while Charles stood inside the glass door, talking with a frowning Russian man. At least the rain had lessened.

"No luck," he said when he emerged, his hat pulled down to keep the scattered raindrops from his eyes. "But I've got another idea, two blocks from here. You still game?"

"Sure," Milly said, though she wasn't sure that she was. Charles seemed more interested in finding the meal than actually talking to her. She hugged her arms to herself and felt the rain sneak inside her collar and down her neck, while she gripped the wine bottle tightly.

"What about that preacher?" Charles asked.

Milly smiled.

"He's staying with us, doing some sort of research. We get word that a young American girl died while in Moscow. Hit by a car, and the poor thing died on the spot. Her parents were in London, and they came as soon as they could. All her family wants is a prayer for their sweet girl before they bury her body in foreign soil. The mother heard about our friend the preacher, so she came over."

Charles again nudged her elbow around a corner, then pulled her to a stop as they waited for a streetcar to splash past. They crossed and headed toward a door with a single globed light reaching out above the entrance.

"The preacher told her no. Religion is banned here, so no. I'm standing right there, crying to hear this poor mother's wish for her dead girl, and all he can do is wring his hands and tell her he won't jeopardize his position. He can't risk violating the ban on preaching, he can't risk getting thrown out. Not with so much research left to do. And the mother is sobbing, begging him to say a prayer over her dead daughter's body."

Anger at the memory filled Milly again, and she clenched her teeth. What a coward. If she ever had to make a risky choice like that, going against the authorities, she'd sure as hell make the brave choice.

"Let me try this place," Charles said, once they reached the illuminated door. "Restaurant," read a painted sign in four different languages.

"I'm going too," Milly said. He opened his mouth to protest, but Milly waved a hand. "How else am I going to learn this damned language, if I don't get to hear people using it?"

He tilted his head, then held out the door for her.

Inside, the restaurant was dark and smelled of sautéed onions. A fat woman stood up from a table where she was knitting, then planted her hands on her hips. A few tables were occupied, but the room was hushed.

Charles asked something quickly, of which Milly understood "beef steak" and "soda pop." The woman nodded and indicated for them to take a table.

"Did he, then?" he asked once they were seated in wooden chairs that creaked with every movement.

"Say the prayer?" Milly shifted her weight, hoping the chair wouldn't collapse. She left the wine bottle on the floor, by her feet. "No. I ended up suggesting another minister, one from Germany. He did it. Gutless phony, my roommate is."

A waiter came and placed two glasses with brown bubbly liquid in front of them.

"Is it beer or cola?" Milly gave Charles a half smile. "I guess at this point I'd take either." She sipped, then tipped her head back in appreciation. Sweet soda pop sparkled in her mouth. "Well done, my champion. This is a rare treat."

"One of the downsides of socialism," Charles said as he put his glass back on the gray tablecloth. "Not much cola to be had."

"Yet. Right?" The Soviet Union was struggling now, but she could see how people's lives were getting better. Already there was a little more food in the markets, and little restaurants like this one were opening. Soon everyone would have soda pop.

"You think socialism's the way the world is going, Milly?" He leaned back in the complaining chair and crossed his arms loosely.

"I hope so. Hearing from friends back home . . ." She sighed.

"I know. It's a damned shame. My brother lost his job at the store where he sells shoes and motor oil and whatever else he could convince people to buy. Sent home without so much as a thank-you or a can of beans to feed his four kids."

"That's rotten," Milly said. She looked at her soda pop with some guilt. Why should she have pop when there were kids going hungry in America?

"This is some talk," she said. "Tell me something funny."

Charles blinked, as if confused, and was saved when the waiter delivered two plates of overcooked beef to the table.

"At least this place gives you a knife," Milly said as she sawed into hers. If Charles wouldn't make her laugh, maybe she could get a smile out of him.

"You mean like that spoon place?" He frowned, then put a small piece of steak into his mouth and chewed. She watched, thinking of Zhenya. Maybe she could find him tonight and get more than a kiss.

An old man pushed open the door of the restaurant and angled himself through, as if opening the door fully was too difficult. His hunched shoulders glistened with rain, and water dripped from the brim of his cap. He reached inside his jacket and pulled out a small bunch of poppies.

"Look at that," Milly said. She inclined her head toward the old man.

"Eh?" Charles's mouth was full of steak.

"He's got to be a broken member of the bourgeoisie. Look how he carries himself."

The old man approached their table and held out the poppies, which had begun to wilt.

"Buy a flower for the lady," he suggested in slow, clear Russian.

"How much?" Charles held an empty fork aloft.

"Twenty-five kopeks."

"That's too much, old man," Charles said. "For one flower? I could buy a glass of wine for that much."

"Bad wine," Milly said in English.

The old man glanced at her, but gave no sign he understood.

"How about fifteen?" Charles suggested. He speared another cube of beef but let his hand hover over his plate.

The man shook his head, and Charles shrugged. He popped the beef in his mouth and looked away from the man.

"I'll take one," Milly said in Russian. She fished the coins from her purse. The old man smiled, and his blue eyes were soft and rheumy.

"Thank you, my dear. I hate to have to ask for anything. Here." He handed her two flowers. "In gratitude." He spoke slowly enough for her to understand, then turned to extend his sad poppies to the other diners. No one else bought one, and he tucked the cluster of flowers back into his jacket and shuffled out into the rain.

Milly shook her head.

"I love this country, Charles. But why? Why should a well-mannered old man have it so rough? Because of who he was."

"It's not like there aren't beggars in America."

She nodded and fingered the red petals. "But this is socialism. They should know how to do better."

"Not yet, I guess."

They spent the rest of the meal mostly chewing, and Milly occasionally tried to elicit some sort of conversation with him by bringing up the censors at the paper, whom usually everyone liked to complain about, or Anna Louise herself, whom people often wanted to ask Milly about—what does she read, where does she go when she travels, when is her next book coming out. But Charles mostly had polite murmurs and the rasp of his knife against the plate.

When they laid their rubles on the table to pay, Milly timed hers so she could brush her fingers against Charles's. But he gave no reaction, and she almost sighed audibly. Zhenya would have taken her hand to kiss it.

They walked the few blocks in the damp night to Anna Louise's street. When they reached the narrow street with Anna Louise's building, Milly paused.

"That looks like an OGPU car," she said, pointing at a black sedan parked one building down from hers.

"Sure does." Charles shook his head. Two smartly dressed officers got out and entered one of the neighboring buildings.

"Poor Ruskies," Milly said in a low voice. "They had the habit of a pampered police, and they couldn't break it. Couldn't do without the Cheka, no matter what they call 'em now."

She shivered in the damp cold, and the wine bottle almost fell from her hands, until she clutched it to her chest.

THE NEXT NIGHT, Milly went to the opera. She wore the only nice dress she had in her closet, which was at least as fine as the feeble imitation European evening dresses some of the other ladies wore, while others, the Communists or workers maybe, milled about the gilded lobby of the Bolshoi in their simple linen frocks or heavy wool skirts. It had been a long day spent tracking down some American professor of economics visiting to assess, measure, and judge Soviet Communism, and since Anna Louise said he was famous, Milly had to interview him. What a stuffed shirt that one was, and she'd had to turn his conceited sniffing into something of a yarn. When Zhenya had called the office to say he could get her a ticket to the night's show, she jumped at the chance. Ruth had overheard and interrupted the conversation before Milly could hang up, so the two of them had orchestra section seats for *Carmen*. Milly reveled in the sloppy circus of it all, the stockings striped with runs, the unshined shoes, the ill-fitting evening dresses, and the pickled smell of vodka.

Zhenya had left their tickets at the box office with a note wrapped around them. The young woman working there winked when she handed over the tickets, and Milly blushed.

"What's that say?" Ruth said, leaning over Milly's shoulder.

"He says he's so grateful that I came."

"Did he call you his baby? What's that there?"

Ruth tried to snatch the paper, and Milly blushed. She crumpled it up.

"He's terribly sweet," she said. She looked at the ball of paper in her fist and hoped he was more than sweet too.

They found their seats and watched as the motley crowd wound its way into the opera hall. The orchestra was quietly whining and moaning as it warmed up, and a few of the yellow lights on the wall flickered in and out behind their crystal sconces, as if they too were preparing for the performance.

Some rows ahead of where Milly sat, a tall, slender woman in a black velvet gown bowed down and whispered something to a man in his seat. After a moment, the man produced a crumpled ruble note and dropped it into a red pail the woman held out.

"They ask for donations here?" Ruth said.

"I've never seen that." Milly squinted, trying to make out any symbol on the bucket.

The woman approached, and Milly envied her elegant ease, the languor with which she bent down to speak to the theatergoers, the grace with which she lifted the pail.

When the woman was at the row in front of them, Milly frowned. The long sleeves of the woman's gown ended above her wrists, and when she moved, a bracelet emerged. A brown and dark orange tortoiseshell bracelet that caught the liquid light. Milly knew that bracelet.

"Subscriptions for the Soviet Red Cross?" the woman said to Milly in English, and Milly looked up at her face with a start.

Zhenya winked.

Milly gaped, then fumbled for her purse and pulled out some coins. She dropped them into the pail, where they thudded on top of the bills lining the bottom.

"Thank you," he said in a sweet tenor, then moved on.

After a minute, Ruth leaned over.

"Was that . . . a man?" Her voice was heavy with anticipation.

"Looked like it, on close inspection." Milly's cheeks burned.

Ruth laughed, but Milly cut her short with a raised hand.

"I don't have any hard feelings toward homosexuals or lesbians or whatever," Milly said, her eyes on the red curtain still drawn tight over the stage.

"I didn't say . . . it's just . . ." Ruth giggled.

Milly waited for the laughter to stop, then changed the subject. Soon, the overture started and the waves of music lifted

Milly out of her thoughts: her worries about the handsome youth who loved to kiss her fingers and twist the bracelet that his friend gave him; her confusion about his invitations to walk the streets of Moscow with Victor, another actor from the opera, while they traded barbed gossip about the opera dance master and both tried to teach her Russian words for the things they saw—crow, maple, sunset; her conviction that Zhenya was the most handsome man she had ever had dinner with; and her fear that he didn't know what he meant when he wrote in a letter to her, "I am only happy when I am with you."

She wanted it to be true.

Now

April 8, 1934

Milly walked to her place in line, according to the number she had obtained yesterday. She knew the routine well enough now that she hardly thought about it. Which gave her chills, when she realized.

Milly gripped her coat sleeves so tightly her fingers ached from both anger and cold, and she wished she could be anywhere else. But waiting here was the only way she could learn more about Zhenya's case. A month had passed since the law had been promulgated, and she'd learned nothing, heard nothing, except for one short letter from Zhenya thanking her for the food and asking for more, but maybe better to send sausages instead of cooked chicken next time. Her face had burned with embarrassment at her foolishness, which he so gently corrected in his note.

A mocking wind whipped down the street where she stood shivering in the watery morning light, and everyone in line around her grimaced and tried to extract some shelter from the building the line snaked alongside. Only the drunk man two people behind her seemed unaffected, his nose glowing ember red and his eyes unfocused. Every so often, he drank from a dented flask, and Milly yearned for a sip too. But she certainly wouldn't step out of line, no matter how much she dreamed of sliding onto a bar stool at the joint she'd spotted around the corner, out of the wind and probably already pouring dishes of vodka.

With her gloved hands, Milly unfolded the note Zhenya had sent. At the end of it, he pleaded with her to get a meeting with Senior Prosecutor Rosonov, the same name Axelrod had gotten when he telephoned at her request. Earlier in the week, when Milly showed Zhenya's letter to Borodin, he'd agreed.

"Take your next rest day and try to find out what's happening," Borodin had said as they bent over the note. His hair smelled like pine and wool, and she breathed deeply, quietly.

"Guess that means you're not letting me go early today," Milly said. Her next rest day was three days away.

Borodin straightened, then stuffed his hands in his pockets. "We've got a paper to put out, Milly. It doesn't wait."

"Neither do men in prison."

"All they do is wait." He laughed, and Milly glowered. "I need you to have a spotless record. There won't be anything to suggest you haven't been useful to the Soviet Union."

She rolled her lips together, then released her grimace with a faint sigh.

"No. There won't be anything." He was right, she couldn't have a blemish on her work record, in case the Foreign Office decided to investigate her. She couldn't help Zhenya from San Francisco.

So she had to wait until today.

Behind her, the drunk man started humming to himself. Like Anna Louise. How strange that he wasn't afraid of getting himself locked up for public drunkenness. Though, Milly knew the OGPU were interested in more serious affairs, and they left the misdemeanors to the city police. Once she had gotten a tour of the city's drunk stations from the chief of Moscow's police. It made a swell article, especially the photographs of the ice-water tanks where they plunged the insensible drunks, to wake them up. But Milly's favorite part had been how, after sleeping off their overindulgence, the drunks were given a hot breakfast and a bill for the cost of their stay. If they didn't have the cash, in true socialist fashion the station chief would let the hungover sods go home, on the promise that they'd fetch back the money. They almost all did, the Moscow chief of militia told her with a proud smile. Milly had thought it charming, at the time. But now, looking around at the shivering grandmother, head bowed under her black kerchief, or the mournful-eyed teenager whose gaze skittered up and down the line as if he were searching for someone, she was less delighted. Perhaps the people returned to pay for a reason other than solidarity.

Milly looked down at her scuffed boots and wiggled her numbed toes, trying to figure out where the icy air might be seeping through. Probably everywhere. When she looked up, a middle-aged woman in a cream-colored coat with a blue embroidered edge stood in front of her.

"Excuse me," Milly said in slow Russian. "The end of the line is that way."

The woman blinked.

"What do you mean?"

"The end of the line is that way. You can't—" She searched for the word. "You can't get in line here. In front of me. Everyone."

"But I've been here."

The woman's voice was firm, but there was a flash of something, fear or defiance, in her brown eyes.

"No. You haven't. I would know that coat."

The line shuffled forward. Behind Milly, an old man chimed in.

"You weren't here," he said in a voice like a brittle fingernail. "You have to wait your turn, like everyone else."

"But it's not fair. My husband . . ." she began to say.

"Everyone waited!" the drunk man bellowed. Milly spun around to see him brandishing a folder. A blonde woman immediately in front of him cringed but then joined in scowling at the woman in the cream coat.

"Do you think any of us want to be here? Get to the back," the blonde woman said.

The interloper's face fell, and she cradled her cheeks in her palms.

Milly's heart wrenched. They were all waiting for loved ones. It wasn't right that any of them should have to wait in this interminable, frigid line. It was worse that they had to turn on one another, all while the people who had created the line, who daily revalidated the line's reason for being by processing papers and filing charges, sat warm and comfortable inside the building that Milly now leaned against.

She wished she hadn't said anything.

The woman slunk away, toward the back of the line, and everyone around Milly fell silent again.

❧

MILLY WAS PAINFULLY hungry by the time she made it to the front of the line. The snacks she had brought had disappeared hours ago, and she had given one slice of cheese to a gangly boy with dirty hands who had come begging. Orphaned, most likely, though he hadn't said anything. He was brave to beg here.

Milly told the secretary she demanded to see Senior Prosecutor Rosonov, as Borodin had instructed her. The young man stared at her, expressionless, and Milly repressed the urge to repeat herself. She was sure she'd been clear.

"You have an appointment?"

"No."

Milly reached into the pocket of her overcoat and ran her fingernail along the edge of Zhenya's letter.

"But this is the day he takes people without an appointment." She lifted her chin.

The young man's shoulders sagged, and he made a note in a large ledger book open in front of him.

"Your name?"

She told him, and he waved her past.

The door behind him led to a stairwell, and at the top of the echoing stair was an open door. Beyond it was a hallway, but the first door was also open.

The sign on the door read "Senior Prosecutor."

Milly rapped her knuckles against the wood but entered without waiting. A thin man with a rounded back stood at a filing cabinet behind a desk, fingering his way through the folders. A door, barely open, led to another room beyond.

"Prosecutor Rosonov?" she asked before she thought. This anteroom would be where the secretary sat.

He looked up, let his eyes range across her body, and then settled his gaze on her face. His disappointment was familiar but no less dispiriting. Milly tugged at the lock of hair behind her ear, as if she could straighten herself into beauty.

"I'd like a meeting with the senior prosecutor, about my husband," she said. "I want to know the details of his case."

He uttered something she couldn't understand, then sat in the green chair behind the desk. On her side, there was a single wooden chair with cracked varnish, and he gestured for her to take it.

"Your proof of identification?"

She rummaged through her purse and found her passport, which she slid across the paper-strewn desk to meet his broad fingers. He flipped it open and looked at each page, particularly the one with her Soviet visa.

"Your marriage certificate?"

Thank god Olga had suggested she bring that. Milly unfolded it in front of the man, and he snatched it away.

"I am the senior prosecutor. What do you want?" he said finally.

"I want to know what he was charged with. Why did they take him away? If it was about me, I—"

"That's enough." Rosonov looked tired as he pushed himself back out of his chair and walked over to the filing cabinet. To his right, a portrait of Stalin gazed serenely into the distance. Milly wanted to cross her arms on the desk, rest her head, and go to sleep.

Down the hall, someone dropped a glass. Rosonov flinched, then returned his attention to the files, where he flicked past dozens while whispering the names written on each tab. Lives overturned.

"Here," he said with a brief, victorious smile that made his face wrinkle like crumpled paper. He pulled out a folder and sat with it on his lap, as if he feared Milly would try to read it or snatch it away. She was tempted.

"Evgeni Ivanovich Konstantinov. His trial was March twentieth, two weeks ago. Convicted of immoral behavior and homosexuality. Sentenced to three years in a work camp."

Milly grabbed the edge of the desk and pulled herself forward. "We've been married for two years. There's no *immoral* behavior." She had sworn she'd stay calm, but already her voice snapped with contempt.

Rosonov jabbed his finger at the file, then lifted a paper for Milly to see.

"That's his signature. Confessing he had taken part in homosexual evenings in 1933."

"Ridiculous. What does that mean? An evening where homosexuals were present? Where they did things?"

Rosonov straightened his mouth into a firm line and returned the paper to its folder.

"I think you know," he said.

"Did Zhenya commit acts of homosexuality? Did he? Tell me what proof you have." To her surprise, her throat tightened and her voice wobbled.

Rosonov said nothing. He stood and replaced the folder. His back stayed hunched, and he massaged one shoulder and winced.

"When you interview your husband, you may get the details."

Milly leapt to her feet.

"Now?" She wanted to see him now, and yet she did not. She wasn't sure if she would slap him or embrace him and cry into his firm shoulder. Her sweet, idiotic Zhenya.

"No. In three days. Come before to get the admission card."

More days of waiting. Milly swallowed back her reflexive American "thank you" and stood. She retrieved her documents from the desk and shoved them into her purse.

"The eleventh of April, then," she said.

He nodded.

Milly turned to go, then paused.

"What of Victor Pavilovich? And Sorokin?"

His face clouded, but he quickly resumed a pose of professional indifference.

"You are not authorized to receive information on those citizens."

"Like hell I'm not," Milly growled in English. Then she took a deep breath and switched back to Russian. "They were released, weren't they? Or they will be. They, how is it, made a deal."

"You may leave now."

"Zhenya's innocent," she said. "I'll prove it. I'll get him out."

Rosonov turned his back to her and pushed the drawer closed with a clang. Then he opened another one.

"You may leave now," he repeated, without turning around.

Milly glanced at his desk, then reached over and pushed a stack of papers to the floor. As they wafted down to the tile, she marched out.

But by the time she reached the street, she was fighting back tears. What a fool she was, to risk ruining Zhenya's chances simply to satisfy her pique.

She hoped that tomorrow Borodin would not ask her how the meeting with Rosonov had gone. How could she tell him she had married a man who . . . who didn't love her, she thought with a tremor. They had married because he wanted her to save him, and she'd failed. She wasn't enough for him, though he had wanted her to be. Or maybe only she had wanted to be his everything. No, it was no good to pity herself. In fact, she should go to the newsroom tonight, since they could probably use the extra hands. If Charles were still on the staff, she could ask him about Zhenya, but Charles had skipped out of Moscow a year ago. Fine, she would buck up, show she wasn't afraid of Borodin and his questions, and maybe work hard enough to justify asking Borodin and Anna Louise to let her spend more of her scheduled workdays coming back here, waiting to help her poor Russian husband.

Or friend.

She stopped and stared up at the gray clouds lurking overhead until the tears in her eyes no longer threatened to spill onto her cheeks.

RUTH HOLLERED OVER at her from her desk.

"You've got a call, Millichka! It's the Russian boyfriend." She gave a wicked grin, and Milly felt the heat rush to her cheeks.

Milly walked to the secretary's desk, where Ruth had answered the phone, and lifted the receiver.

"Milly baby! We must celebrate. It has been a year you have been in Moscow, yes? Let's go out."

It wasn't exactly a year, but close enough, and she was thrilled her Russian opera performer thought of her. Still, she shouldn't be getting social calls at work.

Milly looked up from the phone cord wrapped around her finger, and Axelrod was glaring at her.

"I've got to go. But I can meet you tomorrow night. Restaurant No. 9, the nightclub."

He agreed, and she quickly hung up.

Axelrod coughed, then beckoned to Ruth.

"What's this?" He held up a bound blue journal, the *American Mercury*.

"Looks like a magazine," Milly said, her cheeks flushing.

"Your English getting sloppy, Axelrod?" Ruth usually let Milly do the sharp talking, but when Milly glanced over at her now, her chin was held high.

His forehead bloomed red, and he jabbed a finger at the front cover. "Right there! Your names! 'They all come to Moscow,' it says."

"Do they?" Milly tried to relax against her desk, but her palms were sweating and she slipped a little when she leaned back.

"Why do you think you can laugh at us?"

"It was just good fun," Ruth said, and gave a one-shouldered shrug.

"Saying 'five dollars for a pound of butter' here is not fun," Axelrod growled. He waved the magazine in Ruth's face.

"It's true," she said, her eyes on the marble tiled floor.

He flipped to another page. "'Ah want to have babies. Ah want to have lots of babies, and ah want them all to be born in Soviet Russia!' What is that?" he yelled.

Milly snorted. "Could you read that again? I didn't catch that the first time."

Both she and Ruth devolved into giggles.

Axelrod threw down the magazine, and the slap against the floor silenced the newsroom.

"You." He pointed at Ruth. "I know this was your idea. You're the leader, you make trouble. You are fired."

"But you can't, I am just . . . And Borodin . . ."

Axelrod's eyes glowed. "I have the last word. You. Are. Fired. And you." He turned to Milly. "I'm still thinking about what to do with you."

He kicked the magazine toward them and turned away. Then, he paused, and spun back toward Ruth.

"You will lose your visa this week. Prepare yourself to leave."

Ruth gasped and turned white. Milly hugged her arms around herself and tried to quell the feeling of nausea, luck, and guilt. She hadn't been fired, but her friend had; she was grateful she didn't have to leave, but devastated her friend did. She threw her arms around Ruth.

"I'm sorry," she said, and Ruth's damp cheek pressed against her neck.

❖

THE NEXT DAY, Jack Chen grabbed Milly by her elbow and pulled her aside before she even had a chance to strip down her outer layers.

"Axelrod's out for blood," he whispered.

"I don't know what to do." She walked back to her desk, and Jack followed.

"Apologize for the story," he said. He looked around the room, but all the writers had their eyes fixed on their typewriters or notepads.

She shook her head. "Like hell. It was a harmless story. If we can't laugh at ourselves, what's the point?"

"The point is people's lives, Milly. They're trying to make a new world here."

"All the more reason to be able to laugh. It's a gentle way of telling the truth about some tough ideas." She sat in her desk chair and reached down to tug her sagging stockings up from her ankles.

Milly looked up. Axelrod was standing by her shoulder, and Jack was retreating behind him.

"You scared me," she said as she rotated herself on her chair. Though he wasn't tall, he still loomed over her as she sat. She would have liked to stand too, but he was so close.

"If you're coming to ask me out," Milly said, "I have to tell you I promised your wife I'd bring you home by midnight."

He frowned, and she laughed, nervous but delighted to have confused him.

"You have to buy the gas mask," he said in his thick accent.

"The gas mask?" She blinked, then frowned as she remembered the newest idiotic requirement. "There's no way I'm spending eight whole rubles on a gas mask. You can't really think the fascists are attacking next week."

He gripped the back of her chair and leaned over her.

"It is the regulation."

"Why don't you just mark me down as having done it already? I don't have the money. You'll save everyone the trouble." Her heart raced, and she watched his face as he narrowed his eyes. She could just give him the money, though it would account for nearly every coin in her purse. But this wasn't about the gas mask.

"If you do not buy the mask, we are not . . . in agreement."

"We sure aren't."

"I mean in compliance." His face reddened.

"Look, Axelrod." She lowered her voice. "I'm not buying the mask. It's nearly all the coins I own, and I'm not going to spend them on something useless. No matter what the newsreels say. Mark me down however you like." Then she leaned backward. "I'm glad to help, happy to support the cause," she said more loudly. "What's my assignment today? Not another soccer match, I hope. I can never make sense of those."

He straightened and took a step back. The newsroom ticked with the sound of typewriters and shoes clicking on the marble floors, but still it seemed quiet, and Milly held her breath. He could fire her.

But at least she would have stood her ground.

"Borodin likes your work," he said quietly. "I will let you stay. For now."

He looked at the small notebook in his hand, paused, flipped over a page, then looked up. "Soccer championship finals at two o'clock. Interview both teams beforehand. Get two stories out of it."

Milly groaned, but she wrote down the details.

Axelrod still stood there.

"You are on thin ice," he said. "We got rid of Ruth. We can get rid of you." Then he turned and walked away.

Milly looked down at her notes, which were nearly illegible in her nervous scrawl. She rewrote the address. She should feel victorious, but instead it was as if a dark snake were slithering through her veins, weakening her with doubt. She had stood up for what she wanted, sure, but maybe buying the mask was the way to sacrifice her ego to the building of socialism, or maybe snuffing out her instinct to bristle at authority was the way to get ahead. She took off her glasses and rubbed her eyes. Then, she turned to edit the copy that one of the errand boys had left for her.

A scrawl in her handwriting caught her eye: Restaurant No. 9. She drew a heart around the notation, and her mouth quirked into a half smile. At least she had her evening in the nightclub to look forward to.

❖

IT WAS A few minutes past ten when she showed up on the street outside the restaurant, where the wind gnashed its teeth at her cheeks. Earlier she had gone home to change and splash some camellia perfume on, so now she smelled like glorious summer, the weather be damned. There was no sign of Zhenya. Milly cuddled into her own embrace and relished the scent of her perfume as her nose buried into the scarf.

When Zhenya arrived, a few minutes later, he was accompanied by his friend Victor. Milly sighed but soon straightened herself and smiled. Victor was kind, even if his presence meant she wouldn't get Zhenya on his own.

They walked into the building and down the stairs to the nightclub, where they settled at a table near the frescoed wall, painted to look like a mosaic. Milly scooted her chair a little closer to Zhenya, who lifted her hand to his lips and kissed her knuckles. His kiss brushed her skin like a promise, and she shivered.

"You smell delicious." He held her gaze for a moment. Milly could have thrown herself on him right then.

"I once dated a girl because she smelled so good I could eat her," Victor said with a laugh. His English was nearly as good as Zhenya's. "A peasant girl, in Moscow."

"When was this?" Zhenya rested Milly's hand on the sticky tabletop.

"Maybe two years ago. I was so hungry then. Remember how hungry we were? Almost passing out during rehearsal. I met this girl who smelled like roast beef. I dated her for four months, so I could smell her."

Zhenya laughed and flicked his fingers against Victor's shoulder.

"You're terrible," he said.

"I guess that explains why the shop was sold out of Eau de Boeuf," Milly said dryly. "Next time."

Zhenya wrapped his arm around her shoulders and pulled her tight. The tortoiseshell bracelet at his wrist dug into her skin, but she didn't mind.

"Maybe the secret to winning Zhenya's heart is to win both of you," Milly said, glancing between them. Her pulse raced at her daring, but the confrontation with Axelrod had breached her floodgates, and now her thoughts tumbled out. "We'll all three live together in a little dacha somewhere."

Victor's face burned bright red. But Zhenya threw his head back and laughed, his golden hair shaking like a lion's mane.

"You want all the men to yourself, is that it, Milly baby? But how can I share you?"

"Share and share alike," she said. "I've got practice, any-how—I can teach you."

"Our Milly had a married love," Zhenya whispered in a stage voice to Victor, who was finishing his vodka. "Bourgeois marriages do not dissolve as easily as communist marriages, so the idiot chose to stay with his wife."

"I think so," Milly said. "I got a letter from him yesterday." It wasn't true; the letter had been from a different former beau. But she wanted to see how Zhenya would react. She raised an eyebrow and pulled the letter from her purse. "See?"

"Show it here." Zhenya grew serious. He unwrapped his arm from her shoulders and held out an open palm.

"Private," Milly said with a wink, then she whisked the folded paper back into her purse.

"You are trying to make me jealous," Zhenya said.

Milly kissed his cheek. "Is it working?"

He lifted her fingertips to his lips and held them there until she laughed and pulled them away.

"I told Axelrod I wouldn't buy a gas mask," she said. "It would have been nearly my last fistful of rubles for the month. What should we do instead? Buy all the flowers we can get and hand them out to babushkas? Give all my coins to the first newsboy we see?"

"But how will you eat?" Victor asked, frowning.

"Axelrod didn't care about that, why should I?" Her words came out singed with anger.

Zhenya tapped his fingers against his chin.

"Won't you get in trouble?" Zhenya looked back and forth between them. "For not buying the mask, I mean."

Milly sighed. "Maybe. But he's being a fool. If I'm going to be foolish too, I'd rather it be in the service of a good cause. Here." She took what she had in her purse and pushed it across the table. "Do something good with this."

Zhenya looked at her, appraising, then pushed two of the bills back toward her.

"For your eating. The rest I will give to the family at the end of the hall," he said, referring to a widowed mother and her four children whose drawn faces cringed and turned to the ground whenever the other building's residents passed.

He cupped his hand over hers and a jolt of pleasure raced up her arm as he stroked his thumb against her skin.

"You are like no other woman, Milly baby," he said softly.

And for once her in her life, she believed it.

Now

APRIL 10, 1934

ANOTHER COLD DAY, another line.

Today, Milly needed the admission card so she could come back tomorrow to stand in line again to actually see her husband. She kicked a rock down the sidewalk, and it skittered over the pavement until sailing off the curb. She wondered if Olga would go with her if she got the appointment.

Olga had grown strangely sanguine about Zhenya's imprisonment lately. Maybe since she had read about the homosexuality law. Milly couldn't bring herself to talk about Zhenya's complex desires to his mother, but since the news about the law had come out, Olga's jaw had hardened whenever Milly said Zhenya's name.

"The work will do him good," Olga had said when Milly relayed what she had heard from the senior prosecutor. "That boy lives in his imagination."

Strange criticism from a woman hoarding a box of ancient currency. But Milly held her tongue and silently accepted a glass of tea. Zhenya deserved peace between the women in his life.

When she reached the front of the line, a man in uniform directed her to a desk, where she told a woman in a faded black sweater what the senior prosecutor had told her to do. The woman wrote it all down silently, her lip bitten between her teeth. Then she handed Milly a card.

"Tomorrow, at the address here. You are number twenty-three in line. Next!"

Milly clutched the card to her chest, then placed it into her purse, in the small side pocket that held her spare rubles. She was almost there.

MILLY WAS DIGGING through the pantry at Anna Louise's apartment hoping to find two pans of the same size when then phone rang. Milly scrambled to reach it in time.

"Hello?" She forgot to answer in Russian.

"Milly baby!" Zhenya's bright voice glittered through the phone. "Come out with us tonight."

"To where?" She clutched the phone wire and hoped he would be willing to go dancing.

"Luba is having a name day party," he said.

"But today's not her day." Milly had spoken to Luba about name days during their weekly Russian lessons in Zhenya's apartment.

Zhenya laughed, a lilting, delighted sound.

"Yes, but Victor is calling her Antonia, I don't know why, and today is the day for Antonia. We have to celebrate."

Milly sighed and smiled.

"Does Luba know?" She never knew what the quiet, blond-haired woman found amusing. She'd be silent one moment and pitched over giggling the next.

"Of course. Milly baby, you must come. Get dressed and meet us at the Metropol. Victor says we'll give Luba—Antonia—the best."

He hung up, and Milly stared at the unwrapped chocolate squares on Anna Louise's small counter. She had been about to make fudge, in an effort to be kinder to the confounding woman who hosted her, but that could wait until tomorrow. She put the ingredients away.

Milly arrived at the Metropol in her favorite black dress, the velvet one that hugged her curves and ended at the knee, so she could show off her legs. On her finger she wore a new purchase—one of the pieces of jewelry she had bought from a Russian woman anxious to get rid of the jewels that Communism now declared passé. Milly didn't care. She adored garnets, and this silver ring with the pile of small stones like a split pomegranate didn't embarrass her at all. She cascaded her fingers and let the bloodred stones drink in the light. Maybe Zhenya would notice.

Luba was already there, standing at the ornate bar in her black cotton shirtdress, with the collar rebelling and pointing upward on one side. She ought to have looked uncomfortable in that hideous thing, but she was relaxed, leaning with one elbow against the polished wood and already holding a small glass. The carved wood of the small bar stretched above them like a regal bed post from another age.

"Milly! You came," she said in delighted Russian.

"Luba." Milly kissed her cheeks, then held her shoulders and regarded her friend. "Or should I say, Antonia?"

Luba wrinkled her small nose and laughed. Maybe that wasn't her first drink. Milly raised a hand and ordered two more, then slapped the necessary rubles onto the glossy wood for the bartender to take when he could. Milly had lived in this hotel for a few weeks last winter with Jack Chen's two sisters, and she had all the prices memorized.

"Are the boys coming from the theater?" Milly asked in slow Russian.

Luba's face stilled, and Milly almost repeated the question, certain she must have messed up a word or two.

"I saw them at the theater," Luba said, her eyes fixed on the wall behind Milly's head. "They were . . . holding hands. Said they would meet us. You should know this, Milly."

Milly waved a hand, then grabbed the drinks the bartender had deposited.

"It's nothing," she said, though it wasn't. "You know how affectionate Zhenya is with everyone."

Luba nodded, then took a sip of her vodka. She didn't grimace, unlike Milly, who needed a few sips to acclimate herself to the smooth drink. She had written to her friends, trying to describe vodka, how deceptive and dangerous it was. But like with everything she tried to describe to her friends back home, her words seemed to shrink when they fell from her pen.

"I have another study session tomorrow," Luba said, enunciating. There wasn't much noise in the bar, but the tile floors and high ceilings still made nearly everyone's conversation echo, and even the smallest distortion could make it hard for Milly to figure out what her friend was saying.

Milly started to ask about the young man who liked to loiter outside Luba's study sessions, when the snap of quick steps against the tiles sounded. She turned to see Zhenya barreling toward them, his lean frame rigid. He was frowning, but as soon as he saw Milly, a smile brightened his expression. He caught her in his arms and spun her around, nearly knocking Luba's glass from her hands.

"Milly baby," he said, as if relieved.

He kissed her on the temple, then gave her a dip, cradling her in his muscular arm. Her breath fluttered in her lungs, and she stared into his gray eyes. He held her gaze, pressing his fingertips into her waist, and a heat kindled deep inside her.

"Where's Victor?" Luba asked. She straightened the buttons on her dress.

Zhenya righted Milly, then released her.

"He met a friend. He's coming."

Zhenya turned to the bartender and ordered three more vodkas. Above the bar, a small crystal chandelier sparkled, and the bartender's gloved hands seemed to wink in and out of the light as he moved.

"Did you fight?" Luba asked again, her small eyes hard.

Milly opened her mouth to protest, but Zhenya shrugged.

"Fight, not fight, what's the difference." He downed his glass in one go.

"Luba, it's your name day, right?" Milly said with a broad smile. Maybe it would help if she reminded everyone that this was supposed to be a party.

"And tomorrow I have to go to study group," she groaned. She had faint circles under her eyes.

"Here they are!" The reedy male voice shot toward them, like an arrow.

Victor stood at the entrance to the bar area of the hotel with his arms thrown wide and a golden crown perched upon his brown hair. His face was unremarkable, but his skin seemed to glow with the healthiest of golden light.

Victor marched toward them, and as he walked, a short, stocky man kept pace with him. Zhenya wrapped an arm around Milly's waist.

"Is that the friend?" Milly asked Luba, who nodded and placed her hands on her hips.

"Dear friends! Today we celebrate Antonia." Victor waved for the bartender and ordered a bottle of wine.

"Is he paying for that?" Milly whispered to Zhenya in English.

"He'd better. Unless his friend is." Zhenya released his arm around her waist.

Milly wished she could grab Zhenya and whisk him off to the dance floor. Or better, her bedroom. He just needed to be distracted. But Zhenya, despite performing as a dancer for the opera, never danced when he was out. And neither of them had their own bedroom.

Instead, she wove her arm around his and rubbed her hip against his muscular thigh. He gave her a sly smile.

"Antonia, we salute you," Victor said once his glass was filled with pale wine.

"You salute yourself, you fool," Luba said, but then she smiled. The group laughed, probably more out of relief than humor.

"Sasha is in the military," Victor said. "He knows all about salutes. And digging latrines." He laughed, and Sasha smiled.

Zhenya wrapped his arm around Milly's shoulders. He smelled of vodka, and Milly glanced at the bar, where both their glasses stood empty. She snuggled into the warmth of his ribs.

"Today, Luba. Tomorrow, Milly and I!" Zhenya pronounced the words as if they were lines on the stage, and he finished with his lips slightly puckered, like he did when he was posing for a photograph.

"What do you mean?" Victor took another swallow of his wine.

"I'm done with this fairy business," Zhenya growled, his voice surprisingly sharp. Luba gasped, and Milly pulled away from Zhenya. She looked at him, at the fine structure of his cheekbones, the gray eyes filled with dreams, and the tousled blond hair. He looked at her back, his eyes longing.

"Milly is the only one . . ." he began.

"Don't get any big ideas," she interrupted him in English, her voice low.

He wilted. "But, Milly baby, we . . ."

"You were going to say we were getting married, weren't you?" She jabbed her finger into his chest. His eyes widened.

Milly laughed. Marriages were easy here in Moscow, simply a matter of a few forms and rubles. They were easy to dissolve too.

If a marriage was what this handsome man needed of her, she could give it.

She leaned over and whispered in his ear.

"It's been my dream to ask a man to marry me," she said. Then she coughed and pulled away. Their friends needed to understand this, if the marriage was going to help Zhenya at all.

"Zhenya, let's get married. Tomorrow," she said in loud Russian.

He wrapped her in his arms and kissed her, firmly on the lips.

"My baby," he whispered, his lips tickling the ridges of her ears.

Her insides melted.

The rest of the night he beamed at her, and never once looked at Victor, except in passing.

She had done what Zhenya wanted.

They married the next day, merely by showing up, nursing their headaches at the Vital Records Office, and signing two forms.

"Can you ask Anna Louise to give us one night?" Zhenya asked her when they stood on the sidewalk, blinking in the bright June light.

Milly pulled his hand between hers and kissed his fingertips.

"Really?" They had never had a full night together, though they'd managed some snuggling and petting in his room while his mother slept. She wasn't sure how much he desired her.

"Yes." His eyes burned as he held her gaze. "I am happiest with you. That is the only truth."

"And the others?" She couldn't bring herself to say his other men.

He waved a hand. "We will have a modern socialist marriage. You can still go with your other men." He had misunderstood. Or feigned to. Milly parted her lips to object, but he drew her toward him and silenced her with a kiss.

"I'll talk to Anna Louise," Milly said. Coward that she was, unwilling to ask Zhenya about *his* men.

Anna Louise squealed when Milly told her the reason for wanting the apartment to herself that night.

"Of course! Is he a Party member?"

"No." Milly looked at the floor. "But he makes me feel . . . special, like no man has before. Like I'm his queen." She blushed.

"That's all right," Anna Louise said, oblivious to Milly's confession. "I'll only marry a Party member, I'm sure, but it's not for everyone. And we really should be getting you your own room, shouldn't we. I think I heard of a place, where was it, over by the subway construction site I think. I'll find out tomorrow."

"You'll have a place to sleep tonight?" Milly partly felt guilty for displacing her benefactor, and partly worried the woman had already forgotten her original request.

Anna Louise waved her manicured fingers.

"Don't worry about me."

❖

AFTER WORK THAT night, Milly rushed back to the empty apartment. She had stopped at Torgsin and bought the cheapest bottle of wine they had. It was all she could afford.

She set the bottle on Anna Louise's kitchen table and grabbed two scratched tumbler glasses from the sparsely populated cabinet.

"What a nice surprise."

Milly jumped at the sound of Zhenya's voice, then nervously laughed and turned around.

He stood in brown tweed trousers with a short-sleeved brown shirt that showed the curve of his muscles. His blond hair was combed gently to the side. He smiled and held his arms open.

"My little wife," he said, his voice like raspberry jam.

She cocooned herself in his embrace and nestled her ear to his chest, where the thump of his heartbeat threaded into her pulse.

"Wine?" he said, pulling her away so he could look at her. "It must be a special occasion." His gray eyes twinkled.

"It's not every day a girl gets to celebrate her second marriage." Milly winked.

"To a famous opera star!" Zhenya struck an exaggerated pose, and they both laughed. She wanted to kiss him then, in gratitude for breaking the awkwardness, but she turned to open to the bottle.

"Stand back," she said with a smile. "Who knows what's going to happen when I pop this cork."

Zhenya reached out to cup her cheek in his hand, then stepped back. She extracted the cork without crumbling it and then tipped generous pours into the small glasses.

"A dish for you." She handed it to him.

"*Za zdaróvye*," he said. They both drank.

Behind the silence of their room, streetcars rattled below, and in the room above someone walked with heavy feet.

"You are beautiful." Zhenya put down his empty glass.

Milly tossed her hair. It was the compliment she most wanted and most hated, since she could never believe the words. Her nose was too big, her eyes were too small, her chin jutted too far. Wrapped up in an overcoat she could have been mistaken for a man. But she wanted, so desperately wanted, what other women had.

"I think you mean I've got swell legs." She did a little spin, ending with her ankle turned out and her rounded calf on display beneath her skirts.

"No. I have good legs." He jumped and landed in a firm plié, then smiled. "I mean that you are beautiful."

He reached his hand behind her head, twined his fingers in her thick hair, and pulled her into a kiss.

Milly's shoulders melted as the heat from between her hips rose up, into her chest and neck and then spiraling into his firm kiss. She threw her arms around him and pressed her body to his. Her softness pillowed against him, and she pushed him toward her room.

"Not yet, Milly baby," he said, his voice husky. "I brought you a treat."

He reached into his pocket and extracted a small pouch made of a twisted white handkerchief. He placed the bundle on the table and unwrapped it to reveal five bloodred cherries.

"Sit." He pulled out a chair.

"I haven't had a cherry in over two years," she said, her voice soft. "I haven't seen any here."

He winked and held up a fruit as if preparing to hang it on a Christmas tree.

"Open."

She obeyed, and he placed the cherry between her teeth, then tugged to remove the stem when she closed her lips. Her teeth cut into the flesh and a current of sweetness washed over her. She nipped and tugged at the fruit in her mouth until she had extracted the cherry stone from inside. She lifted her hand to spit it out, but Zhenya stopped her.

"Here." He held his palm to her mouth, and she kissed the delicate skin at the center of his hand as she puckered her lips to produce the stone. Then she closed her eyes as she savored the rest of the fruit.

They repeated the dance for the remaining four cherries, and Zhenya scowled when Milly tried to press him to take a fruit for himself. Then he placed the stones in Anna Louise's trash bucket, and Milly poured two more glasses of wine. She drank hers in a few gulps, while Zhenya took a sip of his and replaced it on the table.

"Now," he said with a half-smile.

He stood tall, as if drawing on his stage presence, and grasped her hand. He led her into her room.

Milly bit back the impulse to crack a joke or make a sarcastic remark. Instead she stayed silent, and Zhenya eased her down onto the edge of the low bed. He got down on his knees, then unbuttoned her blouse, letting his fingers brush her breastbone, her ribcage, her stomach, and finally, her waistband. She shivered and closed her eyes as he eased the sleeves off her shoulders. Then, he frowned and laughed.

"The buttons. You are sitting on them. I'm sorry." He stood, then lifted her to her feet so he could reach around to her backside and unfasten the closure to her skirt. The heavy cotton fell to the floor in a puddle, and Milly slipped her hands under Zhenya's shirt. His torso was firm, but not carved, and she trailed her fingers up his sides.

He sat her back on the bed, leaving her brassier and underpants on. He got back on his knees again and kissed her waist, then her hip bones. She shivered and tried to pull him toward her, but he stayed on his knees and only angled his way between her legs, where he kissed the mound beneath her underwear. She threw her head back and moaned.

Zhenya rubbed and pressed, and Milly's breathing grew rougher. Then he paused, lifted his hands to the waistband of her underwear, and ripped it apart.

"I only have—" Milly started to object, shocked out of her pleasure by the loss of a rare undergarment, but then his mouth was moist upon her, hot and rough, and she collapsed back onto the bed with a roar.

His lips upon her were like nothing Milly had ever felt, and her hands tingled and her eyes flashed stars, and soon she was rocking into him uncontrollably, until the stars behind her eyelids exploded and she shuddered still.

Zhenya crawled onto the bed, curling around her head as she lay, stunned, and he ran his fingers through her hair.

After a few moments, Milly gathered herself and pulled all the way onto the bed, alongside him. She reached her hand down below his waist, where he was growing hard.

"Not now." He pulled her hand up to her lips. "I prefer in the morning."

So Milly pulled on a frilly negligee Ruth had given her before she left, which Milly had thought she would never use, and she curled under the sheets with Zhenya, still in his trousers.

When she awoke the next morning, he was in the kitchen frying four eggs and a sliced sausage.

"More surprises," she said in a sleep-roughened voice, and she pointed at the eggs, though she wasn't sure if she meant the food or the cook.

He lifted the wooden spoon like a wand and waved it in a circle, sending a few splatters of grease onto the floor. Milly picked up a worn rag and wiped them from the wood.

The kitchen was cramped, so she stepped back out to the eating and living area.

"Do you have to work today?" Zhenya called from the kitchen.

"Of course. Why?" She was willing to risk even Axelrod's anger if Zhenya was proposing an encore to last night.

"Next time, then," he said, looking at the pan. "We are organizing last season's costumes today at the theater. I thought you would like to come."

He tipped the breakfast out of the pan and onto two plates.

They sat at the small table and ate a few bites silently.

"Delicious," Milly said. She looked at her husband. What a strange word, husband, and stranger yet that she had found one here, in Moscow. "Where did you get that bracelet?" She pointed her fork at the tortoiseshell bracelet curving around his wrist. The orange and brown colors looked like a stilled campfire atop his pale skin. "You wear it all the time."

He swallowed, then placed his fork down so he could finger the bracelet, turning it around his wrist.

"A friend gave it to me. A school friend, before he moved to Japan. He was my closest friend, and I miss him."

Milly swallowed her last mouthful, then reached over to lay a hand on his arm.

"I would like to give pleasure to you," she said. "If you show me how. You've made me feel . . . like no one else ever has."

Her heart raced as she dared the words. They were treading so close to the swamp that she knew he didn't want to address. She brushed a finger against the fine hairs curling around his bracelet.

"I don't know what you think of me," he said, resting his wrists upon the table. "I'm different from other people. From everyone." He looked up at her, his gray eyes like flint. "I feel— everything."

She took his hand in hers. "I know. And I want to . . ."

She paused. Her own feelings were so tangled. No one had sought her out before, not like Zhenya had.

"I want to protect you," she said. "To be what you need."

He kissed her fingertips.

"No one can."

He stood and brought the dishes into the kitchen, where he washed them in the cold water.

"You are brave, Milly," he said as he stacked the clean dishes. "But I don't think you know how to love yourself. Do you?"

"This isn't about me." She stood up.

He shook his head. "You don't see. I need everything, but I don't need anyone to be everything for me."

Milly stood up from the table and placed her hands on her hips. The flesh there felt round and tender under her fingers.

"I think you, Zhenya, love yourself, but you don't know how to be brave. Why can't you ask for what you want? Why can't I give it to you?"

He shook his head, placed the last dish on the pile, then turned to stare out the window.

"I'm sorry," she said quietly. "I didn't mean—"

"No," he said. "Perhaps you are right. Perhaps I don't know."

He approached and picked up her hands. Then he kissed them and left.

Now

MILLY HANDED ZHENYA'S last crate to Seema, who passed it to her latest boyfriend, Bill. Bill was a newspaperman from Boston, and some in the newsroom seemed to find it scandalous that he, a white man, was dating Seema. No matter that Seema had traveled to the Soviet Union to perform in a movie—*The American Negro*—and was an invited guest of the Kremlin. Milly liked Bill better for his choice in dating partners, but otherwise he was a drag. He stood in the wagon bed and heaved the crate inside. The day before, Milly had seen Zhenya's name on the confirmed list posted outside Butyrka prison. Her finger trembled as she drew it across the letters of his name, as if to strike it out. His sentence of exile was ratified, though it didn't say where he would go. When Milly told Olga that night, the older woman nodded. "We must pack his belongings," she said, as if she had expected the outcome.

"That's it? I thought we were going to petition his case." Milly planted her feet on Olga's scuffed wooden floor, prepared for battle.

"We will. But this is how it goes here. He will get sent regardless." Olga paused and rubbed at her closed eyes. "I have thought, recently, that maybe he deserved the sentence."

Milly gritted her teeth and wanted to growl. Was she the only one willing to fight for him? But she sucked in a breath, held it, then stomped away to pull Zhenya's sweaters from their mothballed boxes at the top of his small wardrobe. He had enough clothes to fill four small crates, and she packed them full. She held in reserve only one pair of pants and a shirt. For when he came home.

Now Bill pulled her and Seema into the back of the wagon, then got down and, with the wagon driver's help, hoisted Olga in behind them.

It was midday and the streets were crowded, filled with horse-drawn carts, streetcars, and pedestrians. Seema tried to engage Olga with pleasantries, but the old woman frowned, and Milly was too drained to try to translate Seema's accent-laden Russian. After a few minutes they fell silent and watched the men and women of Moscow at their business, carrying sack-cloth bags filled with mushrooms and onions, or staring at the monochrome window displays of crates of potatoes or workers' trousers. A teenaged girl with a baby in her arms attracted cooing and baby talk from a knot of grandmothers. A boy stood yelling out the newspaper headlines, and Milly strained to hear if he was yelling in English or Russian; often, it was hard to differentiate through the boys' accents. She was curious to see where the *Moscow Daily News* was sold: often near Torgsin or the embassies, and certainly the Metropol, all places where Americans and Brits passed by.

It was better to think about the newspaper than Zhenya.

Their cart rumbled down a busy avenue, then lumbered up Novoslobodskaya Street for nearly half an hour. The wagon jolted to a stop.

"Where the belongings must be delivered," the driver said in a husky voice with a peasant accent. He must have been among the thousands—or was it millions—who had fled the pains of collectivization for life in the city. Milly clambered down out of the cart and looked around the quiet alley. There was no sign, nor any OGPU personnel visible. She held her pocketbook close to her chest.

A metal gate swung open, and an olive-uniformed man beckoned them through. Milly relaxed her arms.

The wagon pulled into a courtyard filled with boxes, crates, and suitcases. With a few words, the OGPU officer checked Zhenya's crates, made a note on a list he held on a clipboard, and hurried them back out. Olga and Seema remained in the wagon bed, while Milly and Bill worked to help the driver back his wagon out the narrow gate. When they finally succeeded, Bill helped Olga out, Milly paid the driver, who wished her luck, and then she and Olga watched them clatter off.

Milly took Olga's arm in hers and led the old woman around to the front entrance. Milly's hands trembled at the thought that she would finally see Zhenya, and she squeezed Olga's forearm tighter than she had intended to. The redbrick building stretched around the block like a forbidding urban castle, though its three stories of windows were framed in incongruous white, as if to suggest a glowing hope within.

There a few people stood in line, but not as many as Milly had seen in the past. Perhaps they had come too late.

"Wait here." Olga pointed at the end of the line. "This is best left to the old woman." She straightened the black kerchief over her gray-blond hair and walked to the front of the line. She spoke a few minutes with the old man there, then went inside. Milly dug her nails into the nail bed of her thumb, then pushed until it hurt. She needed to see Zhenya. Olga wouldn't visit him without her, surely. Milly strained to see over the heads of the people in front of her, looking for Olga. Sure, Zhenya's wasn't a conventional marriage, but she thought they had a . . . companionship. Once, when Milly was sick and confined to her room in the hotel she was staying at, Zhenya delivered a picture he had drawn of her, and though it was wobbly and primitive, she had never looked so beautiful. She tacked the picture onto the plaster wall.

She would do the same for him. She would let him feel seen and understood. If she, an ugly, brassy woman with more spirit than sense, deserved to be loved, then she could easily let him see how his beauty and generous spirit, his heart that loved more widely than he wanted, deserved tenderness too.

She stood on the pavement outside his prison and frowned.

He had sworn that his dalliances with men were over. But here he was, in prison.

Olga came out the door and made her way down the steep front stair. She gestured for Milly to stay.

"We are in the right place," Olga said. "Here we wait."

This line moved even more slowly than the previous lines had, and so it was not until the five o'clock hour that they left the cold of the street for the interior of the Butyrka prison.

Inside, they told a succession of secretaries that they were there to see Evgeni Konstantinov, a prisoner. Each nodded and waved the women on, until an officer led them down a dirty hall and into a small room. A single lamp rested on a table, and Milly blinked in the dark.

A chair scraped across the floor, and Zhenya stood.

Olga ran to him and threw herself into his arms. They embraced in silence for a moment, and then Zhenya looked up at Milly. His face was a little bloated, and his hands seemed so, too, pressed against Olga's back. Supposedly, such swelling was normal in prison. Milly clutched her hands as she looked at him. His blond hair fell in gentle waves almost to his ears, and his succulent lips curved into a shy smile.

"Milly baby," Zhenya said. He released his mother, and Milly approached. He took her face in his hands and kissed both her cheeks. His dry lips sparked against her skin, and tears quivered in her eyes. Before he released her, he held her gaze. "It is good to see you," he said. "So good."

"Stop speaking English," one of the two OGPU guards sitting at the dark periphery said.

"But we speak in English," Zhenya replied, his voice mild.

"Please," Milly added. She could speak to him in Russian, of course, but that would put yet another layer of distance between them.

The first guard narrowed his eyes and opened his mouth, but the second guard laid her hand upon his.

"We will get an interpreter. No speaking in English until I return," she said. Her boots snapped against the cement floor as she walked out.

They waited in silence. Milly opened her mouth to say something in Russian, but Zhenya narrowed his eyes in such an uncharacteristic reprimand that she swallowed her words. Instead, she looked around the room. The remaining OGPU officer picked at his fingernails, and then blushed. Only when Milly smelled the flatulence did she understand. She turned to Zhenya, ready to laugh with him about it, or at least share a secret smile, but his gaze remained on his feet. His shoes were more scuffed than she had ever seen them, and one of the black laces had been replaced with a too-short brown one. Milly could see, barely, his toes squirming beneath the leather. It was the only part of him that moved. She yearned to fold him into her arms and tuck his face into the crook of her neck, and she even leaned toward him, but she remembered herself and held still.

Beside her, Olga whispered a cadence that could only be a prayer. Milly bowed her head. Her breath seemed to bellow through the silent room as she let her chest rise and fall.

The door shot open, and the female officer entered, followed by another woman in uniform. This woman had a slightly different insignia above her breast, and her eyebrows were furrowed.

"Now you may begin. Hurry, your time is limited."

Milly bit back a retort, then took a deep breath and turned to Zhenya.

"Are you all right? Do you eat?"

The interpreter whispered an echo in Russian to the two officers at the periphery.

"I'm fine," he said. His gray eyes met hers.

Milly squeezed herself, then sat down in a chair.

"Is it true, Zhenya? What they say about you." She leaned forward. The Russian echo sounded, harsh, from behind her. The charges against Zhenya shouldn't matter, they didn't matter, and yet she needed to know. Why was Zhenya taken from her? Or really, what she really wanted to know was in how many ways had she failed him? Her fingers trembled against her thighs, as if her hands were about to dissolve into the cold room. "I wasn't enough," she whispered, so quietly she wasn't sure anyone could hear.

Zhenya sat in the chair facing her, though his expression remained still.

The English-speaking officer leaned forward.

"You may not ask the prisoner about the specifics of his case," she said.

"But the senior prosecutor told me to!" Milly was grateful for someone to snap at. "How else am I to know my husband's situation, how else can I help him?"

The interpreter glowered. "You have been misinformed." She leaned back, alongside the other woman, who seemed to be suppressing a smile. "If you ask about sensitive matters again, the interview will be over."

Milly narrowed her eyes. Hell if this woman was going to stop her from finding out what happened. But then, next to her,

Olga whimpered, confused by the exchange. Zhenya held out a hand toward his mother, whose chair was closer to his.

"It's fine, Mama," he said in Russian. "They treat me fine here."

"Did you get the mended socks? I fixed your favorites, the ones with the silk, did you see?"

"Yes, Mama."

Milly sighed, and the fight went out of her. Maybe she was a coward, letting these bullies tell her and Zhenya what to talk about. But she wouldn't be the one punished if they decided to exact retribution.

"Luba sends her greetings," Milly said in a flat voice. If she could work Victor into the conversation, that would be a clue at least.

"Did she make you her borscht? I've been missing everyone's cooking. And especially your company." He looked back and forth between them, and his eyes glistened.

"We will get you out," Milly said.

"It is only a three-year sentence." He raised three fingers, like a child.

Olga must have understood, for she said enthusiastically in Russian, "The work will do you good, Zhenya. Strengthen you."

"Think of the roles I can get onstage when I have more muscle." Zhenya poked at his arm, bundled in a wool sweater.

"Right. Only three years." Milly tried to sound optimistic. She had been thinking of returning to America this summer, but not now. She needed to stay and fight for him here. "We will write you."

"Please do." Zhenya leaned forward in his chair. "Then it will be like we are talking in the kitchen."

"I will ask Victor to write you too," Milly said.

"And you can visit!" Zhenya scuffled his feet against the floor, as if to gain traction to stand, but a look from the male guard settled him back into his chair. "With the OGPU permission, you can visit."

"Where are you going?" Milly grabbed her purse and rooted inside for a pencil.

Zhenya glanced at the interpreter.

"To the north," the officer said. She sat up in her chair.

"Where?" Milly held her pencil over a notepad.

"That is all you can know. It is not authorized to discuss more."

"What?" Milly's pencil fell to the floor, and she bent down to snatch it up.

"North."

"Now, hold on," Milly said, low. "Other Russian wives, mothers, children learn where their exiles are going. They get to know. Why can't I?"

The interpreter's cheeks darkened in the dim light.

"I will report this," Milly said. "To the senior prosecutor. Or the Moscow police. Or your committee!" She didn't know if OGPU officers had a work committee, but it was worth a try.

"You are a filthy capitalist, with your bargaining," the woman said. The two guards glanced wide-eyed between them.

The interpreter growled, then huffed out a puff of air.

"He is going to a labor camp north of Novosibirsk. Eight days' journey from Moscow."

Milly slid her fingers under her glasses and rubbed the bridge of her nose. Eight days was probably an optimistic calculation, she guessed, based on what she knew of Soviet trains.

"You are wasting your time," the interpreter said. "Return to approved topics."

"Which were?" Milly held her pencil above her paper. She should stop provoking the woman, but she couldn't help herself, she hated witless authority.

"His health. Your health. Matters of the household."

"And how are you?" Zhenya interjected. His eyes were pinched at the corners, and she wished she could let herself fall into his arms.

"I'm fine, Zhenya," she said softly. "Only worried about you."

Zhenya smiled. "If my baby writes me every day, it will be the best thing that has happened to me. I can know everything you are doing."

Milly gave a soft laugh. "You do love letters."

"Maybe not every day. I do not want you to worry. But every week? You will write?"

"Oh, Zhenya, of course I will write you. And I will visit." She shot a look at the interpreter, who was pretending to pick lint off her heavy skirt. "I'll get permission."

She wanted to promise to get him out too. He deserved to be released, she was sure of it. Even if he had dallied, what did that matter to the Soviet state? He had been nothing but loving and kind to her. But she knew enough not to promise. She pressed her lips together into a silent kiss, then listened as Zhenya and his mother spoke about rations and wages and how else Olga would get by. Milly would help, of course, though neither of them mentioned her.

When they were finished, the two guards grabbed Zhenya by the elbows and lifted him to his feet. To her surprise, Zhenya shook them off, then gave each a reassuring smile. He made a slight bow toward first the interpreter, then his mother. He paused, then squeezed the tortoiseshell bracelet off his hand and gave it to his mother, closing her fingers around it. Milly's chest felt like it was caving inward, as if the ceiling of the dark room had collapsed upon her, and her breath grew ragged. He turned toward Milly, who stood. He lifted his fingers to his mouth as if to blow her a kiss, but he let his fingertips hover over his lips until he broke her gaze and walked away. She pressed two hands over her mouth. She barely knew him at all, she feared suddenly, even with two years of their strange marriage. Why hadn't she asked him more questions when they had been alone, when they had walked Moscow's snow-dusted streets and held hands in silence? Why hadn't she found more time to spend with him? Now Zhenya and the guards exited and turned down the hallway, away from the front door.

The interpreter frowned at Milly, who brushed a tear from her cheek and then led the blinking Olga from the room. Outside, the hallway lights strained Milly's eyes, and she closed them for a step.

"I'll see him at that camp," Milly said in Russian, to both Olga and the investigator.

Olga patted her hand.

"He'll be fine. He's a strong boy."

Milly shook her head, then caught herself and walked silently from the prison. Zhenya was hopeful, but that wasn't the same thing as strong. And Milly seemed to be losing her hope day by day. Nothing she had ever hoped for had worked out, and she left a wake of shattered dreams, or lives, behind her. She didn't have Zhenya's optimism. But she knew he needed her, and she would hold on to that. They maneuvered their way through the crowd pressing quietly into the prison, and a man waiting in line held the door open as they left.

14

BEFORE

NOVEMBER 1932

MILLY PLACED HER hands on her hips, but still the woman managed to back her into one of the towering rubber plants that filled the small bedroom. The wide leaf tapped Milly's elbow, as if requesting her attention.

"You have no right to be here!" The woman jabbed a finger into Milly's chest as she yelled in fierce Russian.

"I have the right," Milly said, her words limping as she struggled to find them quickly enough. She'd give this scheming woman her due. Milly had finally found a room to stay in, had paid that driver the atrocious sum of nearly thirty-five dollars in rubles to haul her trunk and couch, and now this woman was trying to kick her out, because she wanted Milly's room for herself.

"My landlady rented it to me," Milly said, trying for a calm tone that might gain her a few more inches of standing room.

"She is a speculator." The woman's round face turned red, and Milly wondered if she was enjoying herself, getting to unload all her pent-up frustration on poor, Russian-hobbled Milly.

"I know you have a . . ." She paused and tried to choose the right adjective. "Room that is small. But Citizen Andreyeva's son bought three rooms, and then he was . . . in the Red Army. It is fair. They rent this house because they must." She shrugged as if it was all an unfortunate misunderstanding. And really, Milly did feel for the angry woman, who was the house committee chief for the building, yet whose whole family was crammed into a tiny room in this same apartment while Milly only had her landlady's plants to share space with. She glanced over at the window, where a purple-leafed spiderwort crept across the windowsill.

"I will call the Moscow chief of militia!" The woman did finally step back, and she lifted her round chin, pleased with herself.

"I would like that," Milly said. Then she added in English, "He's a swell guy. Let me borrow his car once for a story."

"What?" The woman's eyes narrowed.

"Please. Call him." Milly smiled.

"Citizen. Do you think the laws here are made for your comfort?" And without waiting for an answer, the house committee chief walked out and slammed the door behind her.

Milly sighed and collapsed onto her little couch, the daybed she used for sitting and sleeping. The flimsy mattress bowed around her, and she would have liked to fall straight asleep, except she had to go to work soon. She wished she could figure out a way to write a story about Moscow's crowded housing that would get past the censors, or that wouldn't get her in trouble when it was time to renew her visa.

A tepid knock sounded at the door, and Milly didn't bother responding. Her landlady, Ivanna Andreyeva, opened the door and poked her gray-haired head in.

"She won't give up," Ivanna Andreyeva said, her eyes round and sad.

"She wants more space. Is understandable."

"Maybe your lawyer . . . ?" The old woman held her hands, pleading, in front of her chest.

"At work?" Every workplace had a lawyer, or so it seemed. But Milly shook her head. "He's very busy."

"Please ask. For us both."

Milly sighed. She didn't want to go back to Anna Louise's apartment like a forlorn puppy, especially after her last two weeks there, when Anna Louise had spent every night from midnight to two a.m. yelling at someone on the telephone then crying for the hour afterward in heaving sobs. Milly had gone out the first night to comfort her but only received a teacup thrown at her head for her troubles. She ducked and scurried back to her room. Anna Louise was as glad to see her go as she was to leave, she guessed. And here, in this private room, Milly might finally get more time with Zhenya, once she registered him as an overnight guest with the house committee. That would be worth whatever effort the registration took.

That afternoon at work, Milly found the newspaper's lawyer in Borodin's office, and she tried to interrupt, but the lawyer waved her off. The two men were in deep consultation about something—probably some political complication. Milly was glad she didn't have to manage the ins and outs of whose version of socialism they were celebrating today. Axelrod still watched her with a sharp eye, and her decisions would never pass muster with him.

She sat down at her desk and stared at the typewriter, wondering if she could sneak in a letter to one of her pals in San Francisco, when Seema Jones came to sit by her. Anna Louise had hired her a few weeks earlier.

"I've got a story for you." Seema handed Milly a typed page. "I want you to go through the edits with me, so I can learn. You know I'm an art student." She flashed a dazzling smile before turning her long face serious.

"You should ask your boyfriend, the famous writer." Milly nudged Seema, then picked up the paper. She liked the younger woman, who had come over that summer with a group of other black Americans to star in a movie. But after a few months of what was essentially a paid vacation in Russia, the film never materialized. Others in the crew had gone home or, like the poet Langston Hughes, continued to roll around Moscow, but Seema wanted a job. She didn't quite know how to write a yarn, but she had good instincts. Milly was happy to go over the editing with her.

"Who's Wallace?" Seema picked up a stray letter on Milly's desk and frowned.

"Give it here." Milly's cheeks burned. "He's just a fella from back home."

"Just a fella? That's not what those pink cheeks are telling me." Seema winked a long-lashed eye and handed back the letter. "I thought you had a Russian boyfriend."

"I do." She still hadn't told her colleagues that she had married Zhenya. They wouldn't understand, and she wasn't sure she did either, yet. Milly folded the letter into her pocketbook, slung over her chair. "But there's no harm in a few extra friends. Especially across the world, right?"

Milly had expected the other woman to laugh, but instead Seema turned her curved lips into a slight frown.

"If you say so," she said.

"Oh hell, Seema, it's not like that. Look, if you want to talk about men, let's have a drink of something fizzy after we're done with work."

"If you can get my edits done quickly enough." Seema smiled. "Boris is coming to fetch me later." Boris Pilnyak, a famous writer, was already smitten with his American girlfriend, from what Milly could see.

Milly nodded, though she was disappointed. With Ruth gone a year now, Milly was lonely. But friendships can't be forced.

"Another time. Let's get those edits done, all right?"

The night went quickly, with lots of stories to review and an endless number of teeth-gritting translation mistakes from the Russian stories to catch. Seema was long gone by the time

Milly left the office, and Milly considered going to that bar by herself. She buttoned her dog fur coat, then decided against it.

She was bundled against the cold and already four blocks from the office by the time she remembered her landlady's request to solicit the lawyer's help. She stopped on the dark street, and the winter air burned her nostrils as she considered walking back. She pulled her scarf up over her mouth so she could try to breathe some steam into her face. He had probably gone home by now. Lawyers didn't need to stay and put the paper to bed. She could ask him the next day.

But the next morning, a banging sounded on Milly's flimsy door, and she pulled her pillow over her head.

"Go away!" she yelled in Russian, then in English.

There was silence. She smiled and nestled herself deeply into her covers.

Then, the doorknob clicked, and the door swung open. The house committee chief held a small skeleton key aloft while she grinned, and behind her Ivanna Andreyeva cringed.

"You are no longer registered in this residence," the committee chief said, articulating each word with care. "Your presence here is illegal. You are required to leave, Citizen." Her teeth met in an expression that was part smile, part snarl.

❄

FIVE HOURS LATER, Milly was standing outside Zhenya's door. Her trunk was beside her, but she hadn't been able to manage to haul the little couch up the stairs on her own. It languished outside the building door, where she prayed no one would take it.

Milly knocked again, tears forming in her eyes. She had never expected that simply being, having a place to sleep, would be so difficult. She knew her friends in San Francisco were desperate for work, but here she had a job. She earned money.

Yet still no one wanted her.

She wiped her damp cheek with the back of her gloved wrist and knocked a third time.

Victor opened the door.

Milly stepped back.

"Victor, I didn't know you . . ." She fumbled for the right word in Russian, though she wasn't sure she could complete the thought in English either.

He stared at her. His brown hair was disheveled and he wore a sweater that looked two sizes too large.

"Is Zhenya home?" Milly tried to stand straight.

"No." Victor coughed. "I think he had a rehearsal for his scene."

"Could you help me?" Her voice quavered, and she pointed down the stairs. "My sleeping couch is on the street."

"You're moving in?" He ran his fingers through his hair.

"I don't know," Milly said. "Please?"

"Yes, of course." He walked back into the apartment, leaving the door open, and pulled his boots from a small pile of things next to Luba's desk. "Put your trunk there," he said, pointing next to the closed door to Zhenya's room. "Olga Ivanova is sleeping." Then he trotted down the stairs.

Milly dragged her trunk into the apartment as quietly as she could, and when she finished, she sat on its closed top. Within a few minutes, Victor came, panting, into the room.

"You're sure it was on the street?"

Milly jumped to her feet. That couch cost her two months' wages.

"Yes, I—right by the door."

Victor smiled and clapped a hand on her shoulder.

"I am only joking. I came to ask your help in getting it up the stairs." He looked at her, his brown eyes darting back and forth between hers. "I am sorry, I had not meant to alarm you."

"It's fine," Milly said. She lifted her glasses to rub her eyes.

After they squeezed the sleeping couch up the stairs and alongside Luba's cot, they sat at the small kitchen table. Outside, the sky was glistening with a steel sheen that promised snow. Victor dropped coals into the samovar.

"Are you living here now?" Milly asked. She had been so busy recently, at least a week had passed since she had visited Zhenya at his apartment.

Victor bit his lip, then poured the tea into glasses.

"No. Or at least, I hope not. I have slept here the past two nights because a woman in my room has been very sick. Coughing blood. I did not want to stay there. But I had nowhere else to go." He gestured toward Luba's part of the front room, where Milly could now see a pallet of blankets folded on the floor.

"I do not want her to die," he said. "But I want to live in my room. I share it with this woman and her brother, and they are neat and pleasant roommates. My books are there." He shook his head, as if in disbelief.

"Building socialism is hard," she said, and they both nodded, staring at the still-empty glasses. It was what they had to say, but she believed it too, most days. Wrenching society from its foundations, breaking its habits, and teaching new ways—that was all hard. Victor then stood and poured the tea and water.

"I want to believe in it, though," Milly said as he worked. "My friend George Hyde, he lost his job three months ago. In America. He couldn't find a newspaper to take him on. And last week, he put a hose on the car tailpipe. He breathed the air inside until he died." She picked at the wooden grain of the table. "My other friend sent me a wire about it."

"That is sad." Victor handed her the tea glass, and their fingers brushed when she grasped the handle. His hands were rough and dry.

"I have to believe we can do better than that for one another," she said.

Victor pressed his lips together, then took a sip of tea. Milly watched the knot in his throat bob as he swallowed. He had a sort of rough masculinity at times, when viewed at the right angle.

"What?" He held the tea glass near his lips.

"You love him, don't you."

His face flamed red.

"I don't know what you're talking about." He pressed the glass to the table, and the tea nearly sloshed out.

"I think you do," Milly said, her voice husky. "But he won't have you now. Is that right? Because of me."

"I'm not talking to you about this," Victor said. He stood.

"Even if you lurk around, you won't have his heart. You won't." The anger that surged up behind her hot words singed her throat even more than the scalding tea, and the force of it surprised her.

"He loves me," she added.

"What do you know about love?" Victor lifted one side of his delicate nose, then grabbed his coat and left the apartment.

"Some nerve," Milly muttered. Then she sighed and pressed her eyes shut.

"Dammit," she said. She paused, then took both glasses to the small sink to wash them. She didn't know what else to do.

15

Now

APRIL 15, 1934

ZHENYA HAD BEEN imprisoned for over a month, and yet there were moments when Milly could forget and believe he had never been taken. Her work in the newsroom helped. Milly was gnawing at a pencil in her mouth as she wondered how to unkink the particularly bad sentence in front of her, one of the translated pieces that may as well have been left in Russian. If only being in charge of half the translators meant she could fire a quarter of them. The mail delivery boy, a teenager with a splotched face and scars on his knuckles, dropped two letters on her desk before moving on to toss three for Seema.

Milly spat out the pencil and grabbed the letters. Any breath of news from her friends in San Francisco was like an ocean breeze to her, no matter how difficult their news was. The important thing was that a friend had taken the time to write.

The first letter was from a woman she used to write with in San Francisco, and Milly read it so fast she hardly absorbed her friend's stories about her toddling boy, or the gossip about their mutual newspaper friends. She could read it at length and savor it later.

She picked up the second letter and frowned. This wasn't from America, as she had assumed. The return address on the preprinted envelope was for OGPU headquarters. Her hands trembled as she opened and read it, twice to make sure she understood.

Her application to have Zhenya's case reviewed had been accepted. She had an appointment the following afternoon.

❧

THE NEXT DAY, she arrived an hour before the appointed time, in case there was a line to wait in. But she was the only person who presented herself to the senior prosecutor's secretary, so she sat in his room with the filing cabinets, where she had met him before, and tried to read the book she had stuffed into her purse when she ran out of her room at the New Moscow Hotel—*Lady Chatterley's Lover*. Her attention kept wandering to the creaking of the floorboards above, or the furious tapping of the secretary's typewriter, or the urgent whispers that flitted by in the hallway behind her. What fates were being made and unmade here while she tried to read a frivolous novel? She closed the book and set it aside.

Exactly an hour after her arrival, the senior prosecutor opened his door and stuck his narrow head out. He looked around, frowned when he saw Milly, then opened the door wider.

"Citizen Bennett?"

Both Milly and the secretary answered yes simultaneously. Milly glared at the young man, then stood and walked toward Rosonov's inner office.

"Come in, then," he said. He turned away and marched to sit behind his desk. The room was large with two tall windows looking out onto the street. The door shut behind her with a heavy thud.

"Do you have a comment to make?"

Milly opened then closed her mouth.

She took a deep breath, and as she exhaled, she saw a photograph of a stern-faced woman and two children on the bookshelf behind Rosonov.

"You understand marriage, Prosecutor," she said. "You may not see your family much, not with the long hours you work here, but you know your wife. You know how she spends her days, looking down on the playground in the courtyard from your window. In the House of Government, I'm guessing. With no curtains because those are bourgeois, though I'll bet she asks you to buy some for the privacy. But you refuse, as you should. You know your wife will listen." She watched him closely as she spoke, and from the twitch in his eye at the mention of the large apartment complex where the senior-most officials lived, she suspected she had guessed correctly. It wasn't hard.

"I know my husband," she continued. "Even when we didn't see each other often, I know how he spent his time, who he loved, what he dreamed of. I can tell you, the charges are false. He can't be guilty of homosexuality." She had memorized the speech earlier, and now she feared she said it too fast. She wasn't sure, either, that what she said was true, but she would say it if that's what Zhenya needed.

Rosonov nodded.

"I appreciate your commentary," he said. "But our agent at the Bolshoi has very clear information about Evgeni Konstantinov's immoral behavior. We cannot disregard that behavior." He flicked his thumbnail against the nail on his middle finger.

"But what about his wife? Don't you think I know a thing or two about his private behavior?" She wanted to growl and swat all his neat papers onto the floor.

"Our agent has clear evidence. No woman can know everything," he said with a half-smile.

"Your agent?"

"I cannot reveal our sources."

Milly placed her hands on the edge of the desk and dug her fingernails into the wood.

"It's Victor, isn't it? Yes, I see it there on your face. It's Victor, and he's a jealous scheming pig. He claimed Zhenya did things? With him?"

"I cannot comment." Rosonov's face burned red.

"You can't believe his word over mine. Do you want to hear about Zhenya's behavior?" She paused, then glowered at him and reached into her bag. She tossed Lawrence's novel across the desk.

"Read that," she said, trying to level her voice. "You want to know what my life with Zhenya was like? Read that. Then tell me that man deserves to be imprisoned for whatever you claim he did."

She was tempted to follow that with a scream of "who the hell cares anyway," but she knew better than that, at least. What the Soviets had declared illegal was now permanently, incontrovertibly illegal. No matter how absurd the pronouncement was.

"Citizen, have you finished your statement?" His voice was icy cold.

She took a deep breath and wrinkled her nose.

"I got carried away. Forgive me. But the point is true. He is my husband. My testimony should matter too."

Rosonov nodded and, to her surprise, picked up the book. He turned it over, but she could tell he could make little sense of the words. He extended her book toward her.

"This is unnecessary. You may have it back."

She blushed and returned the novel to her purse. He held up a hand to silence her.

"Your passion is understandable. I will review the evidence and send you notice of my decision." He looked at the ceiling for a moment, then back at her. "If you are interested, you may also raise the case with Mikhail Kalinin. It could not hurt to write him a letter. I'm sure you have mutual connections you could mention."

Milly closed the flap of her pocketbook over the novel, though she had to jam the book back down into her messy purse in order to make the latch snap. She should slow down, rearrange her belongings, but she didn't. Her breath coursed shallow.

"Zhenya deserves better than the labor camp. He deserves better than me," she said quietly. "He is an actor, not a brick-layer."

"None of us are above labor," Rosonov said, his eyes narrowing. "But the state will only punish the guilty. I will review the evidence."

He stood.

Milly did too. Her hands were shaking, and she had to bite back a crack about mailing his wife the Lawrence book. She knew better, so she merely nodded and walked out of the office.

"You will receive a letter either way, Citizen," he called from inside the room, as if he had forgotten his standard line.

"Yeah, thanks," Milly muttered in English.

MILLY PULLED HER coat tightly around her to ward off the brisk autumn wind. The season was so short here, and already she could feel winter nipping at her fingertips. This year she really would buy that beautiful embroidered reindeer coat she had her eye on. She'd at least have a fighting chance with that sort of coat, better than the flimsy dog fur.

Brown leaves skittered across the sidewalk as she strode toward the hotel, and one swirled up and snagged on her silk stocking. She bent down to carefully pluck it out. Luba would want Milly to look spotless for the name day celebration; Luba's actual celebration, not the one for Antonia.

When Milly walked up the marble steps just inside the Metropol's revolving door and could see the lobby bar, Zhenya was already there. He had been holding Luba's delicate hand and nodding while she explained something, but when he saw Milly, he dropped Luba's hand and strode over to greet her.

"That dress," he said, giving her an appreciative look up and down. He took her coat. "My Milly baby is the most beautiful woman in the room."

"Thank you." She gave a twirl in the black dress and hoped he wouldn't notice the tiny hole worn in the fabric near her rear. She hadn't had time to mend it, so she wore black underwear in hopes of disguising the tear. She didn't even have a slip.

He gave her a kiss on the cheek.

"What's this? A spritz of perfume?"

"Camellias, of course." Milly winked.

In the spring, she had moved out of his apartment, which had been too small to accommodate the three of them. Now she was in a dormitory where she had, finally, her own room. Over the summer Milly had hosted her friend Marjorie, who was visiting from Constantinople, and Marjorie's presence seemed to clarify Zhenya's relationship for both of them. With Marjorie around, they didn't have sex—and since, had done so only twice. But Zhenya was still the best company, and he took pride in standing by Milly's side or playing host to her friends. He showered her with kisses and held her warm against his body at night. For her part, she tried to take comfort in his pride, and she did what she could to take care of him. In all of Moscow, there was no one's company she preferred over his.

She tried not to wish for more.

"Milly." Luba held out her hand for a kiss.

"Happy name day," Milly said in Russian. "I should write a story about your party, Luba. Americans don't know what name days are, and yours is better than most."

Luba's brows drew together, and she cocked her head.

"Your name means 'love,' right? So each year we celebrate you and love. It's like having a birthday on Valentine's Day, but better."

"You should write it," Luba said, her wide eyes glowing. "I give you my permission."

Milly brushed her lips against her friend's hand. "I was making a joke. This old lady is, as we say it in English, washed up. No one wants my stories. I'm thinking of picking up farming."

Zhenya laughed, and Luba looked between them as if she weren't sure whom to believe. It was true that almost none of Milly's pitches got picked up overseas, and all the editors she knew seemed to prefer the international stringers flitting through Moscow over her; no matter that she'd been here years to their months. But she kept trying. She didn't know how to live if she didn't write, and she needed the money. Maybe she would do a color piece on name days.

"Milly, let me introduce my brother-in-law, Grisha," Luba said, waving for a large man to approach. He had a mass of curly hair springing from his head, and his broad shoulders moved awkwardly in his suit jacket. "He's visiting," Luba added.

Zhenya patted her hand and walked away to talk to a visiting cousin. When Grisha approached, Luba handed them both glasses of vodka she pulled from a nearby low table.

"Milly is a writer," Luba said. "Tell her about life outside the city." Luba nodded, then turned to greet another guest.

"Good evening," Grisha said with an opaque accent that probably hailed from some remote village. He paused, then extended a thick-fingered hand. She shivered to feel how small her hand felt in his grasp.

"Let's sit and you can tell me about where you're from." Milly led him to a bench against the wall. It creaked as he lowered himself to squeeze behind a table and onto the bench, and Milly feared his worn suit would split at the thighs. Then again, maybe he, too, was wearing black underwear. She smiled, then sat down alongside him.

"But you must tell me about the opera," Grisha said. "I love *Boris Godunov*." He clasped his hands together at his knees. "I saw it once and at the end clapped until my hands hurt."

"That is such a good one. Our Zhenya was in it here, did you know?"

"Luba said so. I wish I could have seen it."

They each took a sip of the bright vodka, and Milly relished the warmth in her throat and the tightening at her temples that the drink brought.

Milly glanced at Zhenya, who was still talking to his cousin, but he turned to give an encouraging smile to Milly. He then raised his glass in a salute toward her and returned to his conversation. She took a long sip of the vodka and flinched at the strength of it. He could have been encouraging her flirtation with Grisha, or he could have been oblivious to it. She pinched her eyes shut.

Grisha's calloused fingers brushed against her arm.

"Are you all right?"

She opened her eyes and saw his brown ones crinkled with concern. His skin was thick and weathered, the legacy of a life spent in the sun.

"Do you hunt?" she asked.

"Yes," he said, leaning back. He fixed his gaze on something across the noisy lobby. "Mostly I fish."

Fishing was nearly as sexy as hunting. She leaned forward. "Are you on a collectivized farm?"

He shook his head, and she was ashamed to feel a little disappointed that he wouldn't have a story she could write up. There was no end to editors' appetites for stories about successful collective farmers. There didn't seem to be many of them.

"I work in a factory," he said. "But any moment I can, I'm chopping wood and fishing." He shrugged and looked at her, then lifted a hand to her chin. Heat flooded her core at his touch, and she sucked in a breath.

They poured two more glasses as Milly's head began to swim. She looked over at Zhenya again, who was listening and nodding as Luba spoke, and she nuzzled into Grisha's shoulder. He laughed.

They spent the night drinking and talking, with Milly's ability to parse his burred accent fading as her enthusiasm for his warmth at her side rose.

"You should take me home," she whispered, quite a few drinks in, to Grisha, or at least she thought she did. She wanted his rough hands against her bare skin, pulling and pushing her soft flesh against his. But Grisha didn't react, and maybe she hadn't said it after all, and then she leaned her head against his shoulder and fell asleep.

The next morning she awoke in her room in the dormitory with a pounding headache and a warm body in her bed. Too hot. She pushed herself upright and clutched her head, the heels of her hands pressed into her eyes.

"Awake finally?"

She opened her eyes to see Zhenya propped up on one elbow alongside her. A tightness in her chest released, and she laughed.

"What?" His curved lips pursed in confusion.

"I never know what to expect from you," she said.

He patted her hand, then collapsed back onto the pillow.

"It took three of us to get you up here," he said. "Poor Grisha didn't move all night once you passed out on his shoulder."

Milly rested her head down next to Zhenya's and stared into his long-lashed eyes.

"What kind of marriage do we have, Zhenya?"

He turned to look at the ceiling.

"An interesting one. Like all marriages."

He pulled her toward him and gave her a soft, closed-mouth kiss.

"We are finding our way." He reached to pull up the hem of the dress she was still wearing. With the skirt bunched against her thigh, he began caressing the bare skin of her waist.

"I wish our way had a lot more sex," Milly said, then bit her lip.

He laughed.

SALT THE SNOW • 133

"Always with the jokes, my Milly baby." He retracted his hand and swung his legs out of bed. "Let me brush my teeth."

He winked and took his toothbrush out of the room, toward where the shared bathroom at the end of the dormitory hallway was. The dormitory was a converted stable tucked back behind a large house, and Milly was glad the builders had bothered to put the bathroom inside the dormitory. She took a long drink from the glass of water on her nightstand, then waited.

When Zhenya returned, he locked the door behind him and approached the bed slowly. With his eyes on her, he unbuttoned the cotton shirt he had worn the previous night. Then he shrugged out of his pants, and she could see he already had an erection. Well. She could work with that.

An hour later he left, and Milly pried herself out of bed. She had the day off from the newsroom, where she was now responsible for overseeing half the translator staff, on top of writing her own stories. Today, no matter how much she wanted to sleep, she needed to work on her book. Milly had interviewed a clown by the name of Durov, and she was convinced she could spin a story for American audiences out of his conviction and commitment to entertaining little socialists. She loved listening to the small man with his sparkling eyes talk about how even class consciousness needed humor, and how he used his otherwise unimpressive body to convey a message. She knew about making do with middling physical gifts, and she liked his honesty.

She dressed, then walked into a large room on the second floor of the converted stable, where *Moscow Daily News* had some typewriters and tables, set out for translators. She stayed there working, not talking to anyone as she tried to force her notes into a story, and she left only to get a bland beef stew at a local cooperative restaurant for dinner. When she stepped out of the restaurant, a dingy storefront just a block from her dormitory, she inhaled. The cold bit at her throat, but it was refreshing compared to the cabbage stink of the restaurant. A strong smell of woodsmoke wafted over, and she breathed again.

Then a commotion sounded behind the next house on the street, from the deep yard where Milly's converted stable stood, behind another house.

She ran.

When she reached the yard, four other people from *Moscow Daily News* stood shivering in the grass. Katinka, a tall woman who worked as both a housemaid and a prostitute, stood with her arms crossed as she listened to one of the American reporters howl. Smoke poured out the windows of three of the lower-level rooms.

"What is he saying?" Katinka said to Milly in her deep Russian. She held a telephone clutched in one of her hands, apparently pulled from the wall, judging by the trailing cord.

"Junius!" Milly yelled at her colleague, who pressed a hand to his eyes and sobbed a few words.

"He says his ticket back to America and his passport are locked up in some box in his room," Milly translated for Katinka. At her side, a Russian woman clicked her tongue, as if admonishing the American for thinking his belongings were safer locked up. Or safe at all.

"If he wants help, he should have asked." Katinka laid her salvaged telephone at Milly's feet, raised an eyebrow, then strode toward the burning building.

"Katinka!" Milly yelled, but remained still, and the other woman kept walking. The stable-dormitory still spewed smoke, but she didn't see any flames. Maybe she should try to retrieve her own belongings. Her room was on the far end of the building, away from where the fire appeared to be; perhaps it would be safe enough to rush in and retrieve her papers. Her manuscript about the clown, her letters from Zhenya and her friends and her mother. If nothing else, she could use a warmer pair of stockings. She shivered in the cold.

"I should go—" Milly began.

"No," a Russian woman, probably a neighbor, hissed. "That man was crazy enough."

"Katinka is a woman," Milly said. She looked over at the woman, who had an overcoat buttoned over her nightdress. Behind her rose the house closest to the street, and a few Russian women had thrown open the windows to lean out and watch.

Junius held his head in his hands and cried about his passport, but Seema stepped toward Milly. Her hair was disheveled, pushed up behind her head. It was early to be sleeping, but then she hadn't seemed well lately. Milly furrowed her brow, looking at the other woman's wan complexion, and she tried to find the words to ask if Seema needed any help. But maybe she wasn't sick, just pregnant or something, and she wouldn't want Milly butting in.

"Did anyone call the fire department?" Milly asked.

Seema nodded, but kept quiet as she watched the glowing building.

From inside the dormitory came a loud crash, and Milly jumped. Then a roar, and Milly took a few steps closer. A plume of smoke burned her eyes.

"Katinka! Are you—"

The large woman came bounding out, a wide grin on her face and her hand held high. Some papers protruded.

"I punched through the wall." She dropped the documents in the sobbing Junius's hands with a flourish. "There was no safe, only a small door over the wall. I punched through."

A clanging arose behind them, and they all spun to see a glistening red fire engine pull up under the streetlights. The light cast the engine's winding brass fixings into sharp relief.

"I knew someone had called," Seema said. Milly glanced again at her, and she seemed lost in a daze.

"Seema, are you—"

Then, thick smoke billowed from the building, and the crowd shuffled farther back, coughing. Seema stepped away.

Firefighters dashed past them, carrying two long hoses with golden brass nozzles. Milly was tempted to yell after them, to threaten them with something absurd if they didn't keep her papers dry, but the words stuck in her throat. She hadn't asked, she realized, if everyone had gotten out.

The first hose turned on, and a broad spray of water seemed to push the smoke aside.

"Idiots," Katinka said.

"What do you mean?" Milly's teeth chattered.

Katinka picked up her telephone box and moved it farther from the stable.

"Whoever left his stove burning. And whoever thinks he can stop a fire by putting out the smoke." She spat.

Seema came to Milly's side. "Axelrod is going to kill us," she said in Russian. Sometimes she and Milly preferred Russian over English, partially, Milly knew, out of pride, but also because Russian felt better suited to some things. Like worrying.

"The *News* isn't responsible for the building." Milly watched the firefighters as she spoke. They seemed to be concentrating their efforts on the side of the building away from her room, but still her stomach knotted.

"No, but the paper will have to help everyone replace their clothes. And find us new places to sleep." Seema hugged herself and shuddered. Her dark fingers were bare, and Milly was tempted to grab them and rub them in her own hands. But she knew Seema wouldn't want to be touched.

"Your rooms are safe?" Katinka asked them both.

"I think so," Seema said. She pulled her coat, no, bathrobe, tighter across her chest.

"But—" Katinka pointed at the second floor of the stable, where the smoke now spewed. There hadn't been any sign of fire there a few minutes earlier.

"Those are the offices. Typewriters, desks, no one's personal belongings." Milly shook her head.

"Typewriters?" Katinka straightened. "You would let those burn?"

"Hell," Milly said, though she blushed in the dark. Axelrod had fined her three rubles last month when a hammer on one of the machines got bent. "I am going to get in trouble for that."

Katinka huffed, then bent down to pick up her telephone from the dry grass at Milly's feet. "You have so much money, you can afford to let your tools burn?"

"No, we can't, but what can we do?" Milly's voice slunk out from her throat.

"Someone has trusted you with those tools. And you stand here and watch them burn. Those typewriters must cost as much as I earn in a year. At both my jobs."

"Hell." Milly looked around at her colleagues. Junius had taken his rescued papers and fled to the street, past the main house, and Seema had her arms wrapped around herself for warmth.

"They're not worth dying for," Milly said.

Katinka held up her telephone, as if that proved something. Milly took off her glasses to wipe them clean of the smoke. She replaced them on her nose.

She strode toward the building.

The stair was dark and filled with smoke, but only a little warm. The steps held as she walked up, and soon she heard a clomping behind her.

"At least you have some spirit," Katinka said from over Milly's shoulder.

Upstairs in the workroom, the air was hotter. Milly wondered if the floorboards beneath them were on fire. She didn't know how fire traveled.

"How many can we carry, do you think?" she asked Katinka. Mostly, she was wondering how many Katinka could carry in her well-muscled arms and broad shoulders. Milly would be lucky if she could carry one.

"No time for that." Katinka shook her head. Then she picked up a typewriter, yelled "Look out!" and threw it out the closed window.

The glass shattered, and a distant thump sounded.

"That's not going to save them!" Milly called. She wondered if Katinka had ever used a typewriter.

The other woman ignored her, picked up another one, and threw it out the broken window with a scream. The smoke thickened, and Milly coughed.

"Aw hell." She picked up a typewriter. Then, with a swing, she launched it in a flying parabola out the window.

The typewriter hummed and then crashed as it hit the ground. Outside, someone squealed.

Milly threw back her head and laughed. After he fined her, Axelrod told her to protect the machines no matter what she had to do. She supposed saving them from fire counted as protection.

Katinka looked at her, wide-eyed, then picked up another machine, widened her legs, and swung it low between them before rocketing it out the already-broken window. Milly cheered.

Behind them, the smoke reared up like an angry cobra, and Milly picked up another typewriter.

"This is one way to think of freedom of the press," she said, coughing. She pitched the typewriter out, though this one didn't land far.

"One more each?" Katinka asked. Through the increasingly hazy room, Milly looked at Katinka, who was wiping sweat from her broad forehead, and she smiled.

"No one can say we didn't try."

"Try? We have succeeded!" Katinka hurled a typewriter out of the room.

"To victory!" Milly yelled, and picked up an Underwood. "To truth and courage and hope!"

She pushed the machine into the air and watched it as it sailed away into the dark.

Now

April 30, 1934

Milly stood across the sidewalk from the massive apartment building, which rose some eleven stories at its highest points and occupied an entire block. The House of Government, everyone called it, named for all the senior Soviet officials who lived in the hundreds of apartments built in the demolished wake of the former metalwork and chocolate factory here on the bank of the Moskva River. Behind her, ice chunks still skimmed the fast-flowing river, already swollen with the spring melt-off. Milly took a deep breath, opened and closed her fists, then crossed the street.

The Orlovs lived around the side, at Entryway 10. Not the most prestigious entrance, the daughter had told her, but not far either from the best apartments and their river views. Milly had met Vera, the family's daughter, in a class Milly had taught the previous fall. Now she resurrected the old connection out of desperation. She'd talk to anyone who would help her with Zhenya.

Milly walked past the neoclassicist rectangular columns flanking the riverfront entrances and, following Vera's instructions, turned the corner to find Entryway 10. She walked under a four story-tall breezeway held up by even more massive columns, entered a courtyard, and then found the awning marked "10."

A doorman frowned when he opened the metal-and-glass door upon her buzzing and frowned more deeply when she explained she was there to see Vera Aleksandrovna Orlov.

"Do you have an appointment?" he asked.

"Do eighteen-year-old girls require appointments? She must be more popular than I thought." Milly pretended to frown and bite her lip pensively.

The doorman snorted, but he picked up the phone on the table to his side and dialed. After a hushed conversation, he hung up. He narrowed his eyes, then pointed down the hall at his back.

"The elevator is on your left. Fourth floor."

Milly walked down the tiled hallway, her steps slicing through the quiet of the building. She pushed the elevator button and the contraption clanked in response. Of course, she could take the stairs, but she wanted to see what a deluxe Soviet elevator was like.

The elevator attendant was a hunched woman whose quick movements to crank open the gate and then close the door behind Milly made her think the woman wasn't as old as her lined face would suggest. They ascended to the fourth floor in silence, and there, the woman repeated her rapid performance. Maybe she got tips for speed.

Vera stood waiting in the hallway.

"Welcome!" She threw her arms open wide, both indicating the expanse of their surroundings and preparing to embrace Milly. Milly stepped closer and gave the young woman a quick kiss on the cheek. They hadn't seen each other in months, not since Vera had been hospitalized with rheumatic fever before the class had ended, and before Zhenya was arrested. Their lessons had ceased then, though Vera had written her letters assuring Milly she would be fine. Milly hoped so, though she worried.

"We're that one," Vera said, pointing at a set of tall white doors two apartments down from the elevator, at the end of the short hall. Milly looked around and wondered what Zhenya would have thought of such luxury. Luxury like what his family had had, before the revolution.

"That's Platon Kerzhentsev's family's apartment. He's the chief theoretician for the Bolshevik Conception of Time." Her voice was hushed as they passed.

"He thinks about how to change time?"

Vera looked quickly toward Milly, and she seemed to flinch.

"How to make our use of time more socially conscious." They reached Vera's door, and she smiled. "I think."

The entrance was two narrow doors, and only the one on the right opened. Milly followed Vera inside.

"My father's not home yet," Vera said. She led Milly past a small kitchen and into a sitting room. It adjoined an eating area, which was crowded with one heavy oak table and its stern, rectilinear chairs. The sitting room had two armchairs and a sofa, and bookshelves lined the walls behind the chairs.

"Sit," Vera said. "I'll ask Tania to bring you some tea."

While she stepped into another room, behind a door, Milly craned around to scan the titles on the shelf, covered by a glass door. *Brehm's Life of Animals*, and something by Lermontov, the title obscured by a photograph propped against the book's spine. Milly squinted and leaned toward it, trying to make sense of the scene. It was an urban street from somewhere Milly didn't recognize. Not Moscow, but probably somewhere else in Europe.

A young woman with a square face and a blank expression entered the room and delivered a cup of tea, in thick blue glass, to Milly. She had no saucer and no side table to rest it on, so she tried to balance the hot cup on her knee, alternating the fingers that held it to avoid getting singed.

Vera entered holding her own cup of tea.

"Father will be here soon," she said. "He comes home for lunch on the days when he doesn't have meetings."

"You didn't tell him I was coming." Milly had been about to take a sip of tea, but now she held the cup suspended before her lips.

Vera shook her head. "It's best to surprise him. Say, do you want a tour of the building? There's a movie theater and a performance stage! And a laundry, you can see how they maximize community efficiency by having all these ladies in their white uniforms ironing, like a factory, and—"

"I think I'd better wait. I'll get nervous if we leave. Thinking I might miss him." She finally took a sip, and the tea was cooler than she had expected. Bracingly strong though. "How about we practice your English?" she said in that language.

Vera grimaced but relented, and for some half an hour they groped their way through a conversation about the weather and a comparison of Moscow and San Francisco.

"The bridge is red," Milly said. "You would like it."

"I certainly would," said a deep voice in heavily accented English. Milly looked up to see a short man standing in a khaki-and-olive-colored uniform.

"Father, I didn't hear you come in."

Vera set her teacup on a shelf near the sofa and stood to plant a kiss on her father's cheek.

"General Orlov." Milly stood as well, but still held her cup awkwardly. She might splash the remaining contents on him, she realized, so she gulped the rest of the bitter brew down.

Orlov laughed.

"Thirsty, are we. Vera, who's this?" He continued speaking in English.

"Milly Bennett. My . . . teacher."

Milly worried he would ask what she was a teacher of, but he smiled blandly, to Milly's relief. A senior general in the OGPU might not appreciate Milly's more inquisitive brand of journalism. She wanted socialism to succeed as much as the next gal, and she was sure it would, but all the probing questions still needed to be asked along the way.

"It's a pleasure," Orlov said, his small eyes lighting up. He had a broad forehead exaggerated by a receding hairline, and a narrow mustache bristled over his small mouth. Not an unpleasant-looking man.

"Where's your mother?" he asked Vera.

Vera shrugged. "Still at the office, I guess."

He nodded, as if he had expected as much. He looked again at Milly.

"Are you here to help our Vera improve her English? It is a good skill."

"Your own English is impressive," she said.

"I spent two months in New York." He shrugged, but the pride in his voice was clear.

"General Orlov, I may as well be frank. I'm not much good at being anything but." She cast an apologetic glance at Vera, whose fair skin flushed pink. "I'm here to ask you about Mikhail Kalinin. I've been trying to get an appointment with him, but no one answers my letters."

Orlov exhaled loudly through his nose, then pinched his shaved chin.

"Kalinin. He's in the Politburo. Why would you need to see him?"

"It's for my husband. He's been arrested, and Senior Prosecutor Rosonov suggested I talk to Kalinin about the case. The conviction is wrong, I'm sure. He's a baby, he can't make it—"

"Enough." Orlov's face burned crimson. "I don't want my family involved with criminals."

"But he's not, that's what I'm trying to say."

Orlov glanced at Vera, then back at Milly.

"I don't know Kalinin," he said. "He does not have much dealing with the OGPU. I am sorry."

He turned and walked back toward the kitchen, where Milly could hear him barking orders about the meal in a rounded Russian that she couldn't quite place.

"Hell," she muttered.

"I will talk to him," Vera said, her eyes wide and liquid.

As a part of the class Milly taught, she had taken Vera with her for one interview, about a month after her dormitory had burned down. Only five months ago now, that interview with the American stage actors Alfred Lunt and Lynn Fontanne, but it seemed much longer. Vera had done as she promised, hovering at the fringes of Milly's conversation with the couple, making notes when Alfred said something she could understand. His long fingers, which seemed to dance as he spoke, gesticulating, reminded Milly of Zhenya, and his boyish, handsome face seemed to captivate Vera, whose eyes rarely left his sculpted lips. Milly watched how Alfred and Lynn interacted when she asked them questions: each answering in turn, deferring to each other, tapping each other's hands to indicate whose turn it was, like a precise machine. Milly was fascinated. At one point, Alfred said he liked to call his wife Rich Lynnie for all the money saving she did, and she laughed, perfectly on cue, though surely she had heard the tease dozens of times before. Lynn, who had a prominent nose and eyes like crystal, turned to Milly at the end of the interview, extended a finger toward Vera, and said, in her posh British accent, "That girl of yours is delightful." Then she leaned back in her chair and gave a throaty laugh. "I don't believe a husband and wife should be separated for more than a month. At most. Don't you agree?" And Milly couldn't tell if the question was aimed at her or Alfred, so she focused on the notes she was scribbling in her notebook. Then, Vera had leapt to her feet.

"Milly doesn't live with her husband," she said in English so heavily accented that Milly wasn't sure the actors would understand. But Lynn raised one finely plucked eyebrow, then looked at Milly and winked.

Now, in Vera's sitting room, Milly's stomach clenched. What would Vera say to her father? What little the girl knew of Zhenya was unlikely to help his case. Milly walked to the kitchen.

The small space was crowded with Tania, who had wrapped her blond hair in a kerchief, and Orlov, who was giving her some instructions about vinegar.

"General, I am sorry," Milly said.

He looked at her with narrowed eyes.

"For imposing. My husband is young, and he's too delicate for Siberia. You know what it is to worry, don't you?"

"We all have worries," he said. His words, still in English, were perfectly articulated, like diamonds cut with his teeth.

"Forgive me for imposing. I thought I might help my Zhenya. I don't know what else to do; he's such a sweet boy and now they've taken him for no reason to a freezing place to break rocks and cut down trees and . . ." Her voice snagged, and she pinched her eyes closed for a moment.

"You misunderstand me," Orlov said, now in Russian. "I sympathize, but all criminals against the state must be punished. Do you think I doubt my own state?" He straightened his shoulders. "Vera will show you out."

Milly stepped back, and her arm jarred a frame on the wall. She flushed, then turned to straighten it, only to fumble with the balance. Inside the frame, Lenin's portrait stared distantly over her shoulder. She wanted to cry.

Vera opened the door, and Milly followed her out. In the hallway, their steps echoed against the white-and-black tile.

"I can find my way down," Milly said.

"I'm sorry," Vera said, her voice trembling. Her eyes brimmed with tears, and she was blushing more deeply than Milly had ever seen her before. "My father, he—I shouldn't have surprised him like that. I should have known he'd be like that." She whispered so low that Milly could barely hear her.

"It's fine. I should have thought—"

"No. He's so strict. I hate him, sometimes."

Milly laid a hand on the girl's hot forearm, then withdrew.

"Come around the office when you're ready for some work," she said, though she doubted the girl would.

Without waiting, Milly hurried down the broad open stairway next to the elevator. Tall windows fronted the steps, and as she descended, she could see the children playing in the courtyard below, their bodies getting larger as she reached each floor's landing. Perhaps they were aging before her eyes, growing into the native and pure socialists their country needed. Better than the adults it had now. She rushed into the lobby and waved at the curious doorman in his gray uniform. Outside, the wind bit at her cheeks, even though it was supposed to be spring, and she didn't try to wipe away the foolish tears that fell as she walked back to her empty room.

❖

LESS THAN A month later, on May 22, Milly and Seema walked through the rain to Olga's building. It was Milly's birthday, and Olga was hosting a party for her. In Milly's pocketbook was a letter she had received that day from Rosonov.

He had concluded that there was no compelling evidence to alter Zhenya's sentence. He was guilty, sentenced to three years in the prison camp, subject to reduction in the case of good behavior.

Just as before.

Milly gritted her teeth and tried not to think about the cursed waste of it all: her time and his hope and his life spinning out in the distant labor camp.

She hadn't yet told Olga.

Milly and Seema stood at a streetlight, and Seema giggled. "What?"

"If you want a strawberry so bad, you should just ask." Seema held up the kilo of strawberries she was bringing for a gift.

"I wasn't . . ."

"It sure looked like you were staring at them. Fierce. Here." She plucked out one and handed it to Milly. The fruit wasn't quite sweet, it was too early for that, but still, the burst of juice on Milly's tongue was divine. That's what she needed tonight. Hope.

When they arrived at the apartment, Seema handed the box of berries to Olga, whose lined face lit up. Olga kissed Milly's cheeks three times, then hesitated before doing the same to Seema.

Two of Zhenya's second cousins were already in the main room, where Luba's belongings had been pushed to the side to make room for the long table. Victor was there too, though no one was talking to him as he smoked a cigarette in the corner. Milly hadn't seen him for weeks, certainly not since her meeting with Rosonov, and she scowled.

He was a rotten coward.

Luba was helping in the kitchen, but she dried her hands on a cloth and picked up a bottle of vodka and a pair of stemmed glasses Milly had never seen before. Milly exhaled, relieved. A drink would help.

"Have some," she said to Milly, extending a glass. Seema stood next to her, but Luba said nothing. Milly frowned, then passed her glass to Seema. Russians loved to boast that they didn't have the race problems that America did, yet when faced with an actual human body with dark skin, they seemed to see right past her. Now Luba blushed, handed Milly a second glass, and poured her guests a splash of vodka each.

"Have you heard more?" Luba asked. About Zhenya, obviously.

"He's going to perform in the agitation propaganda group."

Milly swallowed her entire dish of vodka, then held out her glass for another pour, even as the heat of the first one was spreading from her chest down through her limbs. She wasn't ready to tell them about his ratified sentence.

"It's your birthday," Luba said. "Who do you want to kiss?"

"I don't think a solitary kiss is enough to cut mustard with me," she said, then blushed at her instinctive forthrightness. The other two women laughed.

"If you want a tumble, you can find one easily enough," Seema said.

"Yes," Luba added. "I've seen the men watch you dance."

Milly waved the words away, but wished they'd go on. She could almost beg them to tell her about her sex appeal, to tell her enough and then maybe she would believe it.

Olga called them to the table, a long makeshift piece constructed of mismatched tables rammed together, probably borrowed from neighbors, along with the colorful tablecloths patchworking the surface. Milly squeezed past the wall and into a seat toward the middle of the contraption, and one of the second cousins, Kostya, sat next to her. Milly smiled at him. When she and Zhenya had gone out with him before, Kostya tried to net her fingers in his under the tablecloth. Then, she had pulled away. But tonight, she might welcome his advances. Anything to forget about Zhenya. She took another large swallow of vodka.

Seema sat across from her, alongside the other cousin's wife, and Victor was at the far end. Good. She didn't want to sit near him, much less talk to him.

Olga, grinning, placed a large platter of dumplings in the middle of the central table, and then, still standing, she raised her glass in a toast to Milly. The rest of the party followed suit, and then dove into their meal.

Seema nodded and listened to the cousin's wife, who was going on about production quotas in her glass bottle factory, while down the table, Victor had coaxed another guest Milly didn't recognize, a neighbor perhaps, into singing some sort of revolutionary song. But the words didn't sound right, and Milly strained to listen. Something about slop, she heard and frowned. Was Victor trying to get them all in trouble? The neighbor's singing broke into a laugh, and no one else looked concerned. Milly took another drink.

Next to her, Kostya was quietly eating his food. Milly dabbed a napkin to her lips, and when she replaced it in her lap, she let her fingers drift over to his hand, which was resting on the bench they shared. A thrill shivered up her arm when her pinky touched the skin of his thumb. She slid her hand closer.

Kostya held still for a moment, but then Seema said something about quotas, and he laughed and pulled away his hand. He pushed away his empty plate, placed both palms on the table, and leaned forward to listen to the beautiful Seema.

Milly balled her hands into fists, then drained her second glass. Or maybe it was her third. A man might enjoy pursuing a woman, but as soon as she showed a sign of wanting attention, of needing some affection and having the courage to ask for it, he spooked and ran to the next pretty face.

Milly stretched her legs under the table and was tempted to kick Seema, but she didn't. It wasn't Seema's fault her eyes were large and her cheekbones high, nor was it her fault that Milly's chin was large and her front teeth prominent. Her eyes welled up.

The bench shifted, and on the other side of her, away from Kostya, sat Victor.

"It's not the same without Zhenya, is it," he said in a low voice. He held her gaze for a long moment before turning to pick at the tablecloth's rose print.

"Some nerve you have saying that." Milly wiped away a tear that had splashed onto her cheek. "If you had kept your mouth shut . . ." She looked down the table and saw Olga almost smiling at something someone else said. Milly clenched her jaw.

"You don't understand," he said.

"You're right, I don't." It felt good to be angry at Victor. Better the clean fuel of self-righteous anger than the soot-coated self-pity from Kostya's rejection.

Victor opened his mouth, then snapped it shut. He rubbed at his jaw, just beneath the ears.

"Are you going to see him?" he asked, his eyes fixed on his dingy glass.

"How can you ask about him? If you hadn't squealed, would he even have been arrested?"

"I didn't have a choice."

"There's always a choice!" Her declaration attracted a few stares from around the table, and she smiled, holding up her glass. Hell if she'd embarrass Olga for the likes of Victor.

He shook his head.

"You should write about him, Milly. Tell his story, to help him."

She snorted. "Sure, the oh-gee-pee-you would love that." She drew out the name of the secret police, as if lingering on the sounds would make them less terrifying. "Anyway, no one in America will care about an opera actor accused of fairy business." She looked at Victor, challenging him. She wanted to shake him, to ask if he had made love to her Zhenya and then told the secret police about it, to dig into the wounds of betrayal. But she couldn't, not yet, not here.

Victor kept his eyes on the tablecloth.

"It is the same everywhere," he said. "Zhenya is lucky to have you. We all are. Happy birthday, Milly."

He took her hand in his. Before she could pull away, he raised his other hand in a toast, then emptied the glass. Milly yanked her hand free then drained her own glass.

OVER THE DIN of Zhenya's party, hosted in Anna Louise's rooms, Milly heard another knock on the door. She rushed to open it, weaving through the oblivious hot bodies talking and drinking and toasting Zhenya, the most popular supernumerary in the city.

Milly opened the door and smiled to see a salt-and-pepper-bearded man standing in the hallway.

"Captain," she said. "What an honor."

The man bowed and entered, and Milly giggled. He, like so many of the other opera actors and singers, was associated with the former upper classes. In his case, he had been the captain of the tsar's guard.

"Tell me what he would say, Captain," Milly said as she took his wool coat, damp with melting snow, and hung it on top of the other coats piled on the rack.

The former soldier held out his fingers, pinched as if he were a tsar holding a cup of hot tea, and said, "Is it cold in the boulevards today?" Then he switched characters, standing tall with his shoulders thrown back and said, "Sire, you are right, as always. It is colder 'n hell in the boulevards today."

Milly laughed, and threw her arms around the grinning man.

"How delightful you are. Go find Zhenya now, if you can, and wish him happy name day."

Not that Zhenya was hard to find. He was beaming as he held court in the center of the room and laughed at his friends' jokes. As soon as Milly had learned Anna Louise would be in Geneva during Zhenya's name day, she knew she had to do this for him.

A handsome young man with black curls and heavy-lidded eyes stumbled past. The son of a Greek countess, Milly had heard someone say.

"Stop him," a woman called out. "He wants to sleep in the bathtub! And then where shall we pee?" Half a dozen people tittered in laughter, and one redirected the countess's son to a bench by the wall. Milly smiled. What a brawl.

Someone else knocked on the door, and she threw it open, nearly slamming a reedy ballerina in the process.

"I heard you were having a party," said an olive-skinned man in English.

Milly frowned.

"Louis," she said. "Come on in."

Louis Fischer, American journalist and self-righteous pain in the ass, sniffed and then entered, followed by Seema, her boyfriend, Boris, and two others from the newspaper.

"I think I'll have to hang a sign saying we're at capacity." Milly maneuvered among them to take their coats, and they bent over to shuck their winter boots from their feet and add them to the pile by the door. Seema slipped on a pair of heels she pulled from her purse, and she unfurled from her crouch like an iris.

"We found him on the street and thought we'd see if we could give him away to a good home," Seema said, then walked through the crowd to find a drink. Boris shrugged, as if in apology, and followed her.

"The *Moscow Daily News* crowd is exceedingly hospitable," Louis said. He crossed his arms.

"Maybe we'd be more hospitable if you weren't stealing our assignments," Milly said, though she knew she shouldn't—if for no other reason than because she didn't want Louis to know how much it hurt her that the *American Mercury* editors back in the States were so willing to print his byline instead of hers.

Louis looked at her sideways, as if he weren't sure if she was mocking him, then sniffed.

"I tell the stories that need to be told."

Between them, a short woman wearing a blond-braid wig squeezed past with four full glasses in her hands. Milly wanted to warn her not to break Anna Louise's glassware, but she turned to Louis instead. She took a breath and tried to regain her composure.

"I'm going to go check on Zhenya." Without waiting for Louis to respond, she stepped away.

Zhenya was sitting next to Victor on the couch, Victor's head tilted toward Zhenya's. In the months since Milly and Zhenya had married, his friendship with Victor had seemed to stabilize into something easy and comfortable. Now they were both laughing as the woman in the blond wig did some sort of impersonation. Unless Milly someday worked in the theater with them, she would never know even half of Zhenya's life. They had their own language there.

She wedged herself between the two men and laid her hand on Zhenya's knee.

"Let's go find some music to dance to," she whispered loudly into his ear, letting her lips brush the sensitive ridges nestled beside his cropped blond hair. The top of his hair was longer, and she tangled her fingers in his waves.

He frowned.

"You know I don't like to dance in clubs," he said.

"But soon the building curfew will start, and everyone will have to go home." That was true, but she was hoping they could leave even before the house committee chief forced the noisy party out. She wanted to get Zhenya away from the crowd, to snuggle up to him on the dance floor and enjoy the rhythm of their bodies.

He frowned again.

Victor leaned over.

"She makes a good point," he said. "If you wait until the housing chief comes, the party will deflate. People will forget they're having fun."

A cough sounded behind them.

"Are you saying counterrevolutionary things?" Louis said from the other side of the sofa. He had been talking to a Russian man, no one Milly recognized, and Louis looked at her with narrowed eyes.

"Jesus, Louis, mind your own business." Milly stood and tugged Zhenya's hand, then, after a pause, Victor's too. "Let's go," she said. "Someone else will throw these people out."

Zhenya looked at Victor, who flashed half a smile, and then they both stood.

"May as well." Zhenya threw his shoulders back. "I listen to my baby." He planted a kiss on her temple.

The room was hazy with cigarette smoke and loud conversation, and no one seemed to notice as the three of them grabbed their coats and boots and snuck out the front door.

By the time they reached the sidewalk, they were giggling like fugitive schoolchildren. The *Izvestia* headlines flashed through the cold night above their heads, and Milly read one in an exaggerated American accent. The men doubled over laughing. It wasn't really funny, but she would repeat the act endlessly if she could sustain this easy camaraderie.

"Let's go to the nightclub," she said, tingling with happiness. She looked up at Zhenya and held her breath, while he glanced over her head at the street, and the skin around his eyes tightened.

"Fine," he said. He took her cold fingers in his gloved hands and kissed them. "Don't do your crazy things, all right?"

She raised her hand to his soft lips again and smiled at both Zhenya and Victor.

"Let's go have some fun," she said.

When they arrived at Restaurant No. 9, the only nightclub in Moscow, Carol and Jennie, two Americans from *Moscow Daily News*, were sitting at a large table in the dark room, with vaulted ceilings like a wine cellar, and waved them over.

Everyone ordered shashlik, a roasted lamb kebab, and Milly insisted on ordering two bottles of Georgian wine for the table.

The food came quickly, and as they ate, two orchestras set up on opposite sides of the long dining room. One was a traditional Georgian set, with dark-haired musicians in long coats holding instruments that reminded Milly of a string of turnips hung from a rafter. The other band was more Western, she supposed, based on the violin and cello.

"You think they're going to play at the same time?" Carol asked in English. Zhenya frowned, and Victor furrowed his brow, probably trying to make sense of her slanted New York accent.

Milly gestured at the canvas walls dotted in paint made to resemble a mosaic.

"I'm not sure this place knows what it is," she said. "So yeah, I'm guessing it'll be one big mash-up." But it would be better if one group played at a time, so she could get Zhenya to dance with her. She brushed his knuckles with her fingers, and he gave her a half smile.

She drained her glass of white wine and poured another, topping off Jennie's and Victor's glasses afterward. As she did, the Georgian band whined its way into a traditional song, and the other stayed silent. She gave a half shrug to the group.

"Guess not," she said. "And I guess we can't really dance to that."

Zhenya picked at his lamb and leaned over to whisper something in Victor's ear. Victor laughed, and when he did, his lips curled up, almost like an ape's.

The song finished, and the men in their long coats with bullet-shaped pockets bowed to the smattering of applause. Then the other band played a few tuning notes on their instruments. A man with a broom mustache stood at the front of the small stage, below which there were no tables.

"In honor of our American guests," he said in Russian, then gave a bow toward Milly's table.

Milly translated for the other women, who tittered with excitement. Then the band loosed a fox-trot into the air.

Milly jumped to her feet. "We have to dance," she said in both English and Russian. "They want us to."

Carol and Jennie stood, but Zhenya didn't move. She held out a hand toward him. Victor glanced between them, but finally leaned back in his chair. Zhenya crossed his arms.

"Have it your way." She thrust out her lower lip then followed the other Americans to the small space in front of the stage. There the three of them moved an empty table to the side to make more room, and Milly danced. First with Carol, then Jennie, then by herself. She loved the movement and the music, the quick footwork and the tilt of her hips. Maybe she could make Zhenya want to join her, when he saw how fun it was, and how good she looked. When the song finished, the band members gave her red-cheeked grins, and she returned to her table to change out of her boots and into the keen heels she had brought. The men said nothing. Behind her, while she buckled on the shoes, the band started another fox-trot tune.

"Come on, boys," she said when she finished, then poured herself another glass of wine.

"Stop making a scene," Zhenya hissed in Russian. His face had grown pale. "This is not how people act."

"It's dancing." Milly drained her glass. She smiled and wiggled her hips. She hadn't meant to spark a fight. "You're a dancer, you love music. Come on, it'll be fun."

"Look around. You're embarrassing me." Zhenya tilted his head toward the large table of Russians over his left shoulder, all of whom were hunched over their plates and studiously ignoring the pair of dancing women at the back of the room.

"The band is playing these songs for us." More importantly, she wasn't embarrassing. Dancing shouldn't be embarrassing, living shouldn't be shameful.

He crossed his arms. His tortoiseshell bracelet smoldered a rich brown in the restaurant's low light.

She narrowed her eyes, then turned away.

Milly danced two more songs with the other women, and on the third song, a few young soldiers in uniform joined them. Milly glanced over once, and Zhenya's face was as opaque as the frozen river. She looked a second time, and he was gone. She closed her eyes and exhaled, then reached for a half-empty glass she'd placed on a nearby table.

The band concluded and nodded to its Georgian partners on the other side of the room, and the music traded hands.

Milly hooked arms with Jennie. Together they wobbled back to the empty table with Carol following behind. The soldiers laughed and teased the women, but Milly ignored them. One pinched Carol's bottom, and she swiped his hand then planted herself in her chair.

"Rascals," Jennie said, and Milly couldn't tell if she was being critical or appreciative.

Carol reached into her large sack of a purse and pulled out a sketchbook. She propped it on her skinny knee and began drawing one of the Georgian musicians with his onion-shaped instrument.

"Last time she did this she got kicked out," Jennie whispered with wine-perfumed breath into Milly's ear. They both giggled. Maybe it was for the best that Zhenya had left. Milly pinched the bridge of her nose. She hadn't meant to fight with him, not on his name day. But why couldn't he relax with her? He was willing to break other social rules. Only, not the ones she wanted to break.

A grim-faced man in a green sweater came to stand over Carol's shoulder. She sketched away, her pencil flicking across the page. Another man joined the first, and then a woman in a gray wool dress. The Russian trio exchanged a few whispers, but mostly watched Carol draw. Milly emptied the dregs of the thin-tasting wine into her glass.

When the Georgian band finished, Carol ripped the page from her book and stood. Milly squeezed the stem of her wineglass and leaned forward, while next to her Jennie took three quick pulls from her cigarette.

Carol walked over to the musician she had been drawing. But before showing him the sketch, she spun around and displayed the portrait, about two hands' breadth high, to the entire night café.

It was a good likeness for a few minutes' work, and Milly burst into applause.

But she was the only one.

The rest of the café remained silent except for the clicking of plates and forks. Then, a man coughed.

"That is counterrevolutionary!" he yelled. "Bourgeois nostalgia!"

Milly turned to see the speaker was the man in the green sweater. His cheeks were nearly crimson.

Carol shoved the drawing in the musician's hands and rushed to return to the table. Around them, a dust cloud of murmuring rose up.

"Better pay the bill." Milly raised her hand to summon the waiter.

She forked over what was nearly a quarter of her monthly salary, then grabbed her coat. She bent down to reach for her boots, and as she did, a man at another table stood.

"Troublemakers," he called.

"Let's go." Jennie grabbed the other two women.

Up the narrow stairs and out the door they hurried, Milly still in her dancing shoes, and the cold came as a wave of shocking clarity. They clicked their way down the icy sidewalk. Behind them, the nightclub door opened again and the voices of the crowd bubbled, but the group had paused at the threshold.

"You think you're so special," a woman yelled.

"Come dance with me!" a man's voice whined, and Milly wondered if he meant it.

"Where are we?" Carol whispered as they rushed down the cold street as fast as Milly's dancing shoes could take them. A hidden patch of ice snagged Milly's heel, and Jennie caught her by the arm before she fell.

"Not sure," Milly said, panting. "But I think I know that steeple." She pointed at an illuminated dome in the distance.

The air buzzed and a loud thump sounded on the pavement next to them. Milly bent down to see what had fallen, when another projectile crashed into a snowbank next to her. She reached inside.

"They're throwing oranges!" She held one up in wonder. "These are, what, eight rubles? I should try to catch them!"

Jennie hauled her to her feet.

"You catch one of those with your head and you're in the hospital. Come on!"

Another orange skittered past them, and a man yelled something about spreading their legs.

The women ran, short-stepping in their heeled dancing shoes, and trying not to slip.

Milly's heart pounded in her ears, and all she could hear was her feet scratching the slick pavement as she trotted. Her breath was ragged.

Beside her, Jennie slowed to a walk, then laughed. Milly stopped and turned around.

"What a sight we are," Jennie said, panting. "Carol, you should draw us."

They all giggled, nervous and exhausted, and then the absurdity of their shoes and the cruel cold and the quiet night around them tipped the women into uncontrollable laughter.

"The Ruskies sure know how to toss a good party," Milly giggled. She held up the orange still clutched in her numb, gloved hand, threw it a few inches into the air, then caught it in her palm, where the impact stung. "How nice to offer us breakfast on our way out."

Carol snorted with laughter, and Jennie clapped Milly on the back.

"Let's try to hail a cab. My piss is freezing inside my body out here," Jennie said.

"It's not too far to my room," Milly said, though she knew it was probably more than a mile. She wanted to think. "I've got my boots here in the bag. I think I'd rather walk."

"Suit yourself," Jennie said. "I don't have any boots, and that looks like a main street down there." She pointed down a cross street, where on the other end, a few lights wobbled past. "Whaddya say, Carol?"

"There's no way I'm walking." She snuggled her arms around herself. "Come on, Milly."

But Milly had already sat down on a stoop as cold as a block of ice and was working to quickly change her shoes.

"I'll be fine. You go on." She needed the solitude, though she didn't want to tell them that. "I like the city at night."

The other women looked at each other, then shrugged. "If Anna Louise asks, we'll tell her we told you not to. Good night, Milly."

"Good night."

Milly stood and bounced up and down to restore the warmth to her backside while Jennie and Carol trotted toward the yellow lights blinking in and out of the dark. The streets were safe here, as long as she wasn't being chased by a drunk mob, and now that she had her bearings, she knew where she was. She'd be fine walking back to the New Moscow Hotel where she was staying, after the dormitory had burned down. Maybe if she took enough time, Zhenya would be waiting for her.

She shook her head.

No, he wouldn't.

The sides of the shoveled sidewalks were piled high with snow fallen from the leaded roofs of the row houses nearby. In the windows of a few houses a candle or lamp glowed, but mostly the only lights were the illuminated nets cast by each streetlamp, waiting for Milly and then reluctantly relinquishing her as she passed through. There was still enough wine in her for the light to feel indistinct, as shifting as her thoughts.

Zhenya had been right, sure. He was right to be embarrassed of her. She didn't mind looking foolish because, deep down, she thought she was foolish. Ugly, unlovable by anyone except Zhenya. A shiver shot through her gut. For Zhenya, though, there was an element of performance in everything he did. She stopped walking. Even their marriage was a performance. Maybe he could never leave the stage behind, or maybe it was his yearning for applause—approval—that sent him to the stage in the first place. Milly kicked her boot into a snowbank and watched the crystals scatter and reflect the light before falling back into sameness. She knew about wanting approval and love. Wasn't that why she had married him? She tried to remember. That gaping hole of loneliness certainly was why she had let Fred hold her, make love to her, send her to get an abortion, and kiss her scarred body afterward, all while she never even suggested he might leave his wife.

Love was only a plea to be needed. Her lower lip quivered. No one would need her.

In the distance, she could see the headlines on the *Izvestia* building speaking silently into the deaf night. She was getting close.

She turned a corner, and ahead of her shuffled a bundled figure. Milly slowed, cautious. He had a bucket slung over his arm and a sheepskin cap pulled low over his face. He dipped his hand into the bucket, then swung his arm, bent at the elbow, in a circle. He repeated the motion, scattering salt on the sidewalk like seeds on furrowed ground. As Milly approached, she could see the deep lines of his face, worn by the sun. He paused as she passed by, then continued wordlessly sowing the salt upon the snow of the walkway, as once he had surely sown seeds on some farm. Milly turned and watched as he reenacted that vanished life here in the city, sprinkling salt at midnight to keep the relentless snow at bay.

PART TWO

Press Internews Berlin via Northern
Telegraph, July 28, 1936:

young wouldbe girl parachutist
vladivostok
caused crash
plane
her own death and death of two others in it stop
outstepping on wing
preparatory jump
girl lost courage
her hesitancy while on wing
she caused plane
lose balance
entering corkscrew
it crashed.

bennett.

19

IN THE BROAD square, thousands of young men and women danced and paraded past. A man in the viewing stand jostled Milly, and she nudged him back with her elbow. Her hand reached into the pocket of her snappy new white sports dress, a cast-off from the wife of one of the newspapermen in town, and she fingered Zhenya's latest letter. The handsome young people continued to march past, part of All-Union Physical Culture Day. Or, Make Milly Feel Washed-Up Day. She was alone, without her husband or friends—Carol had gone back to New York, and Seema was too busy with Bill these days. Milly left Zhenya's letter alone in her pocket and scratched a few notes about the many colors of the shirts and bathing trunks the youth were wearing. When some young man, perhaps nervous to perform in front of Stalin, wobbled in his ascent of the human pyramid, Milly made a note. She had to turn this spectacle into a story somehow. Two, really, considering how much she could use the extra money she would make from selling another international story to the wire service.

"Milly," a man's deep voice called.

She turned to see one of the newer newspapermen in town, Lindesay Parrott. He handed her a paper cone filled with candied nuts.

"My." Milly licked the sugar off her fingertips. "Thanks. Though I'm thinking this isn't the right snack when we're watching these musclebound youths. Or maybe you're trying to fatten me up for the newspaper slaughter?"

Lindesay laughed, then looked her up and down.

"You're perfect as you are," he said, his voice burred by his slight Scottish accent.

It was as if he had plucked a harp string that ran through her core, and Milly turned away quickly, back toward a row of parading gymnasts. She handed the cone of nuts to a child next to her, and the girl looked up wide-eyed. Then the girl clutched the paper cone to her chest when she realized Milly was serious. Milly stuck her hand in her pocket and ran her thumbnail over the crease in Zhenya's letter, where he repeated how he missed her, and could she please send a different kind of food in the next supply package? Milly gritted her teeth, and below on the street, three young women pirouetted past. She had tried everything she knew how to try, and she didn't know how to get Zhenya out. The worst part was, it was almost like he didn't mind his imprisonment. Sure, she knew his letters were being read by the authorities, and so did he. But as she scrutinized the letters, she could hear his real voice sounding out the words. He missed her, he wrote, but he was doing fine. Could she send some salami? Reading them, she frowned. She wanted to believe the truth was hidden, but perhaps Zhenya's true feelings were right there, scrawled in his looped, rushed handwriting.

"That girl there, she did pretty work with the basketball," Lindesay whispered in English over her shoulder.

"Will you write your story about her? The Russian Amazon who launched a thousand balls?" Milly spoke without turning around, but she knew he could hear her, even over the din of the crowd and the brass band below.

"I'm better waiting to see what you write, then besting that," he said.

Milly laughed.

"You can try."

Truth was, he was a good writer, though she didn't think he was better. He was lucky. He wrote exclusively for international news services and didn't have to bother with the *Moscow Daily News*. The grubby, faithful, ever-derided *Moscow Daily News*.

"Joe Baird and I are going to the Park of Culture and Rest," Lindesay said when the band wheezed into a pause between their songs. "Would you like to join? Try to parachute jump?"

Milly snorted. "These legs are for dancing, not breaking." Then she turned to look at him. He had dark Clark Gable eyes and a nicely groomed mustache. She felt another tremor run through her.

"Will Ursula be there?" His wife. Milly smirked a little as she waited.

Lindesay laughed.

"If she wants, though I doubt she does. I can rarely get her out of the house, and when I do it's to go to Torgsin so she can buy more wool for another dress."

"A girl can't have too many frocks, if she can afford them."

Milly turned back around to watch the parade, and she made a show of pulling out her notebook again to scratch a few notes. In the distance, if she squinted, she could make out Stalin on the grandstand. She tried to figure out which groups he chose to wave at. Or maybe it was merely every third. Not that she could write about that.

"Have you met the man?" Lindesay asked.

"No." Milly wrote down something about some dancers. "You?"

"No. But I want to, before I leave."

"Good luck getting in. You should ask Anna Louise. She'll tell you eight times straight about her one visit with Uncle Joe, and by the end you'll swear you were there too."

Behind her Lindesay blew out a puff of air, and Milly knew he was smiling.

"Speaking of tough broads, are you covering the Mrs. McLean visit?" His voice seemed to brush against her ear.

"Is she rich and American?"

"She owns the Hope diamond."

"Then that's my beat," Milly said, a little mournfully. Writing about rich Americans, not socialism in practice. More and more, Borodin and Axelrod insisted she write about other Americans. After the fire in the dormitory, they'd blamed her for the loss of the typewriters—utterly unfair, she protested—and taken away her management of the translators. Now she wrote glossy pieces about visiting luminaries and sometimes did copyediting.

She shifted her weight and felt the curve of her backside brush against Lindesay's hip. She hadn't realized he was so close, but she didn't shift her weight back. She made another note about the parade.

"I'll see you at the train station, then," Lindesay said, and she felt the pressure behind her step away. "I've got to go file a story on all these handsome youths now." Milly looked over her shoulder again, and Lindesay tipped the brim of his hat in her direction.

"I should do the same," Milly said, but she stood in her place and watched him weave between the people crowded in the viewing stand, and then down the stairs. She knew what he wanted, she wasn't an idiot. Part of her wanted it too. Below, on the street, a young man with bulging arms lifted a smaller man up onto his shoulders so they stood two men high. Even Zhenya might have struggled with that lift, and Milly made a note of it in her notebook. While watching, in the moment, it always seemed like she could never forget any of the details. But she knew they would begin to fade as soon as she stepped away, and would continue to fade the longer it was that she waited to write her story. Again, she thumbed the letter in her pocket. When was the last time a man had placed his hand upon her unclothed waist? She couldn't remember.

That night Milly filed one story for *Moscow Daily News*, but when she cabled her second to the Internews Service, she received a telegram a few hours later that they already had a story on the All-Union Physical Culture Day. Lindesay really did beat her to it. She crumpled the thin blue paper of the telegram message and dropped it in the office wastebasket.

Two days later, the clerk at the front desk at the New Moscow Hotel, where she was still staying, telephoned her in her room.

"You have a visitor," the clerk said, his voice stiff with suspicion. He hung up before Milly could ask any more. She fluffed her hair, then decided to swap the ratty skirt she was wearing for one of the two new frocks her friend in New York had recently sent her. The blue cotton had shrunk in the wash, her friend wrote, so she figured she'd see if Milly could wear it. Happily, Milly had whispered in response.

Now she rushed down the red-carpet hallway and waited impatiently for the elevator. Not many people knew she was at the New Moscow, and she liked the peace and quiet. Usually.

The elevator clanked as she reached the lobby, and the operator took his time in winding back the grate. The lobby seemed louder than usual; someone was having fun at the bar, she supposed. She wouldn't mind a drink either, for that matter.

This lobby wasn't as elegant as the Metropol's, with its geometric tiled floors and its soaring wooden archway near the entrance, but the wooden floors and yellow-painted walls here had their charm.

Milly walked to the front desk, where a clerk with sagging skin under his eyes pointed toward the entrance.

There, by the revolving door, stood Victor, clutching his hands together. Milly's shoulders drooped. The last time she had seen him, she was wallowing in her birthday drinks. And steaming with anger at him.

"What do you want?" she said when she approached.

"Come have a drink with me." His voice was taut, like a wire.

She paused. She didn't want to spend time with him.

"Please," he said. He looked at her with eyes watering over. "I'm ruined. I need your help."

"One drink," Milly said, eyes narrowed. "We don't get paid for three more days."

She turned toward the bar, a room off the main lobby, but the small space was crowded with laughing men in uniform, and a lopsided tune limped out from the piano.

"Not here," Victor said. "Come on." He laid his hand on her forearm, and Milly was surprised by how strong his fingers were, as if her arm were a trout lifted from the lake by his eagle talons. She looked at him as he led her away from the raucous bar, and his jaw was clenching.

Outside, the warm air rustled her skirt as they walked the few blocks to the Metropol. A flock of starlings twittered at them from a tree above. Victor seemed distracted and nervous, and he waved Milly's questions away.

"Not yet," he said, and they waited for the traffic guard to indicate they could cross.

Once they were inside the Metropol lobby, Milly's new dress began to feel shabby. The gilt of the lobby wasn't quite golden enough to reflect her sad image, but the mirrors were. And there, in the small hotel bar, stood a woman in her late forties wearing a velvet gown and a gigantic gemstone resting on her open décolletage, alongside three American marine bodyguards. All four held crystalline dishes of vodka, and Mrs. McLean, whom Milly recognized from yesterday's newspaper photo, was complaining loudly in a voice that seemed sprung from a bullfrog, not her slim body. Her neck was a bit loose, Milly thought as she and Victor slid into a banquette on the other side of the bar.

"That is the famous diamond, eh?" Victor nodded his head.

"The Hope diamond, nestled in her amble bosom. Some gals have all the luck." Milly waved at a waiter, who seemed happy to rush over to a part of the room not dominated by Mrs. McLean's complaints about the American ambassador and his poor manners.

"Two vodkas," Milly said. Once the waiter walked away, she looked closely at Victor, the fine lacework of veins showing in his eyes and the shadows alongside the bridge of his narrow nose. His hair seemed greasy, now that she was closer.

"So?" she asked.

He began to cry, silently.

"You're the only one . . . the only one who misses him like I do."

The waiter plunked two short glasses on the table and spun away. Milly took a quick swallow from hers.

"God dammit, Victor." She hated feeling sympathy for him. He didn't deserve it, when he collaborated with the police, and he was free while Zhenya wasn't.

"Every night I lie in bed wishing I were the one imprisoned and not him. But I was a coward. I can't change that. And now I'm not even allowed to write him letters." Victor wiped a tear from his face. "Would you tell him something for me?"

"Victor. He wrote me . . . he wrote me in his last letter that he was done with the fairy business." She said the last two words in English, partly because she didn't know exactly how to translate it, and partly because she didn't want anyone to overhear. When she had read that letter from Zhenya, she blinked in confusion. The pledge seemed more made to the censors than to her. If he hadn't been done with loving men when they married, she doubted he was done now. But she wouldn't tell Victor that.

Victor shook his head, then retracted his hand to wipe his cheeks dry with the cotton handkerchief folded in his breast pocket.

"I know."

Milly folded her hands in her lap. She couldn't bring herself to ask Victor how long ago Zhenya had left behind the fairy business. Was it when he begged her to propose, to rescue him? She knew he had a special regard for Victor, but had his feelings taken him further than that? It didn't matter now. She took two more sips, nearly draining her glass. Victor hadn't touched his, and she looked at his fingers and wondered if he would. She wondered if he had squeezed Zhenya's bare flesh as she had.

"And carrying on with a nineteen-year-old!" Mrs. McLean's complaints about Ambassador Bullitt wafted over. Milly couldn't see, but she suspected the three soldiers were loving seeing their unconventional boss scorned by this paradigm of wealth. All four of them were probably the sort of people who wanted to believe that wealth was meted out to those who played by the rules. Milly finished her drink.

"He'll be glad to hear from you, Victor." She sighed. It was true, and she couldn't deny Zhenya the pleasure of news from his dear friend . . . or lover. "What should I say?"

He reached into his pocket and pulled out a folded piece of paper.

"Make it sound like it's from you. Just tell him the news about me. The season's gearing up; he'll want to know which shows we're doing."

She looked at the folded letter and wondered what sort of secret language might be concealed inside the names and memories of operas these men had performed together.

"He's in a performance brigade himself. In addition to the labor. He seems . . . pleased about that," she said. It was hard to know what part of Zhenya's enthusiasm was his native spirit and what part was his fear of the censor. She hated that she couldn't tell how this experience had changed him.

A greasy lock of hair fell over Victor's forehead, and he pushed it back.

"When they arrested me—"

"Don't." Milly held up a hand.

Victor ignored her.

"They promised me it didn't matter what I said about him. There was nothing wrong with what we had done. It wasn't illegal then." His eyes were wide and pleading, and Milly wondered when he had last slept.

"I don't want to hear about it, Victor. No matter what you intended, you gave them the information they needed to keep him." His excuses would only make her angry.

"I never thought they would convict Zhenya."

Milly gripped the table and leaned forward. Across from her, Mrs. McLean laughed at something one of the marines had said.

"But you saw them arrest him. You knew how serious his situation was!"

He cradled his head in his hands.

"I was scared."

Milly wanted to throw over the table, or kick him, or scream, but she was stuck alongside him in the banquette against the wall, and so she grabbed his drink and took a large swallow.

"You're a coward," she said.

"I know."

The vodka began to swirl against her temples, and she took a deep breath.

"We're both cowards." She pressed her fingertips under her glasses. "If I were truly brave, I'd write a news story about Zhenya. But who would care? Who would raise a finger to help my beautiful husband once they found out what he was convicted of?"

Victor's chest caved as he slumped into his chair, and Milly pushed the glass back toward him.

"What a pair we are. Drink up."

"You'll tell Zhenya what I wrote?"

"In one form or another. Yes."

The words were hard to say, but she forced them out. She couldn't deny that they both loved Zhenya, and he loved them. That tied her to Victor too, no matter how much she resented it.

Victor drained the rest of his glass.

THE NEXT DAY, Milly, Lindesay, and Joe Baird stood at the foot of the parachute tower in the Park of Culture and Rest. It was some hours after they'd left the office, and they'd already had a few drinks. Lindesay ran the Internews office out of a small corner of the same requisitioned mansion *Moscow Daily News* worked from, and Joe wrote for him.

"It's a long way up." Milly wobbled a little as she craned her neck to look at the top of the wooden structure. It had four sides, like an ancient siege tower, and a ramp winding up the exterior. A wire stretched from the top to the ground, and a woman screamed as she jumped off the platform. Her parachute deployed, and the wire guided her to the ground.

"If only we could parachute up," Joe said, his curly black hair bobbing as he looked up.

Milly giggled, though it wasn't very funny. Lindesay put his hands on her shoulders, and she sucked in a little breath. He turned away from the tower toward a covered stage behind some trees, then released her. She could feel the warmth of his fingers on her skin even after his hands were gone.

"It's too far of a climb," Lindesay said. "Admit it. We're not hiking up that thing. How about some jazz? Or the zoo. I want to hear a lion roar."

Milly clapped her hands like a child, performing of course, but enjoying the act all the same.

"Let's see the lions," she said. "Whaddya say?"

Joe looked wistfully up the tower again, then shrugged his thick shoulders.

"It's all the same to me."

Lindesay needed no further endorsement and set off down the trail, with Milly and Joe behind him. The paved walkways were crowded with families, knots of young girls in yellow and cream dresses, and roving bands of boys chasing pigeons. The manicured hedges disgorged a stumbling man, and Milly shrieked, then laughed as the drunk man doffed his cap. There was a festival atmosphere, with the distant sound of jazz and the intimate smell of candied nuts on the air, and Milly smiled. Then she thought of Zhenya, and she halted. He should be here. She should have tried harder to dispute the charges. Had she wanted for him to be punished? Punished for not being the husband she had thought she wanted. A little girl walked past and then squalled when her ice cream plopped to the ground, out of the dripping cone still in her hand. Lindesay, up ahead, turned and saw Milly standing. He came back toward her.

"It's not your fault," he said, and Milly jerked her head up to meet his gaze. "Here." Then he handed the little girl a ruble note, crumpled from his pocket, and Milly's breath steadied. He didn't know, he didn't know.

"I was thinking of Zhenya," she said, when he nudged her forward to catch up with Joe.

"Do you miss him?" Lindesay bent low so his mouth was near her ear as she walked, and no one else could hear him.

"I need to try harder to get permission to see him. He wants me to come visit."

"That'd make a hell of a story, Milly." He straightened. "American Wife Travels to the Gulag to Visit Husband."

"Like hell it would. I can't write about Zhenya. No one would understand." She hadn't even told most of her friends that they were married, and she usually called him the boyfriend. But one night in the newsroom, when Lindesay was bored with his Internews work and had come to visit her, he had mentioned his wife, so she narrowed her eyes and mentioned her husband. She regretted it now.

Lindesay shrugged. "We newspapermen don't usually think about fair. Just about what makes a good story."

"Newspaperwomen," Milly muttered. Lindesay winked.

They reached the part of the park with the animal cages, and sure enough there was a lion roaring and pacing in his small box.

"Hardly seems decent," Lindesay said.

"I thought you didn't care about decent." Milly nudged him.

"Shouldn't we get a drink?" Joe asked.

"Not yet." Milly hooked her arms through both men's elbows. "Let's go dance first. At the jazz pavilion. I'm counting on you boys to brighten my mood after this dreary place." She inclined her head toward a cage where a black bear sat mournfully on its haunches.

"Just for a turn," Lindesay said. "Then I'll need to get home."

"One turn." Milly pulled them along. She hoped she didn't sound disappointed. "Then I have some OGPU officials to bother."

"A story on the police?" Joe asked, his dark eyebrows raised.

"Nah," Milly said. "Never mind."

But as they walked toward the jazz music, Lindesay looked down at her with those mahogany eyes of his, and she wondered how much he knew. And she hated that she wasn't already standing in line, waiting to make an appointment to wait again, in hopes of getting a meeting. She wondered what Zhenya would do for her. What Lindesay would do. She snorted, and Joe replied with a "Gesundheit." Lindesay looked at her again, and she smiled up. She knew what he'd do—he had said as much. Well, she was better than that, at least. If she wrote about Zhenya it would be to help him, not to earn a few extra dollars. She'd dance a little now, sure, but she'd get to the police offices before they closed.

❁

THREE DAYS LATER, Milly rubbed her aching eyes while she reread the next day's copy under the yellow light of the newsroom lamp. She blinked, and the words blurred then re-formed. She took her glasses off, wiped them, then tried again. She was so damn tired.

She had made it to the OGPU office before closing, but the line was too long, and though she had tried to argue with the officer sent out to shoo them away, in the end she had gone home. Only to lie in bed, unable to sleep, worrying about Zhenya and pitying her own life. She'd even tried, out of boredom or desperation, to rub her hand between her legs, but she couldn't kindle any sparks. Only gloom. And then she was hit with two solid days of work, followed by more restless nights.

"Miss Bennett," the mail delivery boy said, and handed a few letters to Milly. One was a notice from the Writers Union, probably about some upcoming meeting. Another was unmarked. She opened the envelope.

When she finished reading, Milly walked back to her chair and collapsed into the creaking wood. Then she flipped open her calendar.

She had three days to leave for Siberia. Somehow, she had received permission to visit Zhenya.

20

Milly waited on the dirt path outside the tall wooden gate while the guard walked over from his hut to let her in. A grove of aspen trees behind her whispered as he sauntered toward the barred entrance. Every morning for the past week she had followed this routine: walk the ten minutes from the decrepit house she was staying in, then stand here braying at the gate until someone inside the guardhouse roused himself to let her in. She sighed and rolled her eyes as this one took his time looking her up and down, and eventually he opened the gate.

"Breakfast is over," he said.

Milly laughed.

"I'm not here to eat." She held out her rumpled pass. While he scrutinized it, three other women from nearby cabins got in line behind her. Even in Siberia there were lines.

The guard nodded, so Milly snatched her pass back. By now, Zhenya should be in the rehearsal space, in one of the common buildings. She hoped it wouldn't take long to find which one. This was her second-to-last day in the camp.

When she had first arrived, limping and crooked from nine days of train travel, Milly had surprised Zhenya as he walked out of the mess hall after lunch. She almost didn't recognize him, with his face tanned golden brown and his shoulders rounded with muscle under his rough cotton shirt. He had been laughing at something the man next to him said, and when Milly called out his name, he halted, confused. His eyes found her, standing in the shade of the wooden porch of the mess hall, and his mouth fell open. He ran two steps toward her, but then froze, remembering himself, and lunged back into the line from the mess hall.

"Milly baby!" he called, his voice plaintive, and she hurried to wrap her arms around him. He peppered her cheeks and forehead with kisses, while the man behind him frowned.

"You're holding us up," the man growled.

"Yes, yes, you're only jealous," Zhenya said, but he began walking, pulling Milly along with him.

She was so elated to see him that all her nerves about their reunion evaporated under the sunlight of his smile. But as the days wound on, Milly's anxiety grew. A week had passed and she still hadn't been able to have him to herself, not even for a private conversation. Always they were surrounded by at least four or five other men. She wanted time to talk, to hold him. To ask.

Now she walked among the camp's wooden buildings. Some were so weather beaten and warped that they must have dated back to the time of the tsar, but most were newer, square and featureless with a grim determination to swallow the prisoners of the Soviet state.

She saw a prisoner she recognized, a wide-faced man with curly brown hair, and she held up a hand. He squinted at her until she walked a few paces closer, and then he smiled.

"Are you going to the rehearsal?" she asked him as she fell in stride.

"Yes. But we have only morning rehearsal today. This afternoon, more time in the quarry."

"I thought that was finished." Milly frowned. Zhenya had told her, chin high, how he had spent the spring breaking apart and loading rocks, so they could be sent to build walls and bridges all over Russia. He had flexed his muscles for her while she laughed, not sure what to make of his enthusiasm for his own enslavement. He seemed to want to reassure her, so she let him.

"Pavlev, tell me," Milly said as they walked. "Do you like it here?"

He laughed. "Will you take my place? You can have it."

"I wouldn't have believed it if you'd told me a year ago, but yes, I'd live in the camp if the commissar would let me. I spent all yesterday afternoon writing him a letter while sitting outside his own door, which he wouldn't open to see me. And I guess I'll be doing the same today, begging him to let me stay here with Zhenya. So yes, I'd take your spot."

Pavlev shook his head.

"It is hard here. Especially in the winter."

"But I can't leave him."

"Yes, you can."

He walked a little faster, and Milly had to hurry to catch up.

When they reached the common room, Pavlev walked across the bare wooden boards of the floor to take his place in a row of men standing along the opposite wall. A guard glared at him, then saw Milly and lifted his cap, a strangely courteous gesture in the dim brown room.

In the middle, Zhenya stood holding another man's hand.

"But you must understand!" Zhenya squeezed the man's hand, then, still holding it, got down on his knees. He looked up at the other man, a dark-haired fellow about Milly's age. "You must bring in the grain. Your country needs it."

"I do not believe you," the man said, but didn't pull his hand from Zhenya's.

"I will show you." Zhenya stood, pressed the man's hand to his chest, then released it. He waved an arm, and two young men, nearly boys, stepped forward from the wall.

"We are students, training to be doctors," they said in unison. "We will keep our great nation healthy. But to learn, we must eat. We cannot save lives without bread to eat."

Milly leaned against the rough plaster wall and watched as pairs of men took their places representing urban professions and beseeching the peasant for his harvest.

When they all finished, Zhenya turned back to the peasant, who now hung his head and covered his eyes.

"You see, comrade? Together we will build socialism, and a better future for all. Today, we need your grain. Tomorrow, we triumph!"

Zhenya raised his fist and lifted his square chin, then one by one, the men in the chorus followed suit. Finally the peasant stood straight, raised his fist, then doubled over in a coughing fit.

"What the hell, Anatoly?" A uniformed officer stepped toward the prisoner. "We finally had this perfect! And you fucked it up, you goat." The guard closed his fist, but then he looked toward Milly and relaxed his fingers open again.

"Do it again," the guard said, then turned back to take his place against the wall.

Milly sunk to the floor and pulled her knees up under her skirt. She was tempted to rest her forehead against her legs, but she didn't want to offend Zhenya. His face glowed as he puffed his cheeks out to stretch the muscles and then wiggled his eyebrows. She suppressed a giggle. He was taking this so seriously. Perhaps, she realized with a frown, because it was serious. Impressing the guards here was how Zhenya demonstrated good behavior, and thus how he shortened his sentence. She should have understood that more quickly, and she pinched her thigh in punishment.

Two run-throughs later, the guard finally nodded his satisfaction and dismissed the rehearsal. Zhenya came to crouch down in front of Milly, and he placed his hands on her knees.

"We did well, didn't we?" he said, his eyes glittering. His forehead was damp with a fine sheen of sweat, and a lock of golden hair pressed moist against his skin. The warmth of his hand radiated through the cotton covering her knee, and she shivered.

"Perfect, darling."

He stood and extended a hand to pull her up, which she accepted.

"They let me act here. I'm the star, did you see? And I perform best with my Milly baby watching." His cheeks reddened and he looked down at the floor, then looked up at her earnestly. "It's almost better than the opera."

"You could always do better than hold the queen's train."

She kissed the back of his hand, and he squeezed her fingers.

"I think I should stay here," she said in English. "I have a letter to deliver to the commissar, I'm going by today. Whaddya think?" She grasped both of his hands. "We could live like the revolutionaries did in the tsarist prisons. Men with their little wifeys in their own cottages." She had surprised herself how easily, once here, she succumbed to Borodin's vision for her. Or, how thirsty she was to drink in Zhenya's attention.

Zhenya's face grew somber, and he looked down at their clasped hands, then at her.

"But you need money. How would we live here? You cannot work."

She released her grasp and waved a dismissive hand.

"I could still file stories, I'm sure. What American reader wouldn't want to learn about the Siberian taiga?"

Zhenya took a step back.

"You can't write about this."

Behind him, two prisoners were waiting. In the drab uniforms Milly had first thought they all looked alike, but now, after a few days, she found herself more attuned to the details of the men's faces. These two she had seen with Zhenya at meals, and they were both frowning slightly as they waited for him.

"I wouldn't write anything to put you at risk," Milly continued. "Zhenya, don't you want to be together?"

He threw his arms around her.

"Yes, Milly baby, yes. You will ask him. You can work miracles, I have seen them. You managed to come here."

Milly stepped back.

"I thought that was your work. Or they let everyone visit."

Zhenya shook his head. "It was you."

Milly frowned but said nothing.

"Time for chores," one of the men behind Zhenya said.

"Latrines today," added the other.

Zhenya patted Milly's hand. "You do not want this experience. Deliver your letter. See what you can do." Then he gave her a kiss on the cheek and followed the two prisoners out the other side of the room.

Milly walked slowly back to the commissar's office, listening to the sounds of the camp as she did. Hammers on nails, men speaking in low voices, guards barking the occasional reprimand. Above, two dark birds cut across the blue sky, and Milly lifted her fingers to her cheek to touch the skin tightening with a few days' light sunburn. There was an order here that almost gave the impression of peace, and she hadn't found the misery she had expected. If only she could spend two months with a pen and a pile of notebooks. Or better, a reliable typewriter. She would walk around and type up her impressions and slowly she would make sense of the place as meaning accumulated. She shook her head. The authorities would never permit that sort of freedom. At best, she could stay here with Zhenya and write a novel, or try again at that discarded book about the clown. They could be a couple in a way that had eluded them in Moscow, and she could help him prove his good behavior. The wrongness of the charges. Surely he wanted that.

Wanted her.

Dust from the unpaved lane swirled up as a truck loaded with boxes rumbled past, and Milly coughed. She hoped she wasn't catching whatever illness that other prisoner had; she had been feeling run-down even before arriving. She coughed again as she walked up the porch steps to the commander's hut, indistinguishable from the rest of the wooden buildings except for being a little smaller than the common buildings and for having freshly painted shutters by the two front windows.

Milly knocked on the door and then, after a pause, opened it. Someday she was going to catch someone in the act of something scandalous when she did that.

The secretary looked up from his typewriter and scowled. "You again?"

"Good morning. I'm here to deliver a letter." She waved her piece of paper. "In person."

"You may wait." The secretary gestured with a crabbed hand at the same lonely chair Milly had spent the previous afternoon shifting her weight in.

She readied a snappy retort, but she knew not to, not if she hoped to get the commander's time. She sat. She would give the commander an hour.

One hour later, on the dot, according to the wall clock with faded strawberries painted on its wood face, Milly stood and pushed open the door to the commander's office. The secretary sputtered behind her.

The thin door swung open soundlessly, and inside was a simple room with a broad-chested man sitting hunched over a table, which, judging from the papers strewn across it, served as his desk. Behind him hung portraits, printed on yellowing paper, of Stalin and Lenin, and in the corner was a hulking woodstove. Otherwise, the room was bare. It must get frigid during the winter without any carpets or window treatments.

The man was sleeping, Milly realized. She found a single chair against the wall and pulled it toward the table. His eyes snapped open.

"What the hell?" He glowered at her, then wiped his mouth against his sleeve.

"Commander." Milly sat in front of him. "I'm sorry to wake you." She thought about blaming the secretary for sending her in, but decided against it. "I have to leave tomorrow, but I wanted to see you. To thank you. This camp—it's not what I expected. The men are doing good work, and they seem content."

She was laying it on a little thick, but this was more or less true. She was surprised at how content Zhenya seemed, at least, even if some of the other men didn't exude the same glow of satisfaction that he did.

The commander said nothing, but he sat up a little straighter in his chair and adjusted his collar.

"I've heard from the other women that sometimes wives can receive permission to stay too. Stay in the nearby cabins, with their husbands. I would like this. I would even stay in the camp, if necessary. I'd be a good influence on Zhenya."

The commander frowned, and Milly pressed her fingers to her forehead. She had forgotten everything she planned to say, including her own introduction, and now she'd stumbled straight into the middle of her argument. The room seemed to tremble a little, like her mother's aspic.

"Hell. Here's the letter. My husband is Evgeni Konstantinov, and I am petitioning to stay with him. I can support myself"—she hoped that was true—"and would be a contribution to the camp."

The commander did not touch the folded paper, which was nudged up against a messy stack on the table as Milly pushed it toward him.

"Camp life is not for dilettantes," he said, pronouncing the last word slowly, though whether in mockery or caution Milly could not tell.

"I am serious. I have lived in Russia for over three years now. I am accustomed."

"Not to our winters."

The air in the room was warm, but at his sharp pronouncement, Milly rubbed her hands against her arms.

"I'm tough."

He shook his head.

Milly stood, pushed the chair back to its place against the wall, and left. When she passed the scowling secretary on the way out, Milly told him where she was staying, so he could direct the commander's response.

That evening, Milly sat next to Zhenya in the cavernous dining hall, which echoed with the murmured conversation of over two hundred men. Milly had brought her own food—two hard loafs of bread from Moscow and cheese and carrots purchased at the train station here—but still Zhenya insisted she try a sip of his chicken soup.

"Isn't it good?" he said, his eyes wide like a boy's.

"Yes," Milly lied. The soup tasted like onion and water, with a smear of chicken grease. She wanted to ask if Zhenya had been hungry this spring, and if that was why her discerning husband was now eagerly slurping down his yellow broth. But she didn't dare, for his sake. He wanted her to believe in his happiness, and it seemed true enough. Her barbed inquiries would weaken him.

They took a walk around the compound that night, but there were men everywhere. Once, Milly tried to nudge Zhenya down a shadowed alley between two long dormitory buildings.

Her pulse pounded between her thighs as she thought of his caresses, the touches that she yearned for, but another prisoner saw them and called out a greeting. They continued on the main lane.

"I would stay here and be your wife," she said.

"I wish you could." He squeezed her hand.

"I would work to make you happy."

"Milly baby, you do make me happy." Zhenya paused, and looked up at the stars struggling through the white summer night. "But I am also happy with me. With other people."

She tugged at his arm, pulling him closer.

"I don't understand."

He sighed. "Neither do I."

"Are you happy here?" The question seemed fantastical, and she asked it partly out of anger.

He placed his hands on her shoulders and looked at her. In the low summer light, his long lashes looked like those of a movie star.

"Here I can see who I am better than I have before. The life is hard. Hard. But I have the acting, the other men, your letters. These things make me happy. Each day, I am glad to be alive."

"So you don't want me to stay with you?" She clutched her hands together. He wanted her letters, he had said.

"Milly!" He pulled her into a hug. "Of course I want my Milly baby here. You are a flame. I cannot resist."

He kissed her gently on the lips, and then walked her to the compound gate.

When she returned to her little cabin, Milly found her letter shoved under the door. On the exterior, visible as soon as she lit her oil lamp, was one large word.

"Denied."

21

ON THE NINE-DAY train ride back to Moscow, someone stole Milly's red satin slippers, a gift from her friends in San Francisco on the day she had boarded the train for New York. Gained on one train ride, lost on another. She tried to be philosophical about the loss, but as the countryside bounced by and her toes tingled against the cold floor, she merely felt lonely. And when she reached Moscow, the long journey had worn her to a nub. She fell sick. So painfully, miserably sick that Borodin gave her one long look as she sat coughing at her desk, turned to the secretary, and told her to call the Writers Union. Within twenty minutes Borodin had arranged for Milly to have a room in the Writers Rest House, and within an hour he was ushering her out of the office with instructions on how to get there the next day.

The house was hewn out of the same forest that surrounded it, only a few hours outside of Moscow, and Milly sat at the window in her small room watching the rain fall across the bowing pine trees. In the room next door, an old poet tapped her cane against the wooden floor, and Milly tried to ignore the rhythm as she stared at the typewriter in front of her. Of course, each room had a typewriter. A narrow bed, a table, a typewriter, and not much more. Much like Milly's mind, she thought, and jabbed at the letter *H*.

She had dumped her basket of unanswered letters into her suitcase when she rushed, sick and aching, out of Moscow. But now, two weeks into her prescribed four-week stay, she had answered all of them. The only person she hadn't written yet was Zhenya.

When he had said farewell to her at the gate, Milly's throat tightened and her eyes burned with unshed tears while he whispered into her hair that she was his beautiful baby. His voice trembled. But when he released her, she happened to catch a glimpse over his shoulder at the man standing behind Zhenya. Looking at him like Zhenya was a precious gemstone set out on a table, where anyone might pick him up.

Milly understood.

Now, staring at the rain, she understood all of it. That Zhenya loved her and wanted to be the man she saw, but that he could never leave behind the men he loved. She had tried so hard not to see that truth.

She pulled the cover over the typewriter and stood, though her hips complained a little at the motion. She had two choices, live or not live. She took a breath and looked out of the window. Outside, the rain whispered at the trees. Any manner of dying that she knew of would hurt, hurt like hell. Better to run from her pain, bury it like the forest floor under a bed of pine needles. If she didn't feel like living, at least she could fake life long enough until some of her spirit came back to her.

She went and knocked on the door of Andrei, an NKVD officer—as the OGPU now called themselves, though they remained secret police nonetheless—who had nothing to do with writing but had somehow maneuvered his way into a month-long convalescence at the home after his appendectomy.

"Wake up, lazy bones," she called through the door in English. "It's three in the afternoon, you should be dancing," she added in Russian.

The door opened, and the sleep-lined face of a sixty-some-year-old man blinked back at her. He gave a shy smile.

"Or you should be learning billiards," he said.

"No, it's my turn to be the teacher. I've got the fox-trot record, no time to waste. Ditch that bathrobe and meet me in the lounge." She didn't feel like dancing, but it was better than the quiet of billiards or the tomb of her quarters.

He laughed, then closed the door.

He was nothing more than a way to pass the time. Maybe she'd even sleep with him, if she could muster the energy. A tumble would probably do her good. At least if she danced, she didn't have to think about Zhenya. Or the lonely lacuna awaiting her in Moscow.

❧

MILLY STOOD IN the lobby of the Moscow movie theater and stared at the popcorn inside the square glass contraption. She was glad it smelled burnt, since she didn't have the money to buy a bag, but she liked to listen as the kernels burst into life. A few patrons lined up to buy the bags, possibly for the experience, but most of the people filed straight through the lobby to the theater entrance. She hadn't seen a movie since coming back from the rest house, and she had thought she'd wanted to see *Lieutenant Kizhe*. But now she didn't feel like anything except hiding. She didn't want to be here.

She wiggled her toes in her boots, warming her feet, and glanced around the gold-lit room. No sign of Victor. He was the one who had asked to meet, and since she couldn't bear to meet him at the Bolshoi like he had suggested, he agreed to go to the movies. Maybe he liked that this was the theater Zhenya had once worked in, while Milly had hoped that by arranging to see a film, she could get out of talking to him at any length. She had somehow lost, she felt. She was disgraced, and here was a man who had loved her husband, come now to rub her face in it. She didn't even have the courage to stand him up.

No, that wasn't right. She walked up to the poster for *Lieutenant Kizhe* and stared at the missing face of the dancing tsarist military uniform. Victor had no intentions of lording anything over her. Still, she felt defeated.

The lobby quieted, and from behind the closed theater doors came the horns that heralded the beginning of the newsreel. She didn't mind missing that, the menacing news coming from Germany and the depressing scenes of poverty in the United States. She looked down at her ticket, and her stomach tightened. He had probably thought to meet her outside the theater. Maybe he didn't have the rubles to buy his own ticket. She stuffed hers into her pocket and tightened the wool scarf around her neck.

But before she made it to the theater's glass doors, Victor burst in, red cheeked and panting. His face skipped into a wide smile, and he swept his worker's cap off his head, almost a courtly greeting but not too obviously so to any casual observers. That would be bourgeois.

"I'm sorry I'm late," he said. "Shall we get some popcorn?"

"No thanks." She loosened her scarf again but left her coat buttoned. It was chilly inside the theater.

Victor exhaled and stood still, considering her, before he turned to walk toward the popcorn stand. He bought a bag and walked back to her. By now, the lobby was empty except for the two women selling popcorn, one who was stirring the brown kernels, and the other who was midway through some monologue.

"Come look at this poster." Victor pulled at her arm. He led her toward a poster near the entrance, where the cold seeped through the double glass doors, and he regarded the poster's letters cascading across a single figure's body.

"You see how only his face and his accusatory finger are not covered by the repeating text? *The Living Corpse*. It was an excellent film. You should see it, if you can."

"Well, if they bring it back to the theater. What's it about?" Milly hugged herself.

"A man who fakes his death so his wife may think herself a widow and remarry. But then he is found alive, and she is charged with bigamy." Victor ate a piece of popcorn and grimaced, then ate another. "Tolstoy wrote the original."

"I'm not sure I would like it. I prefer to laugh."

"You are in the wrong country, then," he said, but couldn't restrain his grin.

"Russians have the same sense of humor as Americans," Milly said. "We've more in common with you than the British. Should we go? *Lieutenant Kizhe* is probably starting." She took a step toward the theater doors.

Victor laid a hand on her sleeve, and a few pieces of popcorn from the bag in his other hand jostled onto the floor.

"Tell me how he was."

Milly closed her eyes, then took her glasses off and pinched the bridge of her nose.

"Happy. I can't explain it." Her throat tightened. She wanted to tell Victor how unhappy she was, how much she wanted to up and leave the whole damn country, how she couldn't leave Zhenya, who needed her letters and her packages.

Victor frowned, and a line furrowed between his chestnut eyebrows. Then he nodded.

"That is Zhenya's gift. To believe in the future."

"He's not always like that." Milly crossed her arms.

"No one is always like anything. But you know what I mean."

"Maybe he likes summer," she said.

"Maybe." A concession. "Winter will be a different beast."

They looked again at the poster, and behind them, the popcorn vendor rambled on in her anecdote.

"All right, then," Victor said.

Milly nodded, and as she led the way into the theater, she wanted to tell him that she couldn't give him what he wanted. She couldn't give him Zhenya's or her forgiveness. She couldn't.

In her seat, her hands balled into fists. She let the words of the movie wash over her, without paying them any attention.

All she could hear was the easy breathing of the slim man next to her.

MILLY CLOSED THE door to Olga's apartment, and the click echoed down the quiet hallway. Behind her, inside the apartment, Olga was probably releasing the tears she had stoppered up while she and Milly read Zhenya's latest missive, which Milly now carried in her pocket. He was touring with the agit-prop group, telling Soviet peasants whatever fable the Soviet leadership wanted them to know, and he was enjoying it. Or so he said. He had written a separate letter for Olga, which she shared with Milly anyway. He was also doing hard labor, he confessed to his mother. Breaking rocks apart with a hammer and spike. Milly couldn't imagine how cold it must be to do that work outside. Zhenya didn't talk about the weather. Milly folded and refolded her letter as she walked, as if somehow she could multiply the happy words there and send them to vanquish the news in Olga's letter. She felt so useless.

Milly walked down the building stairs and nodded at one of Olga's neighbors. Milly visited once a week, bringing Olga what produce she could find in the Union store and whatever spare luxuries she could afford. An extra pair of socks, a pretty blue candle, a small pot of honey. They didn't speak much, except to read Zhenya's letters—which Milly knew Olga read as soon as they arrived, but she pretended to believe the woman when she acted as if opening them for the first time. The hour or so together was companionable nonetheless, with Milly frying up an omelet or moving whatever pieces of furniture Olga wanted shifted a few inches here or there in her room, while feeling comforted in their partnership whenever one of the more transient residents of the apartment showed up. Together, at least, they could feel his absence, like a bruise they relished probing.

Now, though, Milly was anxious to leave Olga's dark room behind. She had, and there was no other word for it, a date with Lindesay Parrott.

Who was married.

She was a goddamned fool. Especially after what had happened with Fred. But when Lindesay had run his finger across her wrist and asked if she would dine with him sometime—well, she had wanted to throw her lonely bones in his lap right then and there, at Seema and Bill's small Thanksgiving party. She would have been willing to do it if he'd let her. She didn't mind the gossip; what she did mind were the lonely nights. Then, as soon as she thought that, she pinched her eyes shut in disgust. Zhenya was in frigid Siberia, freezing as he traveled to perform "Intervention," whatever that was. His letter hadn't said.

Outside the bitter cold clawed at the inside of her nose and throat, and she ran unsteadily when she saw the tram coming down the street. Panting, she climbed on before the car moved along, and then in the press of bodies, wondered if she would smell of sour sweat.

Lindesay was standing outside his building on the busy Sadovaya-Karetnaya Street, near a strip of public gardens, and he smoked a cigarette in the dark, as if it weren't deathly cold outside. Milly hadn't even asked about his wife when he had suggested coming over before the ten forty-five p.m. showing of *Chapaev*, the only showing they could get tickets for. Milly knew from Seema that Ursula was traveling, visiting her sister in London for the next month. Lindesay broke into a huge grin upon seeing her and dropped his cigarette into the snowbank. Milly's insides trembled with recognition. Still, she hugged her arms against the cold and brushed past him into the lobby.

"Is winter over yet?" She stomped her boots to loosen the snow inside the gray, low-ceilinged lobby.

"Ursula is traveling, so I think it must be spring." He gave a crooked smile.

Milly looked at him and didn't smile back. She knew enough to be wary of a man who professed to hate his wife. What would he say about Milly when she wasn't around?

"Come on." Lindesay took her mittened hand in his. Through the cold wool, the warmth of his palm pressed against hers, and she shivered.

They walked up two flights of stairs and down a long hallway, nodding at a drunk man who was slumped against the wall but still followed them with his eyes.

Lindesay and his wife had the one-room apartment to themselves, and as soon as he shut the door behind Milly, he spun her back against the wood and pressed his lips to her ear.

"Take your coat off," he whispered. "And have a drink."

The warmth of his breath against her ear made her shiver. She wanted to insist on taking more than her coat off, but she clenched her jaw shut. He stepped away, and she shrugged out of her coat and scarf. The wool sweater beneath clung to her breasts.

"I'll have the champagne," she said.

Lindesay laughed.

He pulled a bottle of vodka off the open shelves of the pantry in the corner of the apartment and poured two glasses. He handed one to Milly.

"Cheers," he said. They each took a sip.

Milly dropped herself onto the brown horsehair sofa, next to a curtain that she supposed concealed Lindesay's bed. Her stomach grew warm.

Lindesay sat next to her, close but not touching.

"Do you like it?" he asked.

She frowned.

"What?"

"The drink," he said with a half-smile.

She blushed.

"Sure, I like vodka."

He took another sip.

"I met Ursula young. A group of us went to swim at a set of pools, natural pools they were, where we lived. I must have been fifteen, and I was the only one of them who'd never had an ale before, much less a whiskey. Then I challenged one of the boys, Sam maybe, to fight me for mastery of a rock in the middle of the pool. Sam agreed, but Ursula, who'd had a few whiskeys herself at that point, said he should let a lady have a chance first. So I climbed up on that rock and held out a hand for her to climb up too. She grabbed it, pulled me into the water, and situated herself on the top. That's when I first noticed her. Should have been a hint."

He stood and walked back to the kitchen corner, where he refilled his glass.

"More?" He held up the bottle.

"No thanks. Not yet."

He walked back and sat down next to her, this time a little closer.

"I don't know how to swim," Milly said.

"But you liked Hawaii. How can you live there and not swim?"

"I was doing other things."

She took a sip, set down her glass, then leaned over and kissed him.

His lips were rough, and his mustache chafed at her skin. She pressed herself against his chest, and as they kissed, she felt him stretch to set down his glass. Then his hands were on her breasts, and she sighed with pleasure. Zhenya never touched her there, not like Lindesay was now, caressing her curves then slipping his hand under her sweater to brush his fingers against the bare hill of her skin under her bra.

She pulled away.

"Tell me why you came to Moscow," she said, her voice husky.

"For you." His eyes were heavy lidded, and he reached for her again.

"Cut it out," she said with a laugh, and leaned farther back. They'd have more fun if they paced themselves. "Really."

He raised his eyebrows, gave a slow blink, then took another drink from his glass on the side table.

"Honestly? It was a good career move. Get my name on the international pieces. Maybe next I can cover Whitehall."

"But you've been here a year, had your name on plenty of yarns by now. Why do you stay?"

He looked at her, then looked beyond.

"I want to know what happens next."

She leaned close and gently nipped at his neck, below his jaw. "Next?" she said.

"I surely want to know what happens next."

Then she took his face in her hands and kissed him again, and soon she threw one leg over him, straddling him with her clothes on yet rocking herself against him. He grabbed her buttocks and pulled her tight, so she could feel his hardness through both of their trousers. She could step away now, she knew, now was the last moment, before she surrendered to her hunger and her hopes. He slid a hand back under her sweater, and she rolled her hips against his, miming what it would be to take him inside her. He groaned with wanting.

The phone rang.

They ignored it, letting the rings fade into silence, and Milly maneuvered her fingers under the leather of his belt. She loved unhooking a man's belt, feeling the thick leather slide under the metal clasp of the buckle to lay bare the man who lived inside, hungry, vulnerable, and hard.

The phone rang again.

"Dammit." He rolled out from under her, then stood and went for the phone.

Milly turned onto her back and pushed her hair from her eyes while she tried to calm her racing heart. Across the room, Lindesay frowned.

"What do you mean?" he said in Russian, and adjusted the crotch of his pants. "Go there now?"

Milly sat up. She straightened her sweater.

Lindesay listened, wrote something down on the notepad on the table, then hung up the phone.

"Someone's been shot," he said. "I don't know who, the censor wouldn't tell me, but it must be a big deal. He wants me to meet him so he can tell me in person."

"Aren't censors supposed to keep news secret?" Milly crossed her arms over her chest. A bit of horsehair from the sofa poked at her back, but she ignored it.

Lindesay shrugged, then stood and grabbed his overcoat.

"This one's a friend, or something like that," he said. "And everyone needs someone to tell their secrets to."

"A newspaperman is a strange choice."

"You go ahead to the show, Milly. I'll hang on to my ticket and slip in after it's started."

He took a step toward her, then glanced at his wristwatch and turned back toward the door.

"You don't need to lock it," he said, the door now open. "I'll see you soon."

Milly slowly gathered her jacket and made her way to the movie theater. She showed her ticket and maneuvered through the crowded lobby into the theater, where she flung the coat across the empty seat next to her.

He never showed.

※

THE NEXT MORNING, Milly arrived early at the newsroom, though her eyes were dry and the morning darkness weighed on her like a blanket, begging her to go back to bed. She wanted to know what had happened the night before.

Anna Louise and Borodin were standing in the morning-dark newsroom, talking, and Anna Louise had her fingers in her hair. Axelrod had left the paper four months earlier, leaving the two of them to run the operations, and Milly to finally breathe a little easier. In the low light, the plaster ornamentation on the mansion's battered walls took on gruesome shapes. Anna Louise turned to pace, and in doing so, saw Milly.

"Have you heard? It's terrible," she bellowed.

"What?" Milly left her boots by the door.

"Kirov! He was shot. Killed." Anna Louise shook her head.

"Who's he?" Milly looked to Borodin, whose face was blank.

"Sergei Kirov. A promising Party leader. Senior politician, but young," he said.

Anna Louise shuffled through some papers on the desk nearest her, Seema's, and pulled out an old copy of *Moscow Daily News*. "Don't you read your own paper, Milly? Look. He's an important leader in Leningrad." She held up the broadsheet.

"Was."

"Was!" Anna Louise agreed. "And he was so promising. Rumored even to succeed Uncle Joe someday. Oh, it's such a loss." She clutched the paper to her chest.

"He was a good socialist," Borodin said.

"Are we doing a story about it?"

He glanced at Anna Louise, who pulled the paper from her bosom to look at it again.

"No," he said. "Let the local papers cover this first. The killer has already been arrested."

"Some madman by the name of Nikolaev," Anna Louise said. "May his body rot."

"Before we publish anything, I want to find out if there's more to the story than him," Borodin added.

"Isn't that our job? To find out." Milly walked over to her desk and picked up a red pencil. She tapped it against her knuckles.

"We're not in Leningrad," Anna Louise said.

"I'd go. I will go." The space from Lindesay might be helpful, as dangerous as he was, and she would love to recapture the thrill of chasing a murder story from her old days in San Francisco.

Borodin shook his head.

"Not a chance. We stay put and listen." He walked over and turned on the radio propped against a window. A frantic, crackled voice came on. Milly heard the name "Kirov" easily.

"There will be more to this than one arrest," Borodin said, his countenance sagging.

"The killer can't have worked alone," Anna Louise added.

"Why not?" Milly strained to understand the broadcast.

Anna Louise shook her head.

"There's too much tension now," Borodin said. "In times like this, no one works alone. Every loss has a dozen fathers when there is someone to find them. Not like what you Americans say."

"Failure is an orphan," Anna Louise said with a dark laugh.

Borodin waved his hand. "That's right."

IT WAS MORE than two weeks later when Lindesay called Milly from his apartment.

"Ursula came back early, but she's out with the Swede tonight," he said. "Again. How about we take advantage and have dinner? At your place."

Milly, sitting at the secretary's desk in the newsroom, twirled the telephone cord around her finger. The secretary, another new one, this time from Boston, had winked at Milly when she beckoned her over to take the call, and then the young woman tactfully vanished.

"It's been two weeks, Lindesay." She had glimpsed him in the mansion, coming and going from his office downstairs, but they hadn't been close enough to speak. He hadn't sought her out, and she hadn't gone after him. She wasn't trying to get her heart broken, and if he wanted something, he should be the one to make his intentions clear.

"And I haven't stopped thinking about you. I told you, Ursula came back early. Did you get that wire from the *New York Times* editor I sent over? Are you going to take the job?"

She sat down in the secretary's chair.

"Yes. I told him I'd write the story. Thanks, I guess."

"You guess?"

She could imagine him leaning back to better focus his far-sighted eyes upon her face.

"It feels like you're trying to make me feel better."

"Milly, I am trying to make you feel better. To apologize. Please?"

She looked up at the ceiling, where the light from the fixture splintered into yellow rays across the plaster. It had been so long since she'd had a man in her bed.

"Eight o'clock," she said. "Bring dinner." She hung up the phone.

Borodin approached the desk and tossed his small notebook onto the bare surface. This new secretary was much neater than her predecessor.

"They've arrested Zinoviev and Kamenev," he said, his voice flat.

Milly whistled. "They're high up. Do you think they ordered Kirov killed?"

Borodin rubbed the bridge of his nose.

"They're left oppositionists, the most senior ones since Trotsky left." Borodin glanced around the newsroom, but no one was nearby. "Don't you see what that means? Either they're responsible, and they were making a move against the Party leadership, or they're not responsible, and Party leadership is cleaning house."

"And either way, there will be more arrests."

Borodin gave a wry smile.

"Do we write about it?" she asked.

"What do you think?" He rocked back on his heels, and she couldn't tell if he was testing her or really asking her opinion. Right after the murder, Anna Louise had left to travel again, so maybe he did need a sounding board.

"I think we write something short, with no commentary. So our readers know."

He nodded slowly.

"You write it," he said.

She gulped.

"Can't we get something translated?"

"No. I want to get this right, not to sound like we're coughing up a three-day-old hair ball. You write it. You can call the police to confirm the facts." He scribbled a phone number on his pad and then tore it out to give to her.

She pressed the paper between her fingertips, as if he had handed her a magical feather on a windy day. She wouldn't let him down.

"By tomorrow night," he added, then walked away.

Milly looked at the paper to make sure she could read it, then folded it carefully into her own notebook. The assignment would be one more thing to talk to Lindesay about, at least. She so rarely wrote about politics now, she was more nervous than she wanted to let Borodin know. But if he let her write more sensitive pieces, maybe she could parlay that into more international correspondent work for the wire services.

She looked at the clock. Two hours to finish the slew of editing she had to do tonight, plus write up that story about the poetry competition. She'd better hurry. Though maybe she'd be better off if Lindesay had to wait a little. The thought made her smile.

23

MARION MERRIMAN, THE new secretary after the girl from Boston gave up on Moscow, dropped a sheaf of papers on Milly's desk.

"Come on," Marion said. "Let's get out of here. If I have one more lunch in the cafeteria downstairs I'm going to turn into a potato."

"There could be worse fates," Milly said without looking up from the copy she was editing. "At least men like to eat potatoes."

"Not my Bob," Marion began, but then pressed her lips shut. "Come on, lunch is on me. We'll have a piece of honey cake each at that little place around the corner."

Milly set the editing aside, and Marion's sweet face was looking down at her with a hopeful smile. The two women were like champagne and moonshine, with Marion's refined finishing school mannerisms and Milly's sailor's tongue, but she had had stranger friends over the years. Marion seemed to like and admire her, and these days, that sort of affection was a gift.

"What the hell." Milly grabbed her handbag from under her desk. "I do like honey cake. Better than cabbage, that's for sure."

They passed Borodin's office, where he waved at Milly.

"You've finished already?"

"Nearly," she said. "Just taking a quick break."

He frowned.

"I'll be back in time," she said, her voice thin. Back in December, when she had called the police to confirm the details about the arrests following Kirov's murder, she had somehow botched the interview. Or so she concluded, at least, because the police had called the censors, who called Borodin into a meeting at their offices. The conversation, as he called it, had lasted an entire day. Milly didn't see him until the next, when he summoned her to his office, opened his mouth to explain, then scowled.

"If you could learn to be diplomatic," was all he said.

Since then, she had felt like she was walking on hand-carved matryoshka dolls, thin and round. It was tiring.

"We can't be late," he said, but waved her away.

Outside, the wind stirred up wisps of fallen snowflakes, but the sky was so clear Milly could almost imagine warmth.

"That sun's a treat," she said through the scarf wrapped around her neck.

"See, you're already glad you came," Marion replied.

"Being outside helps me wake up." Milly tugged her collar closer around the neck.

"Tired?"

"Can't sleep these days." She glanced at Marion, who was watching the oncoming traffic, waiting to cross. Her full lips were pressed together in thought, and she looked like a confection. No wonder her handsome economist husband adored her.

When they reached the café, Marion steered Milly to the back, where they claimed a small table.

"Talk," Marion said. "Though you'll have to order for us. My Russian's nonexistent."

"I know it, baby doll," Milly said with a husky laugh. Marion was hopeless on the phones in the office, though she was game to try.

"My sob story isn't one for a proper married lady," Milly said, tracing her fingers on the tabletop. A dark ring was scorched into the wood, as if someone had rested a hot pan directly on the surface.

"I want to listen to what you have to say. It's about Ursula's husband, isn't it? Everyone knows she's been carrying on with the Swede."

Milly looked at her fingers splayed on the table.

"And everyone knows I've been carrying on with Lindesay. I've heard the gossip, in whispers. People calling me a hussy."

Marion frowned. "It's not that bad," she said in a timid voice.

Milly waved away her effort to soften the blow.

"Ursula left her husband, and Lindesay was going to move in with me." She had tried to listen to her better angels, but once she and Lindesay fell into bed together, she was pulled under like a child dragged by the riptide. He was intoxicating, and she couldn't get enough. "Said he loved me, wanted to fight to be with me."

A waiter came, and Milly was grateful for the interruption. She ordered two coffees and two cakes.

"You were saying?" Marion extended her hand to tap her still-gloved fingertips briefly against Milly's forearm.

Milly shrugged.

"These old bones were foolish enough to think he meant it. In the end, he went running right back to her. Hasn't even responded to my letter asking him to send my belongings back . . . my mother's picture, my books." Her throat threatened to close up again. She had trusted him enough to bring one of the only two pictures she had of her mother to his house when Ursula moved out.

"Anyway, that's about it. I'm in a washed-up state. Can't sleep, can't hardly eat." She waved a fork at the square piece of cake the waiter had deposited.

"You're better than him," Marion said.

"You got lucky young—be glad of it. I've made a hash of my life." Milly set her fork down and looked straight at Marion. "Don't tell anyone. Not even Bob. Please? I've had enough of people talking about me. I want this all to go away."

"Of course." Marion set her fork down too and looked at her hands, then up at Milly. "I'm lonely here, Milly. You know this city, these people, the Americans and the Russians, better than anyone I know. I'm hoping you'll . . ."

She trailed off. Milly smiled, then took a big bite of cake. Marion was some thirteen years younger than her, and she didn't know if they could be friends. But she didn't mind trying.

"It's good cake, Marion. Thanks." Milly wasn't used to this sort of kindness, and she blinked back her tears.

That night, Milly stood at the window of her fifth-floor room in the New Moscow Hotel. She opened the window. The cold cut through her nightgown and made her eyes water. Soon the tears streaking her face would freeze, she guessed. He had cast her off, like some whore he had used and paid. Maybe she deserved it. Maybe she deserved to be lonely. She was a terrible wife, a low friend, a mediocre writer . . . The world didn't need her. She stared down the five stories to the courtyard below. Would she die right away? Or lie there in misery until she froze to death? She pinched her eyes shut and felt the pain of the tears biting into her cheeks as they froze.

She closed the window.

When, two weeks later, Lindesay forwarded a telegram from the *New York Times* requesting a story on Moscow's lilac saleswomen, without any commentary from him, she held the paper over the sink and burned it. She wasn't sure what he hoped to get from her, but whatever it was, she wasn't selling. Earlier, while she was at work, he had dropped at the hotel her weekend case, her mother's photograph, and most of the books she had left scattered about his rooms. With no letter, no word of explanation. He had been a good tumble, Milly told herself, and tried to believe that's all she had needed. She looked at the ashes smearing the white porcelain. She didn't need his story leads either. Finally, after long last, she was going to write her book. Except this time it wouldn't be a plaster of paris mold of someone else's life, like her failed effort with the clown Durov. This time, she was going to write her own story. Yes, that was it, the story of her years in Moscow, and her efforts to help her husband. Milly rushed to grab a notebook and jot down a few ideas. She couldn't tell everything, sure, but American readers would be glad to learn how this country could both envision a better world for the masses while failing in its promise for a few. She frowned. Maybe that wasn't the story. She doodled a little flower in the corner, then some speckles of salt along a sidewalk. Well, the end hadn't happened yet. She could leave that part for later.

On the streetcar on the way into the newsroom, Milly crammed herself between an old woman with two curling chin hairs and a middle-aged man who smelled of onions. As she steadied herself to prepare for the jolt of the car, she heard the stout conductor, a woman of about fifty or so, tell the teenaged boy behind her that his ticket expired at the next stop. He muttered something Milly couldn't hear, and the car lurched forward. When it stopped again, a block later, the boy held still.

"Hey, boy!" the conductor called. "Pay another fare or get off."

The boy said nothing.

"You heard me!" she called, then hopped off the crowded car so she could run along the platform back to the entrance where the boy stood. His cheeks were pale but flushed at the center, and he scowled.

"Pay another fare," she said.

"Try and make me," he said. "I haven't got a coin."

Milly dug into her purse but came up empty.

The woman leapt onto the streetcar and tried to pull him out through the open door. By now, nearly everyone on the car had turned to watch the tussle. The conductor blew her whistle to summon any nearby militia, but no one came. Milly looked out the fogged window and saw only blurred pedestrians walking past.

"I won't get off," the boy said, his expression unchanged. "You can't force me."

The car then jerked forward as the driver, oblivious, proceeded to the next stop. The conductor fell against the boy then, red-faced, reached up, snatched the frayed cap from his head, and threw it out an open window.

The streetcar erupted.

"How dare you?" yelled the old woman next to Milly.

"What right do you have to go throwing away citizens' caps?" called someone else.

"She took his hat!" a man exclaimed.

"Some nerve!" Milly added, a pulse of adrenaline racing through her at joining the incensed crowd.

"You should have found a militiaman," the middle-aged man next to Milly said to the conductor. "Let the militia give him the fine."

"You can't take things into your own hands," the old woman added, though Milly could feel the crowd's throbbing desire to do so, the pulse of the mob waiting beneath the frustrated surface. Her heart raced.

Milly's stop came, and after she got off, she thought she saw a plainclothes police officer inside the car, writing down the conductor's badge number. He was NKVD, surely. The energy of the streetcar had faded, quiescent, and Milly shivered and held her pocketbook close to her. The woman shouldn't have thrown the hat, sure. But she didn't deserve that kind of attention. Milly hadn't heard what the labor camps for women looked like, and she didn't know if harassing a teenager would qualify to send someone.

Two years ago she would have scoffed at the notion that the Soviet state would do such a thing.

Four years ago she wouldn't have believed that she could watch such a thing happen and walk away. Milly frowned, and a weight tugged at her heart. She needed to send Zhenya his package this month, and she hadn't yet bought his cured sausages. She stopped on the sidewalk. There were no stores around, and behind her was the conductor, descended from the streetcar and staring at the NKVD officer's little notebook.

Milly walked up to them.

"Excuse me," she said in her mildest, most accent-laden Russian. "Where is the nearest All-Union store?"

The officer blinked as he looked at her, while the conductor's face grew even paler.

"Oh, you are the conductor who helped me the other day," Milly said, and grabbed the woman's pasty hand. Milly took a breath and willed herself to improvise. The conductor's mouth fell slack. "Actually, you helped the three young comrades, and in doing so, helped me."

Milly turned to face the officer. "Three Komsomol youths were lost on the streetcar, and they'd run out of fare. I was going to pay for them, but I had run out of coins too. The conductor, of course, couldn't let them ride for free. So she gave her own coins." Milly mimed reaching into her pocket and pulling out three coins.

The two Russians stood silently, and Milly took a surprised step back.

"I have interrupted something! I'm sorry. What a dumb American. But I am glad to tell this conductor again that she is an excellent comrade."

Milly nodded her head at both of them, then excused herself. Well, she hoped that would help.

It would make a good story in her book, at least, she thought with a half-smile as she hugged her coat against the angry wind.

24

IT WAS THE night before the eighteenth anniversary of the revolution, and Milly stood guard at the door of the *Moscow Daily News* office.

"Thanks, Joe," she said when Joe Baird handed her a wine punch, the third or fourth he'd snuck out of the party for her. Behind him, the party roared so loud in the newsroom's converted ballroom that she couldn't hear the songs streaming from the beat-up phonograph.

"Had to fight 'em off, have you?"

"You know I like a good brawl." She winked at the word play. She had asked to be the door keeper, partly so that if Lindesay and Ursula came, she'd be the first to know. She had seen him a few times around in the past seven months, and it no longer hurt like a sucker punch to see the newly faithful Ursula hanging on his arm. Not that Milly held any of it against the other woman—she had been entitled to her fling with the Swede, and she was entitled to try to win her husband back. All Milly wanted now was to show Lindesay that his rough treatment of her didn't matter. She was fine, fine.

A tall man appeared at the top of the stairs at the end of the hallway, and Milly's heart skipped. Light hair, long neck—but no, it wasn't Zhenya. She had tried to visit Zhenya over the past summer, but she couldn't shake a permission out of the NKVD. She even tried writing Orlov, the father of the girl who she had taught two years ago, and the man to whom she figured she owed her first visitor's pass. But her letters went unanswered, and the summer ticked past.

The man approached the door, and Milly put her hands on her hips.

"State your business, citizen," she said in Russian.

He laughed. "The name's Hermann. I am a geneticist." He waved his wrist in a flourish that was nearly a bow. "Sam invited me."

"Proceed." She flexed one elbow back, like a door swinging open. He gave her an appreciative look up and down, then strode past. She liked the implicit praise, but she wasn't sure she liked being subject to appraisal in the first place. Soon, she knew, she wouldn't pass muster. She'd be too old. And after that, they wouldn't even bother to try to judge her. She wasn't sure which was worse. She drank half the wine punch in her glass, then hollered into the din of the party that Joe must have sucked all the alcohol out. Inside, the crowd had launched into revolutionary songs. Milly hummed along, reminding herself of Anna Louise and her incessant droning, but she didn't feel like singing. Two years ago she had belted out the songs with the best of them, especially the Italian songs, but now humming was the best she could manage. She wondered if Zhenya got a break on Revolution Day. She hoped so.

She took off her glasses to rub a smudge from the lens, and when she put them back on, Lindesay was walking down the hallway, alone. Milly threw back the rest of her wine punch, but there was no more than a swallow left in the dish.

"Ticket, Mr. Parrott?" she said, trying not to sound too harsh. A man could be angry after a breakup, could hold a grudge, but not a woman. Milly didn't want to seem bitter, on top of all the other gossip she had earned.

"Joe invited me," Lindesay said. He stuck his hands into his pockets and looked her full in the face, then beyond her, at the party. His mouth tightened in what might have been disgust, and Milly's hand rose to her throat. She wanted a witty retort, something glamorous and casual, but she felt old and gummed up.

"Joe's a lousy dance partner," she said finally. "But he's yours if you want him. Tell him Bennett needs another drink." Or three. But she wouldn't have Lindesay see that.

A couple came down the hall behind him, and Lindesay let them sweep him into the party. Milly didn't ask them about who invited them, and she didn't care. She'd done well enough managing Lindesay, but she still felt a wreck.

Marion Merriman came out of the party and threw a bare arm over Milly's shoulders. The younger woman's flesh burned against Milly's cold neck.

"I saw Lindesay come in. He looks like he's lost half his hair and gained half his weight since the summer."

It wasn't true, but Milly appreciated the effort. She gave Marion a quick peck on the cheek.

"Thank you for not thinking I was a husband stealer," she said. "After your Bob, or something."

"You'd be welcome to try." Marion laughed. "Keeping that man fed is more than I have in me, sometimes."

Milly nudged Marion with her elbow. If she weren't so darling, her marital bliss would be insufferable.

"Let's go dance," Milly said.

"I heard you wrote a divorce story," Marion said, without moving from the doorway. Her fine-boned face narrowed in thought. "Do you think women were better off when they could pay three rubles and mail the husband a postcard to end the marriage?"

Milly rocked back on her heels and cocked her head.

"Maybe. But men could send divorce postcards too. And what then of Marooshka with her three children and papa nowhere to be found?"

Marion nodded.

"Look, kid, why did you ask about divorce?" Milly looked at her. "You're not . . . ?"

"Us? Heavens, no." She giggled, then cupped Milly's cheeks with her hands. "I was thinking about you. I'm worried you've been here too long, Milly. Maybe it's souring you."

Behind them, the lights flickered off as the power wavered, but the phonograph continued playing. Milly gave Marion a gentle punch to the shoulder.

"I want to help make people's lives better here. I've done a lot of running away in my life, and I'm sick of it. Maybe I can't help Zhenya, but I can still send him packages of cured sausage and socks. And I can still help socialism. I'm not going anywhere. Except to dance." Milly laughed. "Come on."

But as they were walking into the dark room lit only by the glowing tips of cigarettes and the lights from the street signs shining through the large window on the other side of the room, a stone seemed to settle in Milly's chest. She would stay, she would stick this out the way she had intended. Once Zhenya was out, she could return him safely to Olga and then make her own choices.

In the dark newsroom, a calloused hand grabbed hers, twirled her through a few dance steps, then released her back into the crowd again. She strained to find the hand again, or any hand whose fingers would twine with hers. Next to her, a woman purred in pleasure and a man laughed.

Someone jostled her, perhaps the petting couple, and she stumbled a step. The music halted as someone changed the phonograph record to a new jazz number she hadn't heard before. Though it was dark, she closed her eyes and shimmied to the song alone.

25

IT WAS LATE when Milly entered the Hotel Savoy lobby, where she was staying now, and the mild air inside made her glasses fog. She took them off, wiped them down, then put them back on.

She yelped.

In front of her stood Victor, holding his worker's cap in his hands and looking at her with eyes that darted back and forth from Milly's face to the door behind her.

"Milly, can we go up to your room? I'm sorry to ambush you. Please?" He worried at the felt cap with his fingers, and the seam was coming undone.

She tipped her head to the right, regarded him, then sighed.

"Hell, Victor," she said. "You could give a girl some warning."

She had seen him only a few times in the past year, and mostly they seemed agreed to leave each other alone. Zhenya never mentioned his old friend in the letters he wrote, and the letters themselves had grown increasingly infrequent.

They said nothing as they walked up the two flights of stairs to the third floor. Milly shivered in spite of the mild heat the hotel managed to produce. During Moscow's winters, she worried she would never get warm.

When they reached her room, small but pretty, she left her coat on and pulled the bottle of vodka down from its shelf. She poured them each a dish, clinked them both together in a toast, then handed Victor his. She went to go sit on the radiator, where her long coat protected her legs.

"They're arresting more and more people," he said. "Have you heard what Ezhov is saying? About the Zinovievites?"

"Zinoviev was convicted, what, a year ago? What does Kirov's murder have to do with anything?"

Victor shook his head and placed his still-full glass on the small table Milly used for meals. Beneath her, her bottom was beginning to scorch, but the tops of her thighs still felt like ice. She stayed put.

"They're making more arrests. Claiming they are allies of Zinoviev, and that he himself is allied with Trotsky."

Milly snorted. "With Trotsky in Mexico? He's been gone nearly a decade."

Victor waved a hand.

"None of that matters. Aren't you listening? They're arresting people. I'm afraid I'm next."

"You haven't done anything," she said, though it felt like a lie. Victor had helped convict Zhenya, and whenever she thought she could forget that, her resentment surged upward.

"Giorgi was arrested again. He'd been detained earlier, when they were investigating the ballet, but he was released. Like me. And now they've arrested him."

"Giorgi? I don't know him. And you don't know what he did, Victor. Maybe he had secret meetings after rehearsal. The government here can be blockheaded, but I can't imagine they'd convict innocent men."

"You can't?"

Victor held her gaze.

"He wasn't innocent," she whispered, then looked away. "He couldn't stop who he was."

"But how does that make him guilty?" Victor yelled. He threw his cap across the room, then turned wild eyed toward Milly.

"This isn't about Zhenya," she said, low.

"Maybe it should be." He pressed his hands over his eyes. "We both failed him. And now we're going to fail others."

Milly stood, her backside finally too hot. She finished her drink and thought about pouring herself another, but she didn't. Instead she paced in the small space between the bed, next to the radiator, and the wall.

"We're not failing anyone, Victor. You're being hysterical. No one is trying to arrest you."

"Let me stay here tonight. One night. On the floor. And then I'll leave."

"I'll have to register you at the desk."

"No! Just the one night."

For Zhenya, she would have ignored the rules. For Lindesay, in their time, or Olga. But looking at Victor's pinched face, his flushed cheeks, she frowned.

"I can't risk getting thrown out now. Zhenya's supposed to get released this month. Didn't you know? He won't want to stay with his mother, she'll smother him. He needs this room." It was all true, and yet she felt like she was lying.

"Milly."

She stopped pacing.

"Aw, hell, Victor. You want to know the truth? I think you're being selfish. You're trying to believe they want to punish you, so you can feel less guilty about what you did to Zhenya. No one wants to arrest you. I think you're weak, and . . ." Her voice began to choke up. "And Zhenya deserved better than both of us."

She sat on the bed, but not even the release of tears came.

Victor scowled, and walked over to pick up his cap. Without another word, he let himself out of the room.

❖

THE NEXT DAY, Milly went to see Olga. The older woman seemed brighter than when Milly had last seen her, a month earlier, and her hair looked freshly trimmed.

"You are looking forward to having Zhenya back," Milly said, after complimenting her haircut.

"Yes," Olga said, but in a surprisingly casual manner. Milly looked at her again.

"Have you heard from him?" She set her string bag, bulging with potatoes and onions, on the table, then opened the tied mouth to put the produce away in the bins under the sink.

"No." Olga's face darkened. "But he said he would be on the train at the end of February, right?"

Milly nodded. The last letter from Zhenya was a month old, and while his letters had become less frequent since the cold weather set in, going a month without hearing from him worried her. Particularly since in the last two letters he mentioned that his cough had returned. If he was willing to complain about something, it must be serious.

"What are you doing this afternoon?" Milly asked, straightening from the bin.

"What?" Olga's cheeks grew red.

"We should go to the NKVD office and pressure them to tell us something about Zhenya."

"We can't pressure them," Olga whispered. She glanced around the apartment, though none of the other residents were there.

"Ask. I meant ask. There's no harm in asking for his file."

"Not for you, at least."

Milly took her glasses off, then put them back on, without bothering to wipe them down.

"Don't you want to know?" she asked softly.

Olga held up her palms. "Of course I want to know. But I can't be seen to be bothering the police."

Milly nodded, then grabbed the last three potatoes from the table and placed them in the bin. She could understand Olga's caution, even if she hated it. They had done so little for Zhenya. His absence weighed on her like a debt she could never repay, even if she might sometimes forget about it.

"I'll go. I'll let you know what I learn," she said, brushing the dirt from the potatoes onto her wool trousers.

Olga bowed her head.

"Thank you," she said.

Milly bundled up and trudged out to the gray cold and snow-piled streets. The administrative headquarters loomed at the end of Pushechnaya Street, where Olga lived. As she walked, the wall of the shoveled snowbank was so high she could barely see the street, and pedestrians had to squeeze past one another in the narrow sidewalk trench. A uniformed officer in a wool trench coat walked past, said "excuse me" when he bumped into a middle-aged woman. No one said anything, and she wondered if she was imagining the tension that seemed to stiffen the gaze of all the passing citizens.

She made a left-hand turn at the end of the street, and there loomed the massive Lubyanka building, some nine stories tall and all the more hideous for its grim faux balconies and third-story rounded windows, as if those gestures at ornament made up for the decades of misery inflicted. It was so tall you could see Siberia from the basement, Lindesay had once joked. He was disappointed when Milly didn't laugh.

She walked around the block to the main entrance and frowned when she saw no line. Not a single grandmother or young son waiting to send a package or request information.

Milly pulled open the heavy wooden door, and the burnt smell of dense cigarette smoke rushed out to greet her. Inside, a young man sat behind a desk facing the door. He had his overcoat on, and he puffed away at a small cigarette while frowning at a paper in his hand. Behind him, the center of the building opened up to a tall atrium that must have reached all the way to the ceiling, judging from the glow of natural light against the marble floors and columns, though Milly couldn't see that high from the entrance.

"Excuse me," she said. He glanced at her, then put down the letter and began typing something on the typewriter next to him.

"I'm here with the *Moscow Daily News*," she said. "I'd like to get some information about the reeducation camps. The prisoners."

He stopped typing and stared at her, his eyes wide under his brown eyebrows. Milly's stomach twisted, and though she was still cold, she began to sweat. She should have named one of the other papers she wrote for, one of the internationals. Not the newspaper that would get Borodin or her other friends in trouble.

"*Moscow Daily News?* What do they want to know about prisoners?" He stubbed out his cigarette.

Milly puffed out her cheeks, then collapsed them.

"Look, it's just me. Not the paper. I want to know about a friend. If he's due to be released soon."

The man stood up.

"What kind of counterrevolutionary request is that? Give me your name. Our local commissar should know you are making false claims on behalf of the paper. Do you even work there?"

Milly took a step back.

"Aw, shove it," she said in English. Then she turned and ran out of the building.

The young man yelled behind her, something she couldn't understand through the echoes of her feet against the tile, and then the door slammed shut and his voice vanished. She ran all the way into Dzerzhinsky Square, across the street, and then stopped, panting, with her hands on her knees as she felt the cold air rip through her throat.

What an idiot she was.

She straightened and looked at the gray sky. She would have to wait for Zhenya. Just a little while longer.

❄

THAT NIGHT, MILLY splayed the day's copies of *Pravda* and *Izvestia*, the primary Soviet newspapers, across her bed. She was writing wires for Internews, Hearst's wire service, more regularly now, and she needed content. Content they would buy.

A photograph in *Pravda* of a little girl, about ten years old, caught her eye.

"Murdered," said the headline.

Milly crawled onto the bed, the thin papers crinkling and tearing beneath her knees, and she read the article. The girl's schoolteacher had thrown her down a well, breaking the poor child's neck in the process, because the girl had denounced his counterrevolutionary acts. The article did not say what those acts were. Milly read the story two more times to ensure she had understood it, then scribbled down a quick summary. She cut out the picture of the girl, for herself, but changed her mind and folded it up with the rest of the paper. What a terrible story, she should have nothing to do with it. But dead girls sold copies, and maybe both the girl and the teacher deserved to have their stories known. Milly wished she could go interview the man. "Why did you do it, you bastard?" she'd say, like she had back in San Francisco in the twenties. "Was it so bad to have a kid call you counterrevolutionary?"

She wadded up the paper and threw it into the wastebasket. Outside, snow fell, consuming the city silently.

Maybe it was so bad.

She wished she could ask Zhenya.

THE NEXT DAY she went to the train station after sending off her wire. Seven rubles it had cost her to wire her pitch, but at least Internews would repay her that expense, even if they didn't pick up the story. She rubbed her gloved hands against the cold and stared up at the day's train schedule. There were two coming in that she guessed Zhenya could be on, and she waited an hour for the first one. When all the passengers had streamed past, jostling through the station where she stood, shifting her weight back and forth on the tile floor because that was better than sitting on a cold marble bench or leaning against a frigid stone wall, she stared at the door to the platform and willed him to step through. Late but smiling, like her darling of old. He had once waited for her here, when she was returning from that reporting trip and had flirted with the handsome Party member. Then, he had seemed crestfallen to see another man help her down from the train, but now she wondered if it was something else he was disappointed by. Something about Milly herself—her nose, her chin, her bursting laugh—that had made his long wait seem too high a price to pay.

She hugged her arms around herself, then went home.

When she could, over the next few days, she went to wait at the train station. It was silly, of course, to hope she would manage to hit upon his arrival in Moscow, when certainly he would head straight to Olga's, and Olga would know how to find her. But still, Milly clung to the hope that fate would make the past years up to her, to him, and she could surprise him. To be safe, she wrote a letter to him saying she was waiting, and he should tell her if his release date had changed. But it would take two weeks, at least, for her letter to arrive and for him to reply, and that was only if the censors were quick. Or so she assumed. She had never seen a redaction in his correspondence, but she could feel the weight of his fear in his relentless cheerfulness and his vague reports on his life. Or, she thought the undercurrent was fear. It was impossible that he was happy.

After a few days of returning to the train station, she began to recognize some faces: the haggard conductors ending their shifts, the boys selling newspapers and, when they could, roasted chestnuts in small brown bags. The station pulsed with a predictable rhythm, the ebb and flow of passengers and trains like blood throbbing into and out of the heart. She ought to write a story on the station. But she left her notebook in her pocket.

She worked later at the newsroom to make up for the hours she spent waiting, and she woke up early, shivering in the sunless morning, to check the local papers for any possible wire stories. Borodin called her once into his office, raised his hand to say something, then seemed to reconsider.

"Never mind," he said.

After that, they rarely spoke. Milly's stomach curdled with nervousness at the office, and she worked harder to find stories that would interest the editors in London and New York.

Then it was March, and there was still no Zhenya.

Olga called her at the newsroom one afternoon.

"Come over," she said, breathless. "Come quick."

Milly threw down her pen and ran out of the newsroom so fast she was halfway down the stairs before she realized she had forgotten to put her boots on. She ran back, kicked the shoes off and the boots on, and ran out again.

At Olga's apartment, Milly swung the door open without knocking.

Only Olga was there, sitting at her small table. Her face was pale as she looked up. She held out an envelope.

Milly recognized it as her own within a few steps, her boots still on, the door still open. In the hallway, the voice of a mother scolding her child echoed.

Olga handed her the envelope.

On the front, where Milly had addressed it to Zhenya, a wide black mark obscured her writing.

"Return to sender," it read. "No such person."

She screamed.

MILLY STOOD IN Red Square with the Main Universal Store, or GUM, at her back. Somewhere, beyond the sweating marching masses filling the street in front of her, was Lenin's mausoleum.

"His wife's body was displayed there for a few days," she said to Marion, who was fanning herself against the gruesome heat. "I missed it though."

"What?" Marion said back. It was hard to hear over the call and answer of the thousands of workers protesting fascism. A few weeks ago Milly had written in a wire article that Moscow was watching the new war in Spain with reserved detachment; now she would have to revise that description.

"We'll donate a portion of our salaries to defeat Spanish fascism!" yelled a man with a bullhorn. His fellow workers, dressed in blue or red overalls, raised their fists to punch against the sky in unison. As far as Milly could see, their faces remained expressionless. The donation was not their idea.

Still, there was something to the notion of throwing oneself against the fascist military rebels attempting to unseat, by force, Spain's elected democratic Republic. Some of her colleagues had already pulled up stakes in Moscow to cover the fight in Madrid.

She could go, now. She had heard no more from the NKVD about Zhenya, though she had sent a dozen letters. He must be gone, she understood, but still she could not stop herself from seeing his tousled hair or his loose gait on the street. Crowds were the worst, when every ten minutes her heart constricted, thinking she had seen him step behind a worker or turn around a corner. Her mind would catch up and scold her optimism, but not quickly enough.

Marion tugged at Milly's sweat-streaked elbow, then pointed into the crowd of people watching the marchers process past. A thin man with brown hair waved up at her. Victor. She had seen him a few times since she had refused to hide him, and though his fear seemed to have evaporated like the mist over the Moskva River, she regretted her stinginess. Neither of them mentioned it, but she knew Victor's anger—or perhaps shame— still hung between them. She waved back. He nodded, then turned to face the marchers again.

"I've never seen an August this hot," she said to Marion, who nodded. The men in front of them belted out a song about revolutionary fervor, and it would have been charming if it wer- en't for the gas masks hanging from a few of their belts like post-apocalyptic trophies. In July she had traveled to Lenin- grad to witness a mock air raid and chemical attack, and she still dreamt of inhuman gas mask faces fumbling through the haze of canister gas. At the time, the exercise had seemed droll.

"We should go," Milly said closely in Marion's ear. Her friend turned and looked at her, eyebrows raised. Milly had been the one to insist that they attend the march, if for no other reason than to have something to cable to Internews in hopes of getting paid.

"Are you trying to avoid that man?" Marion nodded her head back toward Victor. "He looks harmless."

Milly snorted.

"No. I need a drink."

"You drink too much," Marion said, but she followed.

When they reached a quieter side street, Milly fell in step with Marion.

"Did you see how forced they seemed?"

"Who?"

"The marchers," Milly whispered as they walked. Moscow had grown brittle recently; Victor had been right about that.

"I don't know," Marion said.

"I'm thinking of going to Spain," Milly said, though she hadn't been until the march. Something was turning sour here, she could taste it.

"You can't." Marion paused and grabbed at Milly's bare elbow. "Bob hasn't finished his fellowship, and . . ."

"You'd miss me? Stop it, I'm blushing." She laughed, but then stopped when she saw how serious Marion's face was, her curved lips parted.

Milly sighed and touched the back of Marion's hand in apology.

"You're right, in a way. I ought to see a thing through. I came here to see what the Ruskies could do. I need to stop running."

"You're not a quitter, Milly Bennett." They resumed walking. "I think you're not done here yet."

GRAY-FACED, BORODIN CALLED Milly into his office.

"I'm sorry," he said, then paused and swallowed. One of the light fixtures hanging from the ceiling buzzed in its effort to shed light. "We have to let you go."

"You what?"

He shook his head.

"There aren't as many English-speaking engineers in Moscow anymore. You know how circulation has fallen. The Politburo is thinking of closing us entirely, withdrawing all funding . . . I don't want that to happen. We're shrinking. I'm sorry, Milly."

She sucked in a breath and began to pace.

"I can barely pay my hotel bill as it is," she said. "How am I supposed to live?"

"I know you're writing for Internews," he said without looking up from the trash can he was toeing. "I thought you would have enough money."

"Borodin, I'm working two jobs because I *don't* have enough money! Jesus," she growled.

He held his hands out in front of him.

"I'm sorry, Milly. The decision's final though. We've already informed the commissar and the Writers Union. You'll still have your Union membership. But we can't keep you on."

She clenched her jaw and held back the slew of expletives that pressed at her teeth.

"Why couldn't Anna Louise tell me?" she said.

He shook his head. "She fought for you, Milly. She offered to take no pay herself. You should know that."

"Dammit. Dammit all." Milly kicked her foot into the wooden floor, then exited Borodin's office. She went to her desk, pulled out her few folders of personal papers, and left without another word.

She had lost her job at the *Moscow Daily News*. The laughable, earnest, unloved *Moscow Daily News*.

As she walked home, she let the tears sting her cheeks as they fell. She didn't care who saw, didn't care what they thought. Most likely no one cared anyway. Marion hadn't been fired, none of the men had been fired.

Just her.

❖

BY THE TIME she threw herself on her bed in her hotel room to sob, she already knew what she would do. Have a good cry, and then write twice the stories she had been writing for Internews. They paid her by the piece, and if they saw more from her, they would buy more from her. She needed to stay a little longer, maybe another year, so she could collect enough material for her book. How could the story end now, with Moscow afraid of fascist invasion and the factories just beginning to hum? The Soviet Union was approaching a crucible, or perhaps cresting a mountain, and she needed to be here to witness what was on the other side.

Milly sat up, then got off the bed to kneel next to it. Out from under the bed she pulled a box of papers, her archives, and she hefted it onto the mattress. She lifted the lid and flipped through the carbon copies of her old letters. Her early enthusiasm, her frustrations, her growing sense of mastery. All her letters from Zhenya, including the last one she had received, ten months ago. She looked up at the ceiling and wondered what he would have her do. This was a setback, yes. But life in Moscow was always changing. She replaced that box then pulled a smaller, lighter one out. She didn't need to open it, but rather wanted to weigh the progress of her typed book draft. Not nearly enough.

She would get by. She always had. Like her mother, scrubbing school floors until her knuckles bled. Milly could write fast and clear. She'd find a way to pay for the roof over her head and some bread in her belly. Then, she could publish her book, a truer account of life in Moscow than the fluff that Anna Louise wrote, and a more clear-eyed look at the passions and perils of building socialism than anyone had written before. She gritted her teeth.

The next day, Milly stepped out from the telegraph office onto the sidewalk and fumbled to button the uppermost button of her camel hair coat. Lord, it was cold already. A horse-drawn cart lumbered past in the street, and a black Ford buzzed past it, startling the horse. The poor beast should have been used to such disruptions by now, but Milly sympathized. Change is hard to adapt to. She clenched her gloved fist as she watched.

The staccato patter of the news stories she had just wired filled her head while her stomach rumbled. This was an update to Internews, which they didn't pay her nearly enough for. She wondered which of the four stories in this wire they might be most interested in commissioning a full story for, while on the sidewalk an old woman with a kerchief binding her hair shuffled, hunched over like a comma. Maybe the story about the Soviet impatience with the dithering non-intervention committee, charged with preventing anyone from fueling Spain's war fires by providing weapons. In practice, only the governments who might have helped the democratically elected Spanish Republic were the ones to abide by the agreement, while the fascist powers flaunted it, smiling to the committee and delivering munitions and even fighters to the right-wing military rebels now chewing through Spain's territory. Milly kicked a rock into the street where it disappeared in a slick of rotting leaves. She didn't blame the Soviet spokesman for threatening to disregard the unfair blockade. The fascists shouldn't be able to use their willingness to break rules to overtake another European country. No one should be bound by rules that weren't fair.

She hoped that was the story the editor would pick, but she knew it was more likely to be the arrest of the Soviet officials charged with granting themselves outrageous gifts in advance of next month's revolutionary holiday. Sneering at another country's shortfalls and hypocrisy was a winner for the international papers. She reached up into her coat sleeve and gave the edge of her glove a tug, pulling it up over her cold wrist bone. The city was already sawing away at her body, winter ready to cut her into pieces.

❖

THREE DAYS LATER, Milly was leaving the Savoy lobby when the desk clerk ran up to her.

"Miss Bennett, there's someone here for you. Now." His grip on her arm hurt, and she snatched it away.

"I'm going to work, Citizen," she said. "Can't it wait?" She was already at least half an hour late to the interview she was conducting with the American ambassador, Bill Bullitt, who was finally talking to her. He was growing frustrated with Stalin, and she hoped she might get an interesting story out of him. Maybe a breaking story.

He clucked his tongue and shook his head. No. Then he waved over a stout man in worn blue trousers and a heavy brown jacket still buttoned up to his low-hanging chin.

"Alexei Andreievich," the man said, and the clerk disappeared. "*Pravda*." One of the two official Soviet newspapers. "And here's my colleague, Captain, er . . ." He paused, then mumbled a last name as a uniformed man in a long coat approached. Milly looked at the embroidered lines on the man's coat collar and sucked in a breath. NKVD.

"Let's have this conversation somewhere more comfortable. Your room, perhaps," Alexei said, his bushy eyebrows raised, as if it were a real question.

"Yes." She wrapped her arms around herself.

They led her toward the elevator. She started to protest that they could take the stairs, it was only on the third floor, but then she pinched her mouth shut. As they waited for its clanking descent, her thoughts raced over what was in her room, what notes she might have left carelessly scattered. Maybe this captain was here to conduct a thorough search, exposing her doomed marriage and her foolish affair with Lindesay, and the writer was here to humiliate her by publicizing it. In the elevator, she looked over at the NKVD officer, who was opening and closing his gloved hands, as if to stretch them. Her mouth went dry.

They entered the room without a word, and when Milly closed the door behind them, the captain walked straight toward the small table on the other side of the room from her bed. He paused, frowned at the papers on the table, then took two more steps and went to the window, where he stopped, his arms clasped in front of himself as if he were at attention. Her notes, including the most recent pages she had typed for her book, were scattered on the table.

She unbuttoned her coat and hoped she didn't smell of fear.

"Our contacts tell us," Alexei said, then shuddered with a racking cough. He raised a hand and recovered. "They tell us that yesterday the corrupt Hearst newspapers published a telegram from their staff reporter—that would be you—saying, and I quote, 'The USSR intends by all means necessary to expedite the shipment of weapons and other war materiel to Spain. And the USSR is ready to act against the attempts of other states to interfere with this shipment of Soviet weapons.'" He lowered the typewritten page he had been reading from and glared at her. The captain shifted his weight.

The room was silent.

"'Ready to act?'" Alexei quoted again, his voice dark. "Is that what you meant?"

That quote wasn't exactly what she had wired to her editor, especially not about expediting shipments. But on the other hand, she had reported on the Soviet frustration with the useless non-intervention agreement. That news had seemed interesting but harmless. The foreign ministry was frustrated, her contacts had told her as much, and all she had done was report the truth. Her pulse pounded in her throat, and she looked at the captain, whose face was impassive.

The Soviets were playing a delicate foreign policy game, she guessed. They must not want their frustration with the non-intervention committee known, though she didn't understand why they would pretend to be happy with British and American efforts to dither while Spain burned. Milly swallowed, her throat dry, and glanced again at her table. Her original telegram to Internews from the twenty-seventh lay there, in a stack of other papers, and she suspected she didn't want anyone to see it. It would be harder to deny whatever it was she needed to deny if the NKVD had evidence. She hugged her arms around herself, and her legs began to quiver.

"Why are you telling me this?"

The reporter frowned, then coughed again.

"I am here to discover the truth and correct the record. The captain has come along to deal with the situation in the case that my suspicions are incorrect."

Milly glanced back and forth between the men, who seemed to be ignoring each other. She was the one trying to discover the truth, she wanted to say. She parted her lips, but the captain pulled one glove tighter onto his hand, then looked up at her with a raised eyebrow.

"I am glad you told me," Milly said, the words tasting like ash. "That's not what I wrote."

"I knew the lying capitalist Hearst had fabricated the story," Alexei said. "Now we will publish our own story. The truth. Can you read this and tell me if it is correct?" He handed her a paper.

Milly read out loud.

"I did not send the telegram that was published by Internews dated 27 October 1936. I did not receive such information from the Soviet Foreign Office." Her stomach had soured, and she lowered the paper.

"You can sign at the bottom." He extended a pen toward her.

Behind the captain, the radiator clanked, and Milly gave a small jump.

She took the pen, though she bobbled and nearly dropped it, and went to the small table. The captain nodded and took a step back to give her space.

Izvestia and *Pravda* would surely both publish her "statement," if one newspaper had gone to the trouble of sending a reporter here. She began to sweat. Her editors in London would hear of her retraction, and she wasn't sure what she would say. The editors had mischaracterized her telegram, but she knew that if the Soviet Foreign Office was this angry about the news story, there must have been some truth in what Internews published. That truth, that's what her readers deserved. The Soviet Union was frustrated at the fascists' flagrant violations of the weapons ban, and she had heard rumors that Stalin was preparing something more than a public statement. American readers would need to know Moscow might change its position, and if so, perhaps Washington could also stop its useless non-intervention policy. If she renounced the story, she would be lying to those readers.

She looked again at the captain, who had tipped his head up to stare at the ceiling. Signing also meant preserving her visa. She wasn't happy here, it was true, but she wasn't finished with Russia. If she displeased the Foreign Office, she could be kicked out, or . . . The captain shifted his weight, and the floor creaked. Rose, an Englishwoman who had once worked at *Moscow Daily News* and more recently spent a few years writing on her own, had disappeared. Arrested by the NKVD, the rumors said.

Milly laid a trembling hand against the paper and signed.

"Randolph Hearst is a liar and a fascist," Alexei said as he took her statement and folded it into his coat. "I don't know how you can work for him."

With that, he spun around and exited the room. The captain followed, whispering an apology as he squeezed between Milly and the bed. Outside in the hallway, Alexei coughed again.

"I don't know how you can work for a thuggish propaganda outlet," she muttered in English toward the still-open door. But her stomach clenched, and she sat on the edge of her bed. She did know.

On November 2, both Soviet newspapers printed articles savaging Hearst as a liar and quoting her refutation of the October cable. Her limbs felt at risk of dissolving and floating away as she cut the articles out from the Soviet papers. She typed out the quote and then walked through fresh-fallen snow to the Northern Telegraph office, where she sent a cable to her editor in London. "Statements available if desired," she wrote, her stomach knotted and nauseous. Maybe if she was honest with her editor, that would erase the smear of guilt souring her stomach. Later, she dropped off a letter to Borodin and Anna Louise at the newsroom, offering to explain. She waited outside on the sidewalk for an hour, pacing in the cruel cold, but no one came out of the old palace. That night, she spent half her remaining rubles on a filleted herring, which she fried on the primus stove in her room and ate alone, trying to savor the flesh as she cried.

She was so alone.

Three days later, Milly turned at the top of the stairs toward her floor, and she saw the door to her room was open.

"What is this?" she gasped when she reached the room.

The reporter Alexei Andreievich stood in the room, his arms crossed. The NKVD captain was kneeling by her bed, and upon hearing her, he stood, with a box in his hands.

"Your paper posted our denial," Alexei Andreievich said, his faced narrowed into a grim line. "And said we had pressured you. What are you writing to them, Miss Bennett? Or Mrs. Mitchell? Or Konstantinova?"

Milly took a step back, but her ankle rolled on the uneven carpet beneath her, and her leg buckled, smashing her into the wall. Neither of the men moved to help her, and she remained standing. Her ankle throbbed. She leaned against the doorframe, her eyes on the box in the captain's gloved hands.

"They did not ask me about that, and I did not say I was pressured," she said, silently cursing the London editor for reading between the lines too well.

"We need you to—"

"Look." Milly gingerly stepped on her ankle and moved toward Alexei. He raised both eyebrows. Her pulse raced.

"You have to let it go. Don't give the stupid story any more attention. They are having fun with you, don't you see?" At her expense, no less, and Milly cursed the editor again. Some fellow named Smith, who had surely never thought how his bold gambit from the safety of London would affect her.

"Stupid story?" He narrowed his eyes again, then glanced at the NKVD officer. The captain drew his arms more tightly around the box.

"You know what I mean. You're giving Hearst attention, making it seem like you have something to hide by continuing to deny their claims. Let it go." She was sweating now, probably in rhythm with the pulsing pain of her ankle.

"Just let their lies stand?"

She began to speak, but her voice quaked and broke, so she took a breath and tried again. "Sometimes dignified silence is the best response."

He cocked his head, looked again at the officer, then straightened. "I will speak to my editor."

With that, Alexei Andreievich lifted his chin and paraded out, squeezing past Milly by the door. But the captain remained in the room. His eyes were large and still.

"Is there a receipt for me to sign?" Milly said quietly.

"No," he said.

He nodded and, with the box in his arms like a gift, he walked out.

Milly turned and watched as they walked silently down the hallway, where the captain's long strides quickly caught up with the journalist's waddling. The captain overtook the other man and made the turn around the corner to the staircase first, and then they were both out of sight.

"Shit," Milly said. She limped over to her bed and bent down. As she had suspected, it was her book that had vanished. Slowly, she lowered herself onto the bed and tried to remember every word she had written. Was any of it counterrevolutionary? She hadn't meant it to be, but what was clear-eyed to her was probably blasphemous to an NKVD officer. Once they found someone to translate it. She took off her glasses, rubbed her eyes, then replaced the frames on her nose and limped her way down to the lobby. She would look at the ankle later. Now she had a telegram to send.

She was fed up with letting men yank her this way and that. If Internews didn't make her a full-time correspondent with more money and more control over her stories, well, she'd stop writing for them. And if she was a full-time correspondent, surely they would protect her from any angry secret police who might come for a follow-up interview. As she limped, her resolution stiffened. It wouldn't be running away to issue an ultimatum here, no, that was taking a stand. If they didn't offer more pay and stature, she would be resigning. Effective December 1.

28

MILLY WAS SEATED in the American ambassador's office. Bill Bullitt stood at his desk, his signature red carnation sagging from the buttonhole of his suit jacket as he leaned over to look at the newspaper spread out on the wood.

"Do you see this, Milly?" He pointed at the paper then straightened. "There's a war going on in Spain! After six years in Russia, you should give yourself a gift. A trip to somewhere relaxing. My god, woman. Try Bermuda. White sands, blue sea . . ." He looked into the distance, as if the beach were behind her. Ambassador Bullitt had once been one of the Soviet Union's most steadfast defenders, but since relations between President Roosevelt and the Soviets had soured last year, so had he. Milly sympathized. They both felt, in some way, that the Soviet Union had let them down. Backed away from a promise or, worse, revealed that it never intended to keep the promise in the first place.

Or, even worse, and what Milly worried about as she lay in bed at night, Moscow proved that the promise of a better world was impossible from the beginning. That people would never grow into better selves.

"Bill, you'd go yourself if you could. That Philadelphia blue blood notwithstanding." She forced a smile.

In the past year, Milly had grown more comfortable around the American officials who had once disdained her. The Internews job, which she no longer had, had helped. But so had their appreciation for both her experience and her skepticism.

Bullitt sighed. Then he reached inside his jacket, uncapped the pen he pulled out, and signed her papers.

"There's your safe conduct pass and exit visa," he said. "Don't put yourself in front of any gun barrels, Mrs. Mitchell. It's not becoming to sport a big hole in oneself."

Milly waved a hand.

"Battle will still be better than this place." The bravado felt false, but it was what the situation called for.

"Moscow sets a low bar." He folded up the newspaper on his desk. "If I were escaping, I'd refer Paris, myself."

"Mention it to the president," Milly said as she put away her papers and gathered her coat.

"Oh, I have." The ambassador smiled, and Milly returned the gesture with a half-smile before nodding and leaving. He was fascinating, a mix of rigid upper class and fierce iconoclasm, bound together with a bright intelligence. If only she had known him longer. If only he socialized with newspaperwomen.

Milly spent the next week making her farewells. After Internews had ignored her telegram, there was nothing else for Milly to do but leave Russia. She had no job, no love, and only Marion Merriman for real friendship. Internews didn't want her, nor, it seemed, did anyone else, unless the NKVD had plans for her. But now that it was time to go, she still felt surprised. Undoing her life here was harder than she had envisioned. When the time came, she rushed to give away most of her clothes to the neediest Americans she knew, she scrambled to make sure she had money from her accounts in the States wired to a bank in Paris, and she hopped around town saying farewell to those she could. So many of her friends over the years had left, so she had only the long-term holdouts like herself, and the more recent arrivals, like Bob and Marion Merriman. She even spared an afternoon to say goodbye to Louis Fischer, whose resolute faith in the Soviet Union seemed to be wavering, though he was too proud to say as much. Lindesay she skipped. Anna Louise Strong she took to the ice-skating park on the Moskva River, but Anna Louise kept worrying that someone would see them and judge her as decadent, so they left. Milly gave her an awkward hug and thanked her for all she had done. Their friendship had been rocky, and Milly didn't enjoy Anna Louise's company, but she knew she wouldn't have survived Moscow without the woman's boisterous help.

At Olga's, Milly sat and shared two quiet glasses of tea. There wasn't much to say. Milly had needed to file for divorce so the Americans would change her passport back from married, since the Soviets still refused to provide any proof of Zhenya's death. She hadn't told Olga, and she wouldn't. When they finished their tea, Olga sobbed briefly into Milly's shoulder before drying her eyes on her sleeve and disappearing into her bedroom. When she emerged, she placed her closed fist into Milly's hand, then opened it. Zhenya's tortoiseshell bracelet glistened in Milly's palm.

"I can't," Milly whispered.

"You must." Olga's voice quavered. "He loved you. Take that to America and show people. Tell his story."

Milly nodded, though her hand shook as she dropped the bracelet into her pocket. Her first effort at telling Zhenya's story now sat in NKVD files. Fortunately, in that first draft she had barely touched on his plight, and she'd had the sense to leave Olga entirely out of the narrative. Now she owed them both a second try.

"Could you give this to Victor, please?" She gave Olga a sealed envelope. Inside was a short letter saying she understood. Zhenya had forgiven him long ago, and she did too.

As she left Olga's building, the relentless wind drilled into her chest and her aching heart. She took off her glasses, wiped them, then rubbed at her eyes. This was not the Moscow she had expected, six years earlier. She had gained and lost in equal measure.

❖

TWO DAYS LATER, Milly took a train from Moscow to Leningrad, where she switched trains to board a Finnish train headed to the border. This train gleamed, in comparison to the battered Soviet railcars, and though Milly wished she weren't the type of person who noticed, she was nearly delirious with comfort as she sank into the soft bedding of the clean cabin.

When the train arrived at the Finnish border, all the passengers disembarked and stood shivering in the snow while they waited in line outside the border post. Milly had only three suitcases, two of which were her archive of letters and carbon copies, and she worried as she dragged them forward in line. It was bad enough the NKVD had her unfinished draft. In her letters, she had recorded dozens upon dozens of less-than-flattering stories, and the truth about Zhenya was written across some of those papers too. A cursory glance, like what the censors had surely given each individual letter, would reveal little. But the whole collection, at a time when the Soviets already regarded her with suspicion, thanks to Hearst, could send her right back to Moscow. Or Siberia.

The man in front of her, a German, protested loudly that he was anti-fascist, opposed to Hitler, but still the guards took him and his single suitcase into a back room. Their voices grew muffled. Milly's arms trembled as she held her suitcases.

The soldier turned to her and asked for her passport. He flipped through it, then slung her first suitcase onto a table where he opened it. That case was the one with her clothes: one nice black dress, three pairs of wool trousers, and the few other things worth taking out of Moscow.

The soldier snapped her suitcase shut. Her palms were damp as she looked at him and tried to figure out if it would be better to watch him closely or look away. He shifted his gaze behind her, narrowed his eyes, then stamped her passport. He waved her on.

When the train finally blew its whistle to announce their departure from the Soviet station, Milly pressed her nose against the cold glass. The train rolled slowly across a bridge that spanned a frozen river. When the train, crawling, reached the middle, two dozen uniformed Russian soldiers and NKVD officers jumped off and walked over the thick ice back toward Russia. Inside, the train was silent. Milly wondered if the German man had boarded.

❋

THREE WEEKS LATER, in Paris, she stood inside Brentano's bookshop running her finger down the spines of the books on Europe. Surely there was a good history of Spain, new or used, in this place. She had already checked two of the other English-language bookshops in Paris, to no avail.

"Spain's popular," one of the clerks had said with a shrug.

"Then you should stock more books on it," Milly replied. He shrugged again.

This selection seemed more promising, more books about Spain at least, but no recent histories. She doubted knowing about Miguel de Cervantes would help her understand the current tensions tearing Spain apart. Maybe she should scrap the history idea and buy some Spanish poetry in translation. She'd heard the Spaniards were serious about their poets.

"Milly Bennett!" A familiar voice glowed behind her, and Milly spun around to see the tall Bob Merriman standing with a smile on his young face. The heavy-rimmed glasses that always seemed too serious for him hugged closely to his eyes.

"Studying collective farms in Paris?" Milly asked.

Bob laughed. "If only. No, I'm taking the same plunge as you, in a fashion. Going to Spain." He lowered his voice. "To fight."

"They're taking Americans?" Milly had heard of the fascist military incorporating foreign troops from Italy, and the main rebel army absorbing the colonized Moroccan troops, but she hadn't heard of Americans.

"The loyalists will take anyone they can get to help defend the Republic, from what I hear," Bob said, glancing around the empty store. "Though of course it's still against our own laws to go. Non-intervention committee nonsense. Marion didn't want me to go."

"Marion's opinion had nothing to do with the non-intervention pact, I assure you. Your Marion's a smart girl. You two want to have dinner tonight?"

Bob shook his head, his eyes on the ground.

"She's in Moscow. It wouldn't be safe for her in Spain, and she doesn't have a visa for France. Besides, I won't be in Spain for long. The war will be won by spring."

"Here's hoping, kid." Milly looked back at the bookshelf and spied a promising title. *The Soul of Spain*. Not what she was looking for, but it would do. She grabbed it, then pulled Bob toward the cash register. "Have you bought your gas mask yet? That's where I'm headed next. One for me and four more for the other AP fellows already there."

"Gas mask?"

Milly shook her head. "For a guy with some reserve officer training, you sure are clueless." She smiled, thinking of Axelrod. Maybe she should send him a photograph of her and her masks: proof that, at long last, she had fulfilled the requirement. But only because in Spain, she might need the protection. "Come on. We'll get you a gas mask," she said.

Marion might not be able to be there, but in her absence, Milly would do her damnedest to keep her young friend's beloved husband safe.

Someone deserved happiness in marriage.

PART THREE

The streets of rearguard Valencia are
feverish with the backwash of war.

—MILLY BENNETT

29

FEBRUARY 1937

THE AUTOMOBILE BOUNCED along the macadam road between Madrid and Valencia, and Milly craned her neck to watch the sky while the driver cursed in impenetrable Spanish. In the back, two men, also writing for the Republic's Foreign Press Bureau, dozed. Milly was tired, but she couldn't sleep. She scanned the harsh blue sky for bombers. They still had at least an hour before they made it back to Valencia, that ocean-side city that counted as home these days.

In Madrid, she had tried to sift some good news from the rubble that was the Spanish war. The rebellious fascist generals had stalled west of Madrid, that much was true. But they had seized the coastal gem of Málaga, slaughtering hundreds of government supporters, if the reports were to be believed, and thus deprived the Republic of an important port. Milly could feel the fascist noose tightening around the government, no matter how valiantly the loyal troops defended the Republican holdings. And now, as the writers raced back to Valencia, the rebel forces might as well have been chasing them. There was a battle brewing to the east of Madrid, and Bob Merriman's hodgepodge collection of American, British, and Irish troops was going to be involved. The Abraham Lincoln Battalion, they called themselves, and though they were passionate, Milly had seen them two weeks earlier in their training camp, lunging through frigid mud to try to bayonet straw dummies with broomsticks. There was no ammunition, Bob had whispered as she stood, her notebook slack and her pen capped in her gloved hands. In the cold air, someone yelled for the troops to come in for the sludge they called lunch, and then admonished the men "to study, to fortify ourselves in revolutionary doctrine."

Milly wanted to ask about how doctrine would defend them against bullets, but she saw the pride in Bob's eyes while he watched the tired men listen carefully as the political lecture began, and she kept silent.

In recent weeks, Bob's correspondence had grown vague. Something was happening.

The driver downshifted and turned the car off the main road onto a smaller, bumpier one. Milly groaned. Around them languished rolling hillsides prickly with bare olive trees. In Spain the sun felt closer than it ever had in Moscow, no matter how cold the Spanish air was, and she relished the harsh brilliance. The car circled around a hill and a small gas station came into view.

One of the Spaniards in the back awoke when the car stopped.

"I know this place," Milly said as he rubbed his eyes. She scanned the bright horizon, while the other man slumbered on, or at least pretended to. The curves of the hills beyond the wooden gas station were certainly the same she had seen before. She nudged the sleeping man, since he was the more friendly. "Come translate for me. Por favor."

He said nothing, but opened his eyes and looked at her. Then he got out of the car, and Milly followed.

"I was here last month," she said as they walked across the crunching dirt. "With the American air attaché. Passing through." She hoped he wasn't getting the wrong idea from the mention of her travels; the American air attaché was a quiet man with a wife and son waiting in Virginia. Not Milly's type. "We met some children, and one promised me a drawing. A boy named Peter. Can you ask?"

He rubbed his eyes and nodded before walking into the little café next to the two pumps. Milly waited, then followed. Maybe she could find a cigarette to buy him for his trouble.

Inside, two old men sat hunched over a small table with two streaked glasses of sherry between them. The other writer asked something rapidly, and the men pointed toward the rear exit. Milly followed him, but he turned and held up a hand.

"It is only the outhouse," he said in his richly accented English.

She nodded and waited, watching the old men sip their sherry in silence. Outside, another engine rumbled then came to a stop as a second car arrived. An old newspaper was folded on an empty table in the café, and she was tempted to pick it up, but decided she didn't want to know.

Her colleague came back.

"The boy Peter is dead. All the children were shot when an enemy plane passed over." He shook his head, not shocked by the enemy cruelty, but obviously disappointed by it.

"You're sure?" Her stomach lurched. It couldn't be true, that the wide-smiling boy with a mess of black hair had died, vanished.

He shrugged. "The mechanic, back there. He told me. He was sure." He shook his head again. "Come on. Let's get out of here."

Milly followed him to the car, and on the way, the road drew her eyes to its dark variations. She didn't know where Peter and the children were killed, but still every different shade of the gray macadam, its pressed stone contours, suggested spilled blood, drunk by the paving. She dug her fingernails into her palms. The fascists who could presume to determine that such a sweet boy should die enraged her. The world that could ignore it made her want to scream.

As they drove west, toward the darkening sky, Milly could have sworn she heard the boom and rattle of heavy artillery behind them. She had heard such explosions earlier in the month, in Madrid, when the rebel military was trying to take the city directly. But inside the car, no one agreed.

"I only hear the road," said the man who had gone into the gas station.

"We should go back," Milly said. "There might be a story there, if there's a bombing."

No one replied, and the car continued eastward.

❧

IN A WEEK, the radio reported heavy fighting to the east of Madrid, along the Jarama river. There were hundreds, maybe thousands of dead, people in the Foreign Press Bureau whispered, but the radio made no mention of the casualties. Milly's AP colleagues had no better details either, but when one of them said he was hiring a car to go to the field hospital outside of Murcia, Milly claimed a seat. Having two jobs had some perks, at least. As they drove, she rotated the tortoiseshell bracelet around her wrist, letting the polished surface soothe her fingertips.

They arrived midday, and the bitter scent of blood was overpowering. A truck was unloading men and bodies as Milly walked into the main hospital building, formerly some farm structure, and blood dripped from the bed of the truck onto the frozen ground. She covered her mouth and ran inside.

The wood-and-brick structure did little to keep out the cold, and inside the stretchers and beds lay in neat rows. Silent men watched her as she passed by, and two women in white trundled from bed to bed, rearranging blankets and offering sips of water ladled from a bucket.

Milly extended a hand at a passing man, a doctor, judging from his white coat and stethoscope.

"Are these the Internationals?" She hoped he spoke English.

"Milly? Milly Bennett?" He was balding with fringes of brown hair above his ears, and had a handsome, sharp nose.

She blinked and was reaching for her glasses to wipe them clean when the memory clicked.

"Hermann! Dr. Muller. From Moscow," she added, then giggled at her clumsiness. Of course he knew he had come from Moscow.

He smiled widely, then pulled her into a hug.

"So comforting to see a familiar face here," he said, holding her at arm's length before releasing her. She remembered running into him at a few parties, but though she thought he was handsome, they hadn't exchanged more than a few words.

"What are you doing here? I thought you were a geneticist," she said, risking a glance around at the men in red-stained bandages and dark casts.

"I am still," he said with a wink. "But I am still a doctor too, so I'm here briefly, to help the cause. I'm interested in learning from Dr. Barsky." Hermann pointed across the ward floor to another man in white. "He is doing amazing work with blood."

"Yet he's so clean. I'm sorry, what a dumb thing to say." She blushed. "Hermann, I'm looking for Bob Merriman. Is he here? You might have met him in Moscow too, tall—"

He placed a hand on her arm and interrupted her.

"Bob's here. Hurt badly. I think he'll make it, but . . ."

She sucked in a breath. "His wife, she'll . . . Show me."

He led her through the quiet ward, his confident hands brushing the still blankets of quiet men as they passed. The hospital had two wood-burning stoves at either end of the ward, but still their breath showed in gentle clouds whenever they exhaled deeply. The injured men pulled their covers up to their noses, when they could. A few faces were slack, eyes closed, and Milly wondered. But no, the efficient staff here wouldn't leave dead men in their beds.

Bob was awake when they approached, and his eyes lit up when he saw Milly. But quickly his face clenched in pain. His upper arm and shoulder were encased in a cast, and his tall form looked pinned to the bed like a butterfly in a specimen box.

"We were out of plaster," Hermann said, shaking his head. "We had to use concrete."

"Trying to get me to get my strength back faster," Bob said in a strained voice. His handsome face was pale, even behind his black circular glasses, and he closed his eyes for a moment. Milly's knees felt weak, and she leaned on the metal frame at the end of his bed.

"Marion needs to be here with you," Milly said. She didn't want to ask what, other than his shoulder, might be injured, or if he needed more surgery. The rest of his body lay unmoving under a gray blanket.

"Yes," he whispered. "She does."

"I need a driver," Milly said to Hermann. Her certainty gave her a jolt of energy, and her legs steadied. "His wife has to travel a long way, and I need to get her the telegram now."

Hermann twisted his mouth and looked around the ward. Two nurses in dark blue uniforms, one carrying a stack of blankets, walked from bed to bed unfolding extra blankets over some. Dr. Barsky had disappeared, and there was no other staff in sight.

"Our ambulance drivers are either out at the front or sleeping," he said. "They don't get much of a break. What about the fellow who brought you here?"

Milly shook her head. "He doesn't work for me. And Jim, the other reporter, won't want to leave yet. He's sniffing for a story."

She paused and glanced down at Bob, who had closed his eyes and sunk back into his pillow. His fingers, sticking out of the monstrous cast, were dark and swollen.

"Look at him," she said. "Suffering." If she pressed Hermann enough, maybe he would let her drive the ambulance. She could figure it out.

Hermann nodded. "I'll drive you."

"You will?" She looked at his green eyes, and then quickly away to the soldier next to Bob's bed. He was a darker-skinned man, sleeping with a bandage wrapped around his head. Milly shivered in the cold.

"Absolutely. Let's go before the next batch of wounded shows up."

Milly nodded, then bent down to brush Bob's hair from his forehead. He opened his eyes. "We'll get Marion here," she said. "As soon as possible."

"Thank you." His voice was soft, like a brushed coat.

Milly smiled. At least she could help her friends.

Two hours later, she was in a telegraph office in Murcia. "Come now," she cabled to Marion, and provided her own address in Valencia. Bob wouldn't want any written record that he was injured, since fighting in this war was illegal now for Americans. Marion would understand, anyway. Milly wondered if her friend didn't already have a hunch, hadn't already packed her bag due to some intuitive misgiving. The couple seemed so aware of each other.

"No matter what happens, they're lucky to have each other," Milly said to Hermann as they walked out of the office into the sunny cold.

Hermann put a hand on her lower back and guided her into the passenger seat of their borrowed car. She paused, letting the sensation of his touch linger, then slid into the seat.

"Connections take many forms," Hermann said, leaning over her, with one elbow propped on the open car door. She looked up at him. "Humans make such delightful, varied pairings, don't you think?"

"Is that what geneticists study?" Milly leaned back in her seat and turned out her leg. "You sit around reading Havelock Ellis all day and consider all the . . . different pairings?"

"I don't know that fellow," Hermann said, straightening. "But I'm eager to learn." He smiled, then snapped her door shut.

MILLY'S ARMS TREMBLED as she carried her small suitcase
up the stairs from the entryway of the Hotel Florida's modern
lobby, in central Madrid. She hadn't packed much, only a
change of clothes, a toothbrush, and a small cured ham purchased on impulse right before she got in the car in Valencia.
Now she stood in the tall-ceilinged lobby and wondered why
she hadn't at least packed a nightgown.

After the quick trip to Murcia, she and Hermann had flirted
the whole drive home, then flirted over dinner, and flirted as he
bid her farewell that night. Three days later, a Foreign Press
Bureau photographer returned from a trip to the hospital with
a note for Milly.

"I'm on leave, starting Saturday, for a whole week. Want to
join?"

Milly hadn't bothered to respond. Her heart racing with
anticipation, and her body tingling with excitement, she called
her two bosses, found a ride, and packed a suitcase.

A man in a fine wool suit walked past her in the lobby and
nodded. She smiled automatically, then wondered if she knew
him. Hell, it didn't matter. She wasn't here for work. For the

first time in a year, Milly only planned to please herself. No notes, no deadlines, no public expectations.

She walked up to the desk.

"Could you please inform Dr. Muller his guest has arrived."

The clerk nodded and placed a phone call.

"He says you can go up," the clerk said once he replaced the handset. "Room 526."

Milly looked at the stairs, then the elevator, where there was no operator. She strolled inside and pushed the button herself. Once the door closed, she rushed to pull off her tights and then her underwear, both of which she stuffed into her suitcase, next to the ham, right before the elevator doors peeled open. When the door revealed the hallway, a waiting old woman stared as Milly tilted her head and slipped her feet back into her pumps.

"Perdóname," Milly said, suppressing a giggle, and stepped out.

She walked down the hall, and at room 526, she paused. She took a deep breath. Then she gave her hips a shimmy, and thrilled at the feeling of her bare thighs rubbing against each other. She was too old to feel ashamed of herself, no matter what happened, she decided.

She knocked.

❖

THEY DIDN'T COME out of the room for three days.

At sunset on the third day, the floor shuddered and a crash sounded in the distance. Then another explosion, but closer. Hermann was on top of her, thrusting fiercely at what was the culmination of thirty minutes of play, and he didn't seem to hear. Milly reached up and pulled his head down close to her ears.

"I think they're shelling the neighborhood," she whispered.

He slowed, but continued rocking into her, back and forth. His eyes met hers, and he smiled.

"Let them," he said, then curled down to suck at one of her nipples. She rose up toward him and arched back into the love-making.

When they finished, Hermann collapsed onto the bed and laughed.

"You see how you captivate me?" he said. "I'm glad the fascists have bad aim."

"They're aiming for you, are they?" she said, her head propped up on an elbow.

"I am key to the Republican war effort," he said, and shot out a hand to tickle her soft belly. "Though maybe it's you they're after. Condemning their futile offensives in your scathing articles."

Milly snorted, then got out of bed. She pulled on her trousers, thought about not wearing a bra, then put one on and yanked a sweater over.

"Your hair's a mess," Hermann said, sounding like he was pouting.

"I'm just going to get a bottle of wine," she said. "Surely you can spare me for thirty minutes?" She raised a provocative eyebrow, then waved her hands at his nether regions. "It looks like you're ready for a break anyhow."

He leapt to his feet on the mattress.

"A true man never rests!" Then he collapsed back down. "But a doctor knows how to take his breaks. A good tempranillo, if you can find it, my dear."

Milly gave a little salute, then walked out of the room.

The air in the hallway was fresh compared to the musk of their room, and she breathed deeply. She hadn't been thinking of wine when she pulled her clothes on, but only that she needed to come up for air. She couldn't let herself fall in love with this man. This was a wartime fling, and they both needed the companionship, but nothing more. She walked down the hallway and thought of waiting for the elevator, but decided on the stairs. A few people walking up passed her. One man frowned quizzically, but another man winked. They had gone into the basement shelter when the shelling started, most likely.

Outside in the street there was no damage visible, but smoke smeared the darkening sky in the distance. Milly reached into her pocket to see how much money she had, and she pulled out a scrap of paper. Her notes for how to find her ride home, a car she was sharing with two other reporters in Valencia. Leaving two days from now. Too soon.

No, she should leave now. She was forty, too old to romp in a hotel room for a week, and too old to be falling in love with a man she hardly knew.

A woman with a worker's cap stuffed over her long black hair walked past holding a fistful of almond tree branches, brimming with small pale flowers. The branches would go into some vase or arrangement where, after a few days, the flowers would wilt, shrivel, and die. Yet now they glowed with a springtime beauty Milly was parched for.

She pulled a few peseta bills from her pocket, counted them, and turned toward the little wine and dry goods shop down the street. A tempranillo *would* fit the bill, and when she and Hermann finished drinking, she could throw the empty bottle at the attacking fascists. Let them clean up the mess.

31

IN HER ROOM, Milly dropped a bromide tablet into her water glass and stirred. Her stomach clenched. She hoped she wouldn't vomit again. She needed to get out today, and Valencia's warm, salt-tinged breezes would help. It had been three days since she was able to drag herself into the office, either the AP office or the Foreign Press Bureau, and write a story. Her hotel bill was coming due now; the Hotel Reina Victoria wasn't cheap, and she needed the money.

The sweet liquid did little to quell her nausea, but she choked it down anyway. She had already thrown up the chicory coffee she had tried to make for herself, right down the toilet.

Her monthlies should have come two weeks ago.

It was unbelievable, but she seemed to be pregnant.

Her stomach groaned, and she shuffled over to collapse into the bed. She was sterile, rendered barren by that necessary but ravaging abortion back in San Francisco, and there was no way that she could be pregnant. But now, six weeks after her time in Madrid, she couldn't find any other explanation. In spite of the stomach pain, a bright glow of contentment suffused her. A baby. Her baby. She clasped her hands over her abdomen and curled into a ball on the rumpled bed, where Zhenya's bracelet dug into her skin with a reassuring pinch. He would have wanted her to have this baby too.

An hour later, she mustered the energy to get out of bed. Marion was staying with her, sleeping on a cot they had crammed in between Milly's small bed and the high window that looked into the square shaft above the courtyard, but Marion left each morning at dawn to care for Bob. He was shacked up with three AP men who had agreed to let him stay, since the couple couldn't afford their own room. Marion was so caught in the pain of her husband's recovery she hadn't looked past Milly's flimsy excuse of food poisoning.

Milly had written three letters to Hermann, two gushing with simple affection, ignorant of her condition, and a third referring to their little "medicine ball," the closest she could get to writing the word "baby." It wasn't a baby yet, she knew that. But she had the possibility of a baby, a sweet spark growing inside her, and she wanted it desperately.

He had not replied to any letter, but he had left Spain and returned to Moscow, so she knew the post would take time. There were at least two censors to cross and hundreds, maybe thousands of miles. When she lay in bed at night staring at the high ceiling, she imagined Hermann getting the letter and throwing all his books and suits into a traveling case so he could grab the first train to Paris. But in the morning, she knew reality was more complex. Hermann had to obtain permission from the Soviet authorities to leave his laboratory and, given the arguments he had been having with the political leaders over Lamarck's foolish theories, she wasn't sure he would receive any such permission.

A sparrow landed on her windowsill, pecked, and flew off. Milly propped herself up in bed. No wave of nausea came, so she sat up. Slowly, she dressed and made her way out of the hotel. It was a short walk to the Ministry of Propaganda.

Her boss at the Foreign Press Bureau, Constancia de la Mora, welcomed her with a frown.

"Fix this," Constancia said brusquely. She was usually a charming young woman, a former aristocrat turned dedicated democrat, but sometimes the press of work harried her. Most of the writing Milly had been doing for them recently was cleaning up the translated articles the government wanted to print in the local English-language publication. Similar to what she had done for *Moscow Daily News*, but at least here there was a war. Now, with so many foreigners flooding the Republic, eager to help no matter their lack of Spanish, the government needed a way to communicate with them. She knew how to serve in that role, and this time her writing would be put to better use.

Milly read the piece and groaned. Parts of it were incomprehensible.

"What is this about?" she asked one of the senior editors, a small round man with a broom brush of a mustache. She held up the paper and read aloud. "Women are likely to be spies. Sit at cafés. Talk with soldiers. Reptiles in the rearguard." She flapped the paper in his face. "What in the hell?"

He thinned his lips. "That is what we are worried about. There have been spies. Haven't you heard?"

She shook her head. "There are always spies. Men and women."

"Fix it, Milly."

She glared at him, and held the paper between two hands, her fingers pinched at the edge. But then her stomach roiled, and she placed her hand on her womb and remembered. It was a girl, she decided, a girl who would be born into a world that reviled her, a fatherless female, but a girl with a mother who would do anything to take care of her. Starting with keeping a roof over their heads.

"Fine." She snapped her wrist, extending the article toward him, and he took it. "But the Republic deserves better than this."

"Stop stalling and get to work."

She growled but sat at her desk and put a clean sheet of paper into her typewriter. She would do what she could.

Before leaving that night, the mail boy tossed an envelope on her desk.

"This came for you." He walked away.

She recognized Hermann's elegant handwriting immediately and grabbed the envelope like a wild dog seizing a carcass. But then she saw the date on the postmark, some month earlier. This would have been written before he could have received her latest letter, before she knew about her little burden.

This letter would be his honest thoughts, his feelings before the vise of obligation could constrain him. This letter was about him and her alone.

She slid the envelope into her pocketbook, then stood, placed the cover over her typewriter, and handed the clean article to the boss. She hadn't bothered to find the translator in the end. Anything in the original mash-up that she didn't understand, she had rewritten herself. There were no facts here to get wrong, only admonitions to shape.

"See you tomorrow," she said.

She walked down the steps of the ornate Ministry of Propaganda, once a rich bank, and glanced up as she habitually did at the fresco ornamenting the ceiling of the front portico. In the dark she could barely make out the blue-and-gray medallion, but it comforted her to know it was there. That beauty could persist in a time of war, that the people who came before her gave some thought to beautifying a space you had to go out of your way to see. She pressed her hand to her belly and walked through the park, darkened to conceal it from air raids, and then she continued the remaining winding blocks to her hotel.

When she reached the narrow lobby of the Hotel Reina Victoria, she nodded at the clerk, whose elbows were propped on the desk as she passed. He still wore gloves, though the equalizing forces of war had a year earlier removed the obligation of such class strictures. He nodded back, his face hopeful for a moment that she might approach and chat, then sagging again in boredom as she walked on, winding up the marble staircase with its wrought iron bannister. Ordinarily, she wouldn't mind a chance to practice her terrible Spanish, but now she needed to rush to the safety of her room. The letter may as well have been a hot coal in her purse, glowing and burning with her impatience.

Her room, fortunately, was empty—Marion must still be with Bob. Milly collapsed into the only chair in the room, a brocaded armchair that spoke of another century.

She opened the letter and read.

Her limbs felt weak and fevered by the end. She had misunderstood, he wrote. Their coupling, though tremendously pleasant, was meant to be only a passing affair. Shouldn't people have sexual relations without further obligation, he asked? He had thought she was as modern minded as he was, and he wouldn't have entered into their affair if he had known how attached she would become. He didn't want to hurt her.

He didn't want to hurt her.

❖

THE NEXT DAY, Marion was still asleep on her cot when Milly awoke early. Milly was tempted to wedge her curved body next to the petite one of her friend, to curl into the comfort of her friendship, and to cry her pain away.

But the shame of admitting her folly would hurt more than the pain of bearing it in silence. She was a fool, chasing after men who didn't want her.

Milly sat at her small desk and tried to think of someone to write. Someone who would love her no matter what she said. Her sister, maybe. Milly let her pen sag in her grip.

Marion sat up and stretched.

"How's Bob?" Milly asked, forcing her voice straight, like a limb tied to a splint.

"Better." Marion rubbed her eyes. "He can walk a little."

"Do you need a break? Let's go drink some fresh orange juice and stare at the ocean. I'm sure we can find some."

"Ocean?" Marion smiled.

"If we're lucky." Milly forced a smile back. The beach was a long walk from their hotel, about an hour, but it was worth it when she had the energy. At night, she liked to watch the ships bobbing in the darkness, their lights extinguished for fear of fascist bombers, but their outlines visible in the starlight.

"Sounds swell." Marion stretched again, and her slender limbs glowed in the hazed sunshine coming through the curtains. She was darling, though Milly knew her friend no longer saw her beauty, only her inability to conceive. As if her body were a dried straw doll, Marion had once said.

All the more reason not to confide.

"Up and at 'em," Milly said. "Before everyone else buys the oranges."

❅

Two weeks later, a second letter from Hermann came. Now he had read her news about the little medicine ball, and though he already had a teenaged son from his first marriage back in America, his words hummed with optimism.

"What agony you have gone through, my Milly," he said. He bemoaned her sickness, and though he said nothing about his dismissal, he urged her to take care of herself. He might be able to take a vacation in Paris, he said. One week.

She hugged the letter to her breast. It was pathetic, but she would accept the comfort from his letter. She didn't care. Her morning sickness had continued to rack her, and she was losing weight. Even Marion, occupied by her own sadness, had begun to look at her searchingly.

Milly pulled a clean piece of paper from her desk, while around her, the other editors at the Propaganda Ministry typed away on their clattering machines.

"Yes," she wrote. "Just say where."

She sealed it up and dashed his address on the envelope before she could reconsider.

"How's the exhibition coming?" Constancia said when she dropped her letter in the box near Constancia's desk. Milly was collecting an anti-fascist show of Spanish children's artwork, drawings done by kids that showed their villages demolished by fascist bombs or their families' blood flowing into the soil. The project reminded her of Peter, the little boy who died in a bombing somewhere near a petrol station, and she did the work in his honor. Once she had all the drawings, she would take them to Madrid for the government to display to the foreign press.

"Rosy," she said. She didn't have the words to explain how the children's anguish tore at her heart, and yet that same heart glowed with the hope that Hermann would embrace her and this little life. She picked up a drawing done in charcoal stick and looked at the bowed, childish lines of a house that seemed to cow in the face of a line of massive bullets. What place was there in this world for innocence? And yet.

"The exhibition's coming along great," Milly continued. Maybe the children's art would make a difference.

"Perfect," Constancia said. "After all, the children are our future."

Milly restrained the urge to touch her belly. She wasn't sure if she'd lose her job over the pregnancy, and she certainly wasn't going to risk her employment yet.

"Indeed they are," she said, smiling.

32

THE WAR HAD started a year ago, and every day the fascist rebels seemed to gnaw more territory away from the Republic. Milly kept a map tacked up on the wall of the small apartment in Valencia she now rented, much cheaper than the hotel, and she sketched the evolving front onto it. Her stomach sank with each government loss. In May, while she was in Paris with Hermann, the Republican leadership had fled under the cover of night from Madrid to Valencia, and now her seaside town was the capital, though Madrid still held, thank goodness. And even Valencia didn't feel safe. The diplomats were starting to flee, and each night, the British were rowed out to their destroyer the *Resource* to spend the night safely in her bunks. Soon, Milly feared, the capital would shift again. Each time she looked at the map, she thought about taking it down. All the map did was remind her of the strength of evil.

It was nighttime, and though it was a mournful anniversary, the Spanish spirit remained undaunted. Mandatory blackouts began at ten p.m., but men and women capered in the streets with flashlights and candles afterward. Milly sat in a café with Kajsa, a Swedish woman who had fought with the Internationals last fall, when women were allowed to do so. Now Kajsa stayed in Milly's apartment as she figured out what else she could do to help the Republic's cause. The leaves of the orange trees planted along the sidewalk rustled in the dark.

"Are they celebrating or protesting?" Kajsa said, watching a band of teenaged boys walk arm in arm down the street crowing revolutionary songs.

"I don't know." Milly took a small sip of her wine. She didn't drink much, now that she cradled her little medicine ball in her belly, which was swelling with a comforting tightness against her pants. Soon she would have to tell people, though she suspected Kajsa and Marion, who had found her own apartment, had their suspicions.

"Have you heard from your doctor? Hermann?" Kajsa asked. Her blond hair glowed in the candlelight shed by the taper on their table.

"He sent some sugared violets from his trip to Toulouse," Milly said, though the violets had come weeks ago. Their visit in Paris had been pleasant, but Hermann had been so solicitous of her health that he refused to make love, no matter how often she tried to throw her legs around him. Since then, his letters had been full of paternal affection and concerns about his laboratory in Moscow. She fretted.

"And the soldiers?" Kajsa giggled. She was delighted with Milly's love life, or what she imagined of it, and she made much of an American from the International Brigade who had stopped to flirt with Milly outside the Ministry of Propaganda once.

"I'm sure they're at the front." She picked at a piece of hardened wax that had splattered on the circular table. She wondered if she should tell Kajsa now. Milly had prepared her resignation papers, to be effective August 1, from the Propaganda Ministry. Her appetite had only tiptoed back, and she hardly had the energy to manage half the information bulletins her editor was constantly asking her to write. But still, she hadn't filed the papers. Hermann had insisted he would pay for her to return to the United States, but she couldn't peel herself away from Spain. As if the Republic couldn't stand to lose a single ally. In the street, a woman in trousers swirled an anti-fascist banner and laughed. A bearded man, or so he seemed in the dark, caught her in his arms and dipped her back as if dancing.

Then, a twinge that had been scratching at Milly's stomach seized into a spasm. She gasped.

"Are you all right?" Kajsa paused, her wineglass held suspended before her pale lips.

Milly nodded, but then another spasm gripped her all the way around her midsection.

"Oh god," she moaned. The pain subsided, and she took a breath, only to find another cramp clamping her down. She doubled over. Kajsa leapt up, nearly toppling the table, and ran to her side.

"What is it? Do you need a doctor?" She squeezed Milly's hand.

"I'm fine . . ." She gasped again. "Home. I need to lie down."

Kajsa threw Milly's arm around her tall shoulders and hefted her out of her chair. Haltingly, they made their way back to the apartment. Milly's pants grew slick, but she told herself it was sweat. Sweat from the Spanish heat. When she lay down, she kept her pants on and refused to look closely at the damp circle spreading along her thighs.

In the morning, the baby was gone.

❖

SHE SPENT A week in bed, with Kajsa cooing over her and dabbing her forehead with a damp cloth. There was no fever, but that was Kajsa's remedy for heartbreak. At the end of the week, Milly pulled herself out of bed.

"There's a war," she said, her prepared words feeling stiff in her mouth. "People are dying at fascist hands. I'm here for a reason, and it's not to lie in bed."

"But you . . ." Neither of them could say what had happened.

"Could you bring me some paper? I have a letter to write." She needed to tell Hermann. To relieve him of his burden. And to reassure him that she would keep it a secret. He was fighting a legal case to gain custody of his teenaged son in Texas, and word of an illicit affair in Spain would undoubtedly count against him. She would tell no one.

"And then?" Kajsa handed her a sheet of paper and a pen.

"I'm not sure." She took the paper and placed it on a closed book on her lap. She had a hole she needed to stop up before her life and soul gushed out of it, leaving her empty and alone, but she didn't know how.

Kajsa took Milly's hand in hers and pressed it against her cheek.

"You have had a difficult thing."

Milly snatched her hand away.

"I cannot pity myself when I'm lying in bed in a country at war. Where bombs fall and children die and mothers starve."

Kajsa looked down.

"I'm sorry," Milly continued. "It's not you I'm angry at. I think . . . I think I need to be serious about this war. I'm not committed enough."

"I don't know what you mean," Kajsa said.

"You will."

She gritted her teeth and lifted her pen.

33

Milly sat in a small room overlooking the flat walls and carved portico of the old church across the plaza. Santo Domingo, she thought it was. At the desk across from her, a young man with straight black hair cropped carelessly above his ears coughed.

"Citizen," he said, making her wonder for a moment if she were back in Moscow. "Did you hear the question?"

She had, but she needed the moment to think. She had already botched the answer on dialectical materialism, and she wasn't sure what he had wanted her to say when he asked her views on private land ownership. The Communist Party of Spain had been making noises as if it supported private ownership, but she wasn't sure.

"What is the role of the Party in the bourgeois democracy?"

She drummed her fingers on the desk. She had wanted to get in, wanted to subsume herself to someone else's leadership. This morning she had continued past her office and walked the additional block and a half to the Communist Party Headquarters. She had filed her intention to apply a week ago, and she wanted to see if she had earned an interview.

She had.

"The role of the Party is to nudge the society through its bourgeois phase." She was sure "nudge" wasn't a Marxist word, but hell, she'd still never had a chance to study the man's writings. She'd just have to wing it, based on the dozens and dozens of cocktail conversations she had overheard.

He held his pen aloft, waiting, then made a quick note.

"I want to get in, join the Party," Milly said, unprompted. She was nervous. "It's the only thing bigger than myself that I can believe in these days. There's just so much nonsense out there, so much horror, death, and you people are the only ones trying to make a difference." She shouldn't have mentioned death. A dry darkness began to suck at her core when she mentioned death, as if in an echo of what she had lost. She pinched her eyes closed.

The young man cleared his throat.

"Were your parents workers?"

She snapped her eyes open. There was another echo, and she rubbed her head.

"They asked me that in Moscow," she muttered.

"What?"

She parted her lips to answer, to again tell the story of her mother's sacrifices, but then thought better of it.

"Why does it matter?" she said.

"How could it not matter? Your class history informs you."

"Does it?"

The young man placed his notebook on the desk.

"Will you be answering the questions that are part of this interview?"

Pique rushed in a heat to Milly's face, and her cheeks burned. She slapped her palm on the table, and was about to tell him what to do with his interview, when she caught herself.

She took a deep breath.

"I wanted to be a part of something bigger," she said. "But I guess that's not for me."

She stood, gathered her purse, reached over to lift her application card from his desk, and walked to the door. As she passed the wastebasket, she crumpled the card and dropped it in.

"Thank you for your time," she said.

When she reached the street, she breathed the hot, salted air and gazed up at the sun-bright sky.

If only her father could see her there, controlling her temper and making a split-second decision.

Maybe he would be proud after all.

She walked over to the park, which also faced the Ministry of Propaganda's requisitioned building, and sat on a bench facing a marble statue of a man sitting on a bench while cherubs cavorted at his feet. A pediatrician, honored by the city nearly two decades earlier.

She wondered if he had children of his own, and if it was different for men when they didn't. Hope was the cruelest master, hadn't someone said that? Or maybe it was simply true. She hadn't expected to foster a life, so when her little ball began glowing inside her, she didn't have her defenses up. Milly wrapped her arms around herself as she looked at the white stone doctor, his legs crossed, his eyes downcast. She mimicked the position. But copying someone else didn't make her feel better, so she unfolded herself and stared at the palm fronds splitting the sky above her head.

She was late for work. By another life's timeline, she would have resigned two weeks ago. She would have a baby growing inside of her, and she would be on an ocean liner bound for the United States. Well, that future didn't come to pass. But it didn't mean she had to stick with her old future, the one she'd been plodding through before the pregnancy. She could resign from the Foreign Press Bureau.

The thought alone made her smile. Maybe she could go somewhere. She didn't have to be here, in Valencia, if it didn't suit her. She loved the city with its pastel and stone buildings and its ancient cathedrals sprinkled everywhere, but she didn't have to stay.

She stood from the bench, brushed her skirt straight, and walked to the train station. She would just look, she thought as she was walking. Maybe she would get an idea. Or maybe she would go happily back to the Foreign Press Bureau to edit translations and help people understand what Spanish democracy was suffering.

The station must have been from about the same era as her marble pediatrician friend in the park. While she was dancing on beaches in Hawaii and dodging bullets in China, this city was going about its serious business of building railroads and healing sick children. Maybe Valencia wasn't the place for her.

Inside the long station hall, the windows rattled with the noise of hundreds of passengers scuttling to and fro. Milly nudged her way through a crowd of soldiers so she could see the train tables.

"Excuse me," a man said in New York English when he bumped into her. "Sorry about that, lady."

She looked at the group more closely.

"Is Bob Merriman here?" she asked.

"Captain Merriman? Nah, he's at the front already. But you want to see our commander?" The man turned away. "Major Amlie! Some broad here to see you!"

Milly held up a hand to tell him not to worry, but then let it fall to her side. Maybe she could get a good story out of this. It had been a while since she'd filed anything with the international editors.

The commander approached them, his face stern.

"McCarthy, I was worried." The commander towered over the other man, but he hunched his shoulders, as if to make himself shorter.

"I'm sorry, Major Amlie. I didn't mean to be late. But listen, this lady here wants to talk to you."

The tall man nodded. "I'm glad you're here, McCarthy. Steve Nelson over there needs some help with the artillery, could you help him organize it?"

Milly was surprised that the officer framed his request so mildly, but the soldier merely dipped his chin.

"Yes, sir," he said.

"Hans, you mean. You go on leave with a pretty girl and you forget all your solidarity?" He gave a half smile in Milly's direction.

"I wish she were mine," McCarthy said, and flashed a smile at Milly before walking off.

"I'm sorry," Hans said, blushing. "I hadn't meant to scare your boyfriend away."

"It's all right. I just met him. I mean—" She caught herself when he blushed even more deeply. "He's not my boyfriend. Just someone I ran into here a minute ago." She looked up at the commanding officer. "I'm Milly Bennett. With the AP and the Foreign Press Bureau. I guess I'll be seeing you around."

Hans took a step back. "Will you be writing stories about us?"

"Do you think I should?"

He looked over at the men, sitting on packages of clothing tied with string or huddled in groups, smoking and laughing.

"I don't see why not," he said. "They're a brave bunch."

"Where can I find you?"

Hans shook his head. "That's not my information to give out, Miss. But if you contact the Brigade authorities, they'll let you know. It was a pleasure meeting you." He doffed his cap, then turned and began calling out requests to the other men meandering through the echoing hall.

Milly watched for a few minutes before she left to head to the Ministry. It was a good idea, going out to cover the Internationals. Maybe she should. But for now, some mindless writing would clear her head, some hours spent crafting sentences that someone else wanted her to write. Information bulletins that shaped the world according to the wishes of her superiors, rather than translating the chaotic and painful world that she saw. A world where blackout orders only made Valencia's star-washed nightlife more romantic, as couples nuzzled by candlelight in cafés even while shrapnel-scarred trucks limped past, in from the front. A world where airplanes could drop bombs on Valencia's port and the movie theaters played on. A world where a group of men willing to fight and die for someone else's cause could make Milly forget, for a moment, her pain.

34

THE FIGHTING CAME fast and hard, according to what news they heard in Valencia. The Aragon front had exploded, and the Internationals were scrambling to retake—or was it hold—a little crossroads town called Belchite.

"I want to write about it," Milly told the new senior editor at the Foreign Press Bureau, a sallow-skinned man with perpetual bags under his eyes. She wondered if he slept. She certainly wasn't sleeping, not much. That was part of the reason she needed to travel.

"A front-line story?" He rubbed his chin.

"That's right. We'll tell people how it really is." And if he wouldn't let her publish it, maybe she could sell it to AP.

He pulled out a notebook from his back pocket, wrote a few words, then shoved it back into his trousers.

"Go ahead. Get a pass from the third floor"—an administrative office— "and head out to the front. Write something interesting."

"That's all I do." She laughed. What lies. She thought interesting thoughts, but it had been months since she had written a solid story. But now was the time to try. If she couldn't be happy, at least she could be a decent newspaperwoman. There were stories out there only she could tell.

It took nearly the whole day to get the pass, but eventually she had all the signatures she needed, and the driver of a propaganda truck headed north was willing to give her a ride. The truck was constructed like a gigantic megaphone, with a massive cone on the back that amplified whatever messages they were trying to send to the enemy troops to get them to desert. Mostly opera to the Italian fascists, or so she had heard. She scribbled a few impressions in her notebook.

They arrived after nightfall, and Milly tried to sleep in the truck with the windows open. But even at night, the air blowing across the plains felt like the wafts coming down from one of Hawaii's volcanoes, and her now-chronic insomnia kept her tossing and turning. At least at home she had the London *Times* correspondent who lived on the floor beneath her and read her passages of *Romeo and Juliet* at night through the air ducts. His unrequited affection helped, somehow. As if his yearning balanced her own, even though they couldn't ease each other's pain.

She must have slept a little though, because she woke in the morning with her hair sweaty and plastered to her forehead. While she was sitting up and trying to arrange herself, one of the soldiers banged on the door.

"The major wants to talk to you," he yelled through the aluminum.

"I'm coming," Milly said, then cringed as a volley of gunfire sounded in the distance.

"Better hurry, before things get bad," he yelled.

Milly plucked at her dress, hoping to generate a little cool breeze. If a battle was unfolding here, she could be the first to write about it. She could tell the story the way she wanted to, and no one could force her pen otherwise.

She approached a grove of olive trees where men in tattered uniforms were crouching, some tending the wounds of others.

A lanky man emerged hunched over from under a bower of branches, and when he straightened, she recognized the tall commander she had met at the train station.

"Major," she called, hoping she'd remembered his rank correctly. He didn't react, so she yelled again. Frowning, the man looked at her, then he brightened.

"Just call me Hans, Miss Bennett," he said. In the distance, artillery exploded and a stream of machine gun fire flew. "You're here to see the battle?"

"Yes. And it's Milly." She didn't want to sound like a tourist. "I'll write a story, tell the Americans how their brave men are fighting to keep Spain free."

His eyes softened. "I don't know about brave, but we'll take whatever attention we can get. Be careful." He gestured for her to follow him.

"We're trying to take this town," he said, pointing south at the moderate-sized village. Two church towers reached up from either end of the long rows of houses. An explosion sounded in the town, and a cloud of dust burst up. "The defenders don't want to leave, though. In the last town we saw graffiti painted on the wall that said 'Kill a red, get one less year in purgatory.' I hear it sounds better in Spanish."

Milly wrote down a few quick lines, but the zipper of the machine gun fire made her hands tremble. She hoped her notes would be legible later. Assuming there was a later.

"Why do we need this town?" She pointed at the expanse of low hills stretching all around beneath a large blue sky that gave the impression of presiding over a flat land.

"The short answer is, because headquarters said so." He smiled, and she noticed his eyes crinkled at the edges like fresh gingerbread. "The longer answer has something to do with a crossroads and trying to recapture Zaragoza. But that feels awfully far away."

She didn't write that part. In town, an artillery shell screamed and exploded upon the wall of a building, which collapsed in a pile of bricks. Milly flinched.

"I wish they'd just surrender," Hans said. His shoulders sagged as he gazed over at the battle, just a few hundred yards away. He looked more sad than keyed up, and Milly wondered how a gentle man like himself had fallen into command in war.

"I'd better get back to it," he said. "Will you be all right back here?"

"Sure," Milly said with more conviction that she felt. It seemed unlikely that the rebels holed up in those beat-up buildings would come cascading out to assault the improvised camp in the olive grove, but she wasn't sure she wanted to bet her life on it. Still, she didn't want to let the major down. "I'll be fine."

He turned back to look at her and gave her a quick smile.

"Tomorrow's my birthday, you know. Let's see if we win a town as my present."

Milly returned to the relative safety of the olive grove, where she sat for the rest of the afternoon, peering around the trunk of a tree while the International machine guns spit bullets from their positions at the front of the grove and the men in the town crept from building to alley to house. The sandy orange bricks spit up a regular storm of debris that the wind carried north, back to the olive grove, and by the time night fell, Milly was fingering the dust out of her hair.

She spent the night in the truck, though she hardly slept through the sound of artillery and guns cratering the night. Before dawn, she had a meager breakfast of thin porridge. She hated to take even that from the soldiers, but she knew she would be grateful for the food later. The machine gun fire coming from town made it hard to swallow, but she tried.

A tall young man with jaundiced skin came and crouched next to her.

"We captured the church yesterday, did you hear? What do you think of it?" he said.

"The battle? I'm hardly a military expert."

"Not like we were before we showed up, most of us." He snorted. "You're a reporter, you must know stuff. You've been places, right?"

Milly looked at the horizon, which was starting to brighten with the rising sun, defining the soft hills like the curves on a dancer's muscled thigh.

"I have been places. It's easy to forget sometimes, when you're in them. That they're places, I mean. Worth journeying to."

He nodded, which was generous, since she knew she was making a hash of her thoughts.

"I've never had anyone write about me before," he said. "Will you write about me?"

"Sure." She pulled out her notebook. "What's your name? Only if you want me to publish it, I mean."

"Phil Detre. Captain."

He told her a story about an alleyway he had assaulted the day before, and the grenades he had thrown at Captain Bob Merriman's command.

"Merriman is here?" Milly sat up straight. It would be wonderful to see her old friend again.

He nodded. "Somewhere. Probably directing the assault down there." He pointed toward the town. Most of the soldiers were based out of some sort of warehouse at the edge of town. "I'd better go see if I'm needed."

Dawn was still breaking, and an airplane buzzed overhead. Everyone around her cringed and hid. One soldier, closer to the warehouse, pulled a flashlight from his pocket and flashed it up to the sky.

"What the hell is he doing?" hissed a soldier near Milly. "Mark, cut it out!" he called, but the man couldn't hear or ignored him. She wanted to make a note of the scene, the trembling soldiers, the mad man with the flashlight, the hush that fell over the guns while everyone hoped for the airplane to pass, but her hands were shaking too much to hold a pencil. She nearly threw her breakfast up. The man with the light was only one hundred yards away.

Something hissed through the air, then crashed into the ground near the signaling man.

A brown lump lay inert.

A second crash, and a large unmoving shadow.

The man with the flashlight grabbed the two wrapped crates and dragged them up to the olive trees. The soldiers tore into them and laughed.

Inside were cured hams hocks and bread, packed above small bags of letters.

The man who had signaled the plane threw back his head in laughter. "The fascists have supplied us, boys!"

Then he began handing out lumps of bread. He reached for Milly but recoiled when he looked at her.

"What's a gal doing here?" he asked. He looked around at the other soldiers, who were tearing into their crusts. "Paul, you sure hired an ugly whore. Send her back." He scowled at Milly and thrust the bread he had been about to give to her to someone else.

"I'm not—" she began to object, but the man grabbed his gun and ran back toward the village, where the fighting had swelled up again. Someone yelled behind them, and most of the other men ran too. Two soldiers hanging back, both with bandages wrapped around their arms, dragged the fascist supplies back deeper into the olive grove.

Milly turned and threw up the runny porridge she had been trying to hold down all morning. Reflexively, she glanced around, worried someone would see her. Especially that man, so high on his theft from the fascists that he could cut her down. No one was looking. Her hand shook as she leaned against the small tree, and she sunk to the ground. She tried to conjure some rage, but all she could feel was defeat and the burden of her losses—the men she had loved who hadn't loved her, the baby who couldn't find a home in her womb, the friends who forgot to respond to her letters. Maybe she should die here. Maybe this was what her life had led her to, all her running and dreaming of writing stories and trying to save two broken marriages, all that was leading her to Spain where she could take a bullet between the eyes and martyr herself for the Spanish cause.

It would make a swell story. She was pretty sure she'd be the first newspaperwoman to die in combat. Her blood would water the roots of this tree and season this dry earth beneath her knees.

She stood up.

Behind her, the propaganda truck with the massive horn mounted on its roof sounded, calling on the Spaniards to surrender, and she sat back down. Even her grandiose gestures were idiotic.

Against the olive tree, she watched the battle and took no notes.

After a few hours, the gunfire and artillery began to slow and grow more sporadic, as if the fighting were a massive flock of starlings landing, leaving the sky quiet. Behind her another truck drove up.

Constancia de la Mora got out, and Milly ran over to her. She nearly embraced the younger woman, but collected herself as she approached on the dusty, rocky earth, and instead gave Constancia a nudge on the shoulder.

"Come to see the action?"

"I couldn't let you have all the fun." Constancia's eyes glowed, and she looked over Milly's shoulder at the caved-in roof of the church. "They really did a number on that church."

"It's been brutal out here," Milly said.

"You'll have a good story, then."

Milly nodded, though she knew she wouldn't. There wasn't much she could write about this slow demolition of ancient brick buildings, all to extricate some stubborn fascists. This hardly seemed heroic.

Another artillery shell exploded, and Constancia fell to her knees. Then, it was silence.

"Nearly over, girls," said a man behind them. "You here to help us celebrate?" He leered at them.

"Come on," Milly hissed. She grabbed Constancia by the elbow. A fringe of the woman's black hair, cropped below her ears, shined in the sun where it billowed out from under her gray cap.

Milly pulled her toward the town. Down a hill from the olive grove, across a dirt road, and then through an alleyway that led between two bullet-scraped buildings.

"What are you doing?" Constancia hissed. The area near them was quiet, but a few guns fired some blocks away.

"We're here to observe the battle, so that's what we're going to do. Up close," Milly said. Then she stopped. "Go back, Constancia. I didn't mean to drag you here. This is me being bold and mad and loony."

"But . . ." Constancia looked around, her eyes wide.

"Go." Milly turned her back toward the olive grove, and Constancia ran.

The town was nearly in ruins, and a sickly rotting smell rolled over the heat emanating from the bricks. Milly walked a few more steps, until the alley led to a larger street. The buildings there must have been stores and fine homes, but now they were mostly gaping mouths filled with piles of brick at the back of the throat.

Something moved in the shadows, and Milly froze. The scraping sound of a brick sliding then falling came from inside one of the houses.

"Don't shoot," Milly said, then repeated it in Spanish. She held up her hands.

Silence.

She looked above the hole smashed through the building's frontage and saw a poster proclaiming, simply, "Spain!" The symbol decorating the poster was probably some sort of fascist propaganda, but she didn't recognize it. She probably should have.

She took another step forward.

"Don't shoot," she said again, though she had probably imagined the sound. If she could just pull down the poster, that would be enough to take back and prove she had been here. Had been brave. She could look at that poster and know that once she hadn't run away.

She crossed the street toward the damaged building, and as she did, the smell lashed at her. She gagged and covered her nose with her sleeve. Down the street, she saw a huddle of Internationals lighting cigarettes. The fighting must truly be over.

She used her foot to tip over a large piece of cement, probably a cornice from a building corner, all while keeping her sleeve over her face.

She stepped up on it.

A woman shrouded in a mantle stepped out of the building.

Milly shrieked and toppled.

She threw her arms out and landed, wobbly but without injuring herself.

"Don't shoot!" she said again to the woman. But when she looked up, she saw the woman held a baby. The dusty black mantle on the woman's head fell back from her forehead, and her cheeks showed the streak marks of tears.

Milly took a step closer.

The infant in the woman's arms was dead. A crust of dried blood coated its small head, and a gray arm fell limp from its body. The baby's fingers were curled inward, like a little fist wanting to nurse.

The woman sobbed. She stood perfectly still, holding the baby close to her chest, but not squeezing it. Her thin cheeks spasmed as she wept, but she made no sound other than a gasping for breath.

Milly wiped her sleeve against her own cheeks, and as she did, she felt the nub of the tortoiseshell bracelet. She slid it from her wrist and extended it toward the woman.

"You can sell this," she said in Spanish, or she tried to say. In English, she added, "The soldiers won't hurt you. I know they don't want to trouble the civilians. Just the fascist troops."

The woman had stopped sobbing, but still the tears ran down her face.

"*Hice nacer a la muerte*," she said.

Milly understood. I gave birth to death.

"Me too," she whispered. She took a few more steps closer, until she could reach the woman. She slipped the bracelet in between the woman's fingers and the bundle of her dead child.

"You can sell it," she repeated. "Zhenya would be glad to help."

He would. She pressed her eyes closed and imagined his smiling gray eyes and his blond hair, tousled by the breeze. He wouldn't have known what to make of Spain, but he would have tried to ease this woman's suffering.

Blinking back tears, Milly turned around and walked back to the alley.

As she crossed the main street, she saw a tall figure regarding her from the end of the block. In the bright sun it was hard to tell, but she thought she recognized Hans Amlie. The man tipped his cap at her. She raised a hand to wave, hoping her tremors didn't show.

She found Constancia interviewing the man who ran the sound truck. Milly joined their huddle but said nothing.

Behind them, the sound truck whirred to life and began projecting calls to surrender. "Your leaders are lying to you," a voice said in slow Spanish. Milly put her hands over her ears and still the voice pained her. "You will get no reinforcements. Come over to us and live."

And live, she thought. She ran her fingers over the lines of her face, caressing her large nose, her jutting chin, her smooth cheeks. How glad she was to be alive.

"We should go," Milly said to Constancia.

To her surprise, the other woman agreed.

"It reeks of death here," she said. "I hadn't expected that."

Milly shook her head slowly.

"I hadn't either. But now we can tell people, so everyone knows."

❈

ON THE DRIVE back, Milly wrote furiously as the car bumped along the road. She described the battle, the sacrifices of the men, and the destruction the fascists left in their wake. She was unstinting in her evaluation of the loyalist troops' offensive: all that sacrifice for a hollowed-out town with no strategic significance. None that she could see. She wrote and wrote.

A day later, she typed up the story and handed it to the senior editor at the Foreign Press Bureau. She stood and watched as he read.

His face grew pale.

"You are mad," he said in a low voice. The skin under his eyes grew even more green tinted as he blanched. "We cannot publish this. I cannot allow any newspaper in the world to publish this."

"You don't understand. If people know the truth, they will fight harder. The Americans will change their policy, they'll abandon non-intervention when they learn how bad it is here."

"They'll throw their money after a losing cause?"

He gasped as soon as the words left his mouth. The admission hung in the air between them, and in the quiet, Milly heard the gentle patter of typewriter keys in the next room. Like the distant fall of gunfire.

The editor reached into his desk, pulled something out, then held Milly's pages up. Before she could say anything, he lit them on fire.

The flames surged, hungry, and leapt up the paper. Quickly, he dropped the burning pages into the metal wastebasket by his feet.

"Don't pull a stunt like that again," he said, articulating each word carefully. "That is not how we win a war."

"What do you know," Milly said.

"More than you." He glowered at her.

She turned on her heel and stormed out.

Outside, a girl in a yellow dress held up a bunch of flowers and called out a price. Her hair was divided into two braids, each slinking down the back of her browned ears. Milly blinked back a tear.

"Here." She pulled out the smallest peso note she had and handed it over. The girl wouldn't have change, no one could find any coins these days, but Milly didn't care. At least she was doing something to help. The girl handed out two branches of white blossoms, not a flower Milly recognized.

"Gracias."

The girl trotted off, happy with her sale. Milly grasped the branches tightly, then noticed she had crushed a few of the flowers. She loosened her grip and tried to straighten the blossoms. Two of them fluttered to the ground.

Back in her apartment, she pulled the notes she had made from her notebook and rewrote the story. It wasn't good, but it was something. She couldn't mail it, the censors would filter it, but she could give it to one of the correspondents passing through. Tucked into their luggage, the story would escape the notice of all except the most diligent border guard, and the guards had more worrying things to search for than sad news stories. She would find someone to give it to.

Months earlier, during one of her visits in Madrid, Milly had found Ernest Hemingway in the lobby of the Hotel Florida. The great man was sitting alone, so Milly had taken a deep breath and invited herself to join him at his table. He nodded toward the empty chair.

Over the course of one whiskey, Milly had told him about her writing, and the novel about her time in Moscow that she wanted to write.

Hemingway had nodded.

"If you write how people think it was," he said, "it'll be rotten writing. You have to write it true. The way it happened."

Now she looked at the story she had written. It was true. That much she knew.

A MONTH LATER, Milly packed her bags and talked her way into a car heading north, to Quinto. She'd had enough of the Foreign Press Bureau, so she rattled and bumped through the ride north, until she showed up in the headquarters of the Lincoln Battalion like Little Orphan Annie.

"Is Major Amlie here?" she asked.

The adjutant who greeted the car full of reporters frowned at her request.

"I'm here to be the battalion secretary," she said. "He's expecting me." It wasn't true, not yet at least. But what was true was the fight happening here, not the stories being spun in Valencia. She needed to be here, on the front, where the action was. This was where Spain's future was being written, not by the bureaucrats—however well-meaning—back on the coast.

The town was nestled against a hill, alongside the winding Ebro River, and the battalion headquarters was on the outskirts. Milly lifted her face to the autumn sun, and she breathed in the crisp scent of rotting leaves and cook fires. The two other reporters in the car had already disappeared into the camp, made invisible by their maleness, while Milly stood and waited. She hated that she needed permission to be here.

Eventually, Hans strode out of a large tent in the middle of the camp, followed by Bob Merriman and, to Milly's delight, Marion Merriman. Milly threw herself into her friend's arms.

"We've been needing another woman's touch around here," Marion said.

"You know that's my specialty," Milly said with a snort.

Milly stepped back. Her eyes were unexpectedly damp, and she smiled to see Marion's concerned face.

"Come out of the wind," Marion said, taking Milly's hand. She shot a look at Bob, who seemed about to object. "I meant it. This place could use another straight-thinking woman."

And with that, Milly found herself at home in the Lincoln Battalion.

❁

SHE SLEPT IN an old wooden shed outside the circle of tents, and though she trembled at night while thinking of fascist scouts, she was glad to have the protection against the rain and damp ground that the tents couldn't offer. Each morning, Marion showed up in their outdoor mess hall, pale-faced and shivering, as if she had spent the night damp. Milly, though, slept better than she had in months.

During the day, she wrote. She followed the men as they played cards or cleaned their rifles or came back from patrol. She made notes about the way they spoke and the contradictions that wove through the battalion like veins of mold in cheese. The men wanted a voice in military decisions, but they knew the unit needed discipline. They yearned for home but scorned deserters. They professed egalitarianism but rarely sat down alongside men whose skin color differed from their own. She wrote it all down.

In early November, the two American military attachés surprised the battalion by rolling up in a sleek black car with small American flags snapping from the front. Milly ran down to greet them, her calf-length pencil skirt shortening her strides as she hurried down the hill. She laughed as Colonel Fuqua, the military attaché, and his colleague Major Griffith, unfolded themselves from the car.

"Well, well," she said, laughing. She had met Thomas Griffith, the air attaché, in Madrid, back when she was writing only for the AP, and he had proved an interesting source of information about the German planes bombing the city. Back then, no one was willing to admit the level of German involvement in Spain's war, but she wanted to force the world's eyes open.

Major Amlie, Bob, and Marion all joined them and showed the men around the camp. One of the senior International Brigade commanders, a man most of the men despised, took the opportunity to show off and present Bob with a ceremonial watch in honor of his bravery at Belchite. Bob was now deputy commander in the battalion, second to Major Amlie. Everyone clapped politely, and Bob passed the watch around. Milly handled it quickly, and as she passed it to the next person, her eyes caught on Hans, who stood round shouldered at the back of the crowd. Then, Colonel Fuqua, not to be outdone, offered Bob a leather jacket that Fuqua said had been his own in the Great War. Milly watched Hans, whose face remained blank except, she thought, for a slight pinching at the corners of his eyes, as if the sun shined too brightly. No one was honoring him, though he had fought too. No one even mentioned his leadership.

She walked over to him.

"I think we're alike," she said.

"What?" He turned to her in surprise. Around them, everyone clapped for the leather jacket. Bob flushed with pleasure, then announced that Marion, his beautiful wife, was soon traveling to America to make speeches for the cause.

"We see things, but others don't always see us." Milly took her glasses from her face and wiped them clean. She replaced them and looked back at him. "Am I right?"

"I don't know," he said slowly. "I think people look at you quite a lot."

She shook her head.

"It's not the same, being looked at and being seen. I used to think it was." She thought of Zhenya, parading with the soprano's train in his elegant hands, hundreds of eyes upon him. It had taken her so long to understand him, and she was ashamed.

"But you don't think so anymore?"

"No. I don't want to be looked at now."

He laughed. "Hard to avoid that, in a camp full of men whose eyes drink in a woman's every curve." Then he blushed. "The point is, you're an interesting lady. People want to get to know you."

Around them, the crowd dispersed, though the American officials still stood talking to Bob and Marion.

"Are you going to join them?" Milly asked.

"No," he said. He looked at the ground. "Would you like to go for a walk?"

"I think they're serving us lunch," she said, nodding her head at the Americans. "It wouldn't look good for the battalion commander to disappear before the meal."

"That's true." He fiddled with the button on his coat. "Maybe afterward?"

"Yes, I'd like that. Afterward."

36

MILLY AWOKE THAT morning in Hans's tent. They had, after two weeks of talking and flirting, finally escaped to his tent to make love on a pile of blankets on the dirt floor. His long, lean body seemed to fit into her soft one, and she wrapped herself around him as they slept. Now he was already up and dressed, ready to begin his morning's duties, but he glanced over when she yawned. His blue eyes were warm with affection, and her heart puddled, like snowmelt. The first night they had stayed up late, sitting around a banked campfire, he had asked her about her parents. No man had ever asked about her parents. Unless she counted the interviews to enter the Writers Union or the Communist Party, but she didn't.

"I had not expected to find a woman like you," he said quietly in the morning dark. "Not anywhere, and certainly not here."

"You should have most expected to find me here." She propped herself up on an elbow. The blankets slipped low on her breasts, barely covering her nipples. "My whole life has been leading me to Spain, I think. This is what I was meant to see, to write about. Where people are fighting to be free and make other lives better, but it's so hard to do it right." She thought of the woman with the dead baby.

He got down on his knees and kissed the tip of her nose.

"I'm glad," he said. Then he stood and walked out.

She dressed quickly, knowing how embarrassed he would be to be seen with a woman in his tent. But she hoped this wouldn't be the last time he let her spend the night. Being together felt right, fitting in a way that she hadn't fit with a man in years. If ever.

The day was cold, and when she emerged from the tent, the wind stung her eyes and nearly swept her glasses from her nose. A few gunshots echoed in the distance, but those had been sounding for some weeks now, and she didn't make much of it. Their scouts were telling them the fascists didn't intend to launch an offensive on this part of the line; they were more likely to move south, closer to Valencia.

She walked to the mess tent, where the cooks were ladling porridge into tin bowls. She had forgotten the cup she usually brought with her, but one of the other men lent her his. No one acted different, or otherwise acknowledged her night with the commander. Hans himself was already gone, probably inspecting the fortifications outside the camp.

A few more gunshots sounded, this time closer. Milly glanced over at the soldier next to her, a man she recognized from her weeks with the battalion, and raised her eyebrows. He shrugged.

"Maybe we got some fascist scouts."

She nodded and sipped the chicory-flavored coffee filling the tin cup. Terrible stuff, but at least it was hot.

A man sprinted into the camp, sweat streaming down the side of his face.

"They've been shot!" he yelled. "Major Amlie and Steve Noll, they've both been shot!"

Milly ran.

SHE SAT NEXT to Hans's bed in the field hospital. She had ridden in the ambulance with him, some three hours south of Quinto, to this ward filling the former country estate of some Spanish princess. In what must have been the princess's dining room, a long row of mostly empty beds waited for the war's injured. Hans had been hit in the side, and he had been incoherent during the transit. But now, a few days later, he was recovering well. Milly held his hand and watched him sleep.

A young doctor, probably English, stopped by the bed.

"He's going to be fine, you know," he said. "You should get some sleep."

"I have," Milly said, though she had only slept a few hours at a time. Each time her mind succumbed to darkness, her dreams grabbed hold of her and whispered that Hans would be lost, that his wound would grow infected and no one would notice until too late. So she shot awake and shuffled to his bedside, where she kept her vigil.

The doctor clucked his tongue.

"Here." He pulled the sheets back from Hans's side and then lifted the nightshirt covering his body. "See? The wound here is healing well. Redness around the stitches is normal and healthy. There's no excessive swelling, no sign of infection. We removed the bullet, clean." He replaced Hans's shirt, and as he did, the patient flickered his eyes open.

"Milly?"

"Tell her to go get some sleep," the doctor said. "She can't heal you with the force of her presence."

"Don't be too sure," Hans said, his voice scratchy. Milly handed him a cup of water that she had already poured.

The doctor shook his head and walked away.

"But he's right," Hans said. "You do need to rest. You could get sick if you don't take care of yourself."

"I sent a telegram to your brother," she said. She had learned, during their long walks, that Hans's brother was a US congressman from Wisconsin.

"You told him I'm fine?"

"More or less."

Hans squeezed her hand.

"I need to get back to the fight. The men need me."

"No, they don't. You need to heal."

Hans closed his eyes. He worried about the men, constantly. He wondered if they had enough spare spectacles, and he had tried to order more. He asked Brigade headquarters if they could improve the mail deliveries, so the men could have better word of their sweethearts at home. He chased down the quartermaster, so he could make sure they were getting the best food the battalion could possibly afford.

But when the young man had run up saying Hans and the other soldier were injured, no one had seemed concerned. Hans was no Bob Merriman, instinctively commanding the love of his soldiers. Just like Milly was no Marion, easily finding the love of her life. Milly squeezed Hans's hand.

"You need to take your time," she said.

❖

A WEEK LATER, more injured men started to pour in. The fighting had restarted, now around Teruel, close to the field hospital. Sometimes Milly had to tread carefully as she led Hans on his short walks around the ward, since the floor might be slick, newly washed to clean away the blood of a recently arrived man. Once, she walked outside for a breath of fresh air and gasped to see the corpse of a young man lying on the ground where the ambulance had left him, gaping at the sky. War was creeping closer.

She had left all her notes about the Lincoln Battalion behind when she rushed into the ambulance with Hans, and when her belongings arrived at the hospital, her notes and books were not among them. Her letters to Quinto produced only apologetic responses. Her writing was lost. Frustrated, Milly started writing again, but describing the moans of injured men and the blue sky over the red-tiled roof of the princess's seized manor felt hollow.

Then, a writer from the Ministry of Propaganda visited. He had a small notebook and a wide smile, and the English doctor led him around the ward. Curious, Milly followed at a distance.

"Innovative care will restore our men for the fight," the doctor said, his eyes bright as he pointed out the transfusion equipment that Dr. Barsky had helped design earlier in the year, with Hermann's help.

"What fight?" Milly said from behind them. Both men spun around. "Without international support, how can the Republic possibly fight? How can the bodies of our men stop the fascist guns? What will blood transfusions do to stop that?" Her chest heaved.

"Transfusions keep men alive," the doctor countered, his gaze narrow.

"For one more turn at the battlefield, until the fascist guns can really cut them into pieces. Write that," she said, turning to the newspaperman. "Write that their lives are a finger in the goddamn fascist dike, nothing more than a stopgap, so long as the democratic countries of the world starve Spain."

The man picked up his pen, put it to the paper, then let his hands fall to his sides.

"That won't pass the censor," he said. He had full cheeks: the face of a man who had been eating well for the past few months. Milly rolled her eyes.

"You want to make a difference?" she demanded. "Tell the truth. Tell the goddamn truth."

In the ward, Hans angled himself up in bed. His side still pained him, but he was regaining his mobility. He watched her, his blue eyes deep and unknowable. She swallowed.

For so long, she had been as men had wanted her. As she thought people had wanted her to be. When she was a little girl, Milly had taken the cork from her mother's ink bottle and gone out into the apartment building's hallway. There, crouching in front of the wallpaper, she carefully stamped circle after circle onto the yellow pattern. Making it so much prettier, making the pattern deeper and more meaningful. But then one of their neighbors had come out and screamed. "Look at that brat!" she yelled. "We'll all have to pay to replace the wallpaper!" Suddenly, a blow shattered Milly's cheek. She held her ringing face and looked up to see her father, her beloved father, red-faced and looking down at her. "You're a disappointment, Mildred," he said. She dropped the stamp and wept.

He hadn't understood.

Now she walked over to her lover.

"Hans," she said. "Let's get married. Let's be a team, and together we'll tell the Americans what it's really like. We'll convince Roosevelt to change his tune. What do you think?"

"You can't get married," the Ministry newspaperman said from behind her. "Men in the Brigades can't get married if they're not already wed."

"They can if they're dying," Hans said quietly. He looked at Milly. "Am I dying?"

She reached out and held his hand. His knuckles were knobbed and rough, and his grip was firm.

"You tell me."

"Doctor," Hans called. The doctor stepped closer. "I need a deathbed marriage."

The Englishman looked back and forth between them. Milly pressed Hans's hand to her forehead and closed her eyes.

"Indeed you do," the doctor said softly. He was a good man. Milly kissed Hans's fingers.

37

MILLY CLOSED THE lid of her suitcase and looked around their Barcelona hotel room. Not only had they managed permission for a wedding, but Hans had received discharge papers, due to his wound, and they had made it to Barcelona for two days of honeymoon. She tried to memorize each flocked fleur-de-lis of the gold wallpaper, and each tassel on the lampshades. Here, they had gotten to know each other in ways that they hadn't managed in Quinto. Here, Milly felt joined to her husband in a way that she had never felt before, not with any of her previous lovers. Hans was a serious shadow to her flitting candlelight, a quiet pause to match her chattering birdsong. She was almost surprised to find how much she loved him.

"Let's stow the luggage at the train station and spend one last day seeing the city," she said. They had a train to Paris that evening, and from there they would make it to port to catch their ocean liner back to the United States.

He buttoned his cotton shirt and bent over to give her a kiss on the forehead.

"Perfect," he said.

They deposited their luggage with the porter at the train station, then found a café for lunch. Milly laughed at Hans's silly jokes, and he looked into her eyes as if he were drinking deeply at a well. When they paid the bill, she blushed at the heart she saw the waiter had written on the receipt.

They stepped out onto the sidewalk, and Milly flagged a passing boy hawking the newspaper. She hoped to bring as much news as she could back to New York, real news that she could interpret for American audiences. She handed him a five peso note, all she had, and told him to keep the change. He grinned.

Then, the air raid sirens sounded.

The sirens screamed, rending the air, and Milly and Hans ran. They scrambled down the stairs to a subway entrance, and behind them, the earth shook. Milly and Hans fell into each other's arms at the base of the stairs, then stumbled into the tunnel entrance, while outside explosions rocked the street. Crumbled mortar spattered the stairs. They ran down the steps.

When the noise subsided, and the all-clear bells rang, Milly and Hans emerged tentatively into the daylight. Dust still clouded the air, and they coughed. The café where they had lunched was blown out, its glass shattered and tables overturned. Rivulets of blood ran out along the floor, and a dead woman lay sprawled next to the threshold. Milly turned to gag.

"We were there," she said.

Hans nodded.

"This war." Hans stood, the words stuck in his throat. Milly understood. What more was there to say? The horror was unspeakable. A man staggered from the café, clutching his gut and moaning. Hans ran to him and helped him into the middle of the street, where soon a medic with a stretcher arrived to carry him over the rubble. Milly helped a black-haired woman with a gash in her arm pick her way over the piled stones toward an ambulance at the end of the street. There was nothing to do but help.

That night, as their train pulled away from Barcelona, Milly leaned into Hans's shoulder. She held her breath, wondering if the German and Italian planes would return, obliterating their escape. But the train rattled on, rocking its way through the darkness.

"We're doing the right thing, aren't we?" She couldn't help but doubt herself. She hadn't thought she was running when she decided to leave, but maybe she was.

Hans ran his thumb down her temple and along her jaw.

"I don't know," he said. "I'm following you."

She nodded. She could stay, but in Spain her stories would be stifled. The censors thought they knew how to protect Spain, but they were wrong, and they needed people like her and Hans. Out in the world, talking about Spain's war.

"We're doing the right thing." She looked out into the dark night, where she knew invisible Spanish farms and mountains and rivers lay. "We'll tell people the truth."

"And we'll live our lives."

"I don't mind that," she admitted. "We'll live our lives."

Then, she reached down into her valise and pulled out a notebook. There was an empty divot on her right wrist where the bracelet used to rest when she pressed her hand on paper, and she caressed the absence with her finger.

After a few minutes of staring into the gilded dark, she began to write.

HISTORICAL NOTE

Milly Bennett, born Mildred Bremler, nosed her way into my life all the way back in 2003, and she hasn't left since. I found her story when I was researching the Spanish Civil War for my master's degree capstone project, and I was captivated by this brave, vulnerable woman who reported on the Spanish Civil War. In writing this novel I hope I have done her justice and created a Milly whom she would recognize and appreciate.

Like any story, my reflection is sure to have its distortions from the original. Milly's voluminous correspondence and papers, in the Hoover Institution Archives, are a boon to any researcher—but also a challenge. I chose to simplify some aspects of Milly's story, in hopes of keeping this novel to a reasonable length. Milly had more flirtations and lovers than I could keep track of, so I focused on her most significant affairs. She also flirted with Communism all her life, but she was too independent-minded to bind herself to the Party in the way that many of her contemporaries did. She never became a Party member.

I also simplified the workplace politics of *Moscow Daily News*, notably by combining some of the editors and reporters and by disregarding the paper's first years of life, when it was not daily. Until 1932 the paper was called *Moscow News*, and it competed with the English-language *Worker's News*.

For those interested in learning more about the lives of elite Bolshevik leaders in the 1930s, I highly recommend Yuri Slezkine's *The House of Government*. Platon Kerzhentsev wasn't the chief theoretician of the Bolshevik Conception of Time when he lived in the House of Government (when Milly visited, he had moved on to being chief administrator of the Council of People's Commissars), but I loved the title and how it reflected Soviet efforts to reconceptualize the world.

We are all engaged in reconceptualizing the world, since this crazy, complicated world of ours resists any one definition. During my graduate school studies in international relations, Professor Eliot Cohen argued that wars often don't end. They linger in the bodies of veterans, the resentments of the defeated nations, the distorted maps, and the world's collective memory. Both the Russian Revolution and the Spanish Civil War had legacies that lingered well beyond the tidy dates that marked their conclusions, and in some ways, we are still feeling those legacies today. Milly lived in the shadow of both wars, particularly as they sowed the seeds for the fearful Cold War that followed. After Milly returned to the United States to pursue her writing and advocacy for Spain, the FBI grew increasingly interested in her. Periodically, over the rest of her life, she endured interrogations and even harassment by a paranoid FBI convinced she was a Communist agent. She never gave up fighting for her independence, however, and she resisted their attempts to intimidate her, including berating an agent who came to her house. She continued to withstand what she deemed FBI harassment until she died in 1960.

Upon her death, she gave her extensive personal records to two friends from her years in Russia. Milly knew she had witnessed and done extraordinary things, even if she didn't succeed in publishing her own book-length account in her lifetime. Her friends, in turn, donated the records to the Hoover Institution Archives. In 1993, A. Tom Grunfeld published the part of her memoirs that Milly had completed, taking her from her early years through her adventures in China. Readers looking to learn more about Milly would be wise to start with that fascinating book, which Grunfeld titled *On Her Own*.

Maybe Milly was alone for many of her years, but she found the courage to believe in herself, even when it seemed like the world didn't. I'm so glad she did.

ACKNOWLEDGMENTS

First, reader, thank you for reading books, including this one. Milly's story would be incomplete without your participation.

Her story, as I've rendered it, would never have taken flight had it not been for my passionate, insightful agent, Shannon Hassan. I'm eternally grateful for her guidance and faith.

The team at Amberjack continues to make me feel at home, and I'm so glad to be a part of their family. Thank you to Justin Mitson, Madison Perdue, Katie Erwin, Dayna Anderson, and Cassandra Farrin for all your hard work. Particular thanks to Cherrita Lee for her patience, wisdom, and editorial skill in pushing me to make this book better. Kerianne Steinberg is a goddess of detail, whose close attention corrected my many inconsistences and comma splices.

I've taught a workshop on how to edit your own writing, and I preface it with a confession: the premise is false. I rely on the keen eye and masterful feedback of my writing crew, and I don't know what I would do without them. Thanks to Mary Aceituno, Felix Amerasinghe, Suzie Eckl, Jeanne Jones, Terri Lewis, Melody Steiner, and Kathryn Wichmann for reading an early sample. Particular thanks to brave souls Mara Adams, Richard

Agemo, Meredith Crosbie, Andrea Pawley, and Samantha Raja-ram for reading the entire manuscript. My Authors18 crew helped teach me the ropes of this whole author thing, and they were the best company a new author could have.

Writing about Russia was a massive leap of faith for me, and I'm grateful to Aidos Bekturganov for his generosity in trans-lating numerous letters and answering my many questions. Ksenia Coulter helped me with naming conventions, and Kseniya Melnik and her parents generously explained regional pronunciation. Elga Zalite was the researcher of my dreams, and both Julia Mickleburg and Lisa Kirschenbaum were kind to lend their deep expertise to this novelist's quest. None of this would have been possible without the Hoover Institution Archives's commitment to preserving Milly's records.

My family and friends continue to astonish me with their love and support. There are too many to list (I tried), so I merely bow my head in appreciation.

The writing life is hard, and sometimes the brunt is borne by those who are the closest. I'm grateful to my children for all the times they played independently while I worked, and for their patience with their mom and her ever-present books.

Finally, my eternal love and gratitude to my husband, Pat-rick. He makes it both possible and worthwhile.